CORAL RED

A. L. HAWKE

PHANTOM HEART, LLC

ISBN: 9781953919106 (ebook)

ISBN: 9781953919113 (paperback)

ISBN: 9781953919403 (hardcover)

Library of Congress Control Number: 2022904624

This is a work of fiction. It comes directly from the author's imagination. The book also includes fictitious names, characters, places, and incidents. Any public names are used solely for creative purposes. Any resemblance to actual people, living or dead, or to companies, institutions, or locales is entirely coincidental or accidental.

Line edited by Stephanie Ward

Proofread by Alexa B., alexabooks.wixsite.com/authors

Cover & Map Design © 2021 by Sean Counley

Published by Phantom Heart, LLC

27702 Crown Valley Pkwy D-4, #201

Ladera Ranch, CA 92694, USA

Printed and bound in the United States of America

First printing April, 2022

Learn more about A.L. Hawke at www.alhawke.com

Correspondence: contact@alhawke.com

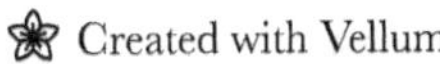 Created with Vellum

MOUNT AMBITUS
THE STRATOS RIVER
Napea
AZUR
THE CRYSTAL PALACE
Tartarus
Elysium
River
THE UN

The Hinterlands
RE BLUE
THE STYGIAN HOLE
STRAIT OF AZURE
THE LANDS OF ATALA
Mangoria
Mount Ambitus
Plum Caves
UNDERWORLD

MOUNT AMBITUS
NAPEA
Azure Blue
Crete
CRESCENT
SHADOW POINT
AZERBAN
SUN KING
CRYSTA
KIT
THE CONTINENT OF ATALA

BLUE
ADELIN
MOON DESERT
DOM
FOX KINGDOM
CATANIA
TAL LAKE
KINGDOM
LOGENAS
RIVER OF TRINIZ
HERIA
SINTERIA
CLIFFS OF ZONOOH
TELERIA
PORDUNN
HARKIST
EDITHIAN
Strait of Aethiopia
Egypt

1

RETURN OF THE FIREBIRD

A LINE OF MEN WITH EYES OUTLINED IN KOHL, SHIRTLESS, wearing linen skirts, came down the boulevard, cocking their arms up and down with elbows straight, turning their heads and arms to the beat of drums, sistrums, and cymbals to a crowd of cheery faces watching the Atlantean sea barge. The barge was carried aloft on the shoulders of the pharaoh's foot soldiers. And lines of women in narrow white sheaths walked beside them waving. Behind the float performed dancers and singers, some even running up to the crowds breathing fire. Thousands crowded the streets as the barge sailed through the roads of downtown Wasset.

The masonry and decorations surrounding the square stone buildings were no less magnificent. It seemed every section of stone and column was painted with strange figures—men and women painted red and blue with animals' heads: some had bird heads, some dogs, even a strange lizard. And on the rooftops, wealthy men adorned in gold necklaces, wearing long kilts with black paint along their eyes, wrapped their arms around women adorned in rubies, sapphires, and gold.

"Wondrous," Sol said, laughing to his companions. "Wondrous. Isn't it incredible, Cambria?"

Cambria sat to his left and nodded, but she tapped a bow on her lap. She wore the red hoplite armor of an Amazon, but her long blond hair flowed without her helm. Sol's daughter, Cassandra, sat on his right. She wore very thick blue makeup, in the tradition of her ancient nymph ancestors, with a matching blue peplos. Cassandra was so enthralled that she didn't even turn in response to her father's comment.

"Only a wonderful opportunity to kill the emperor of Atlantis," Cambria finally quipped. "Why you agreed to this parade with so little defense is beyond me."

Then, as if on cue, a dirty, wild-eyed man, wearing only a skirt, started screaming "*Nefertiti! Nefertiti!*" and climbed into the barge. He tried to pull Casey off, but he was quickly taken down by three Egyptian soldiers.

"You're perfectly safe," reassured Sadiki, an Egyptian advisor sitting behind her.

Cambria rolled her eyes and sheathed a knife she had removed from her scabbard.

"Permit me a little joy, Cambria," Sol said bitterly—a bit more sadly than he intended.

Cambria resumed scanning the crowds.

Cambria was Solinair's chief general and guard. Sol remembered her joyous spirit many moons ago. But since the death of his wife, the Amazon queen, Avivae Ambrosia, she had been somber.

"Enjoying the festival, Pharaoh?" asked Sadiki, tapping Sol's shoulder from behind. "This time of year, it's temperate. Perfect for our celebration."

Sol nodded.

Sadiki was a thin, bald man with a tan complexion and a single ponytail. He sat behind Sol with three other men. All four of them wore long white kilts decorated with gold and jewels. They were all shirtless, but each wore a leopard skin over his shoulders to mark their positions as high priests and advisors to the pharaoh. They laughed and waved. The people were cheering for them, along with the rest of the royal cavalcade.

"Aye," Sol said, aboard the barge, with a nod and a smile. "Aye. Wondrous, Sadiki. Wondrous."

"I presume nothing is like this at home?"

"We hold wonders of our own," remarked Cambria.

"Of course, General," Sadiki said with a bow and a chuckle. "Pardon me. So I've heard."

Cambria didn't smile. She folded her arms and resumed tapping her bow.

It was then that rainbows of cloth streamers rained down from the ceilings of the buildings, showering them with all sorts of vibrant color. Cassandra chuckled as the transparent linen fell over her blue dress.

"Wait until you see the temple, my queen," Sadiki said to Cassandra. "It will dazzle you. I promise. Simply dazzle."

"Father, look!" cried Cassandra. She pointed to a bird soaring over their float. The bird was black but had multicolored wings. It was the first thing that had turned Cambria's eyes from the crowd and made her smile. The large bird soared above the falling streamers and landed on the bow of the boat. The crowd, thinking it was part of the spectacle, raged more loudly.

"Cambria, it's a phoenix!" said Cassandra.

"I've never seen such a bird," said Sadiki in wonder.

"It's not just a phoenix, Casey," Cambria said, permitting a smile for the first time. "That's Mainax."

The bird perched on Cassandra's shoulder.

"Impossible," said Cassandra. "We're over a hundred and fifty leagues from home."

"There's only one phoenix I know of," answered Cambria.

Sol stared at the magnificent bird. Suddenly all the raucousness became meaningless to him. This phoenix was the Amazon nymphs' standard. And when his wife, Avva, had fallen into the Stygian Hole, those that had witnessed her fall into the abyss said that the phoenix burst into flame and fell with her. Yet here the bird was. Many had assumed it died with the queen. Now Mainax perched on Cassandra's shoulder as if nothing had ever happened.

"How are you, firebird?" Casey asked with a chuckle. "Have you seen Cora? Hmm?"

"Bennu," said Sadiki. "We call him Bennu, Amazon Queen. May I?" he asked, reaching to touch the bird.

Cassandra nodded.

Sadiki petted the bird and Mainax cooed. "Magnificent."

It grew dark.

"We're entering the temple," Sadiki said, sitting back. "I suppose with a new friend. Perhaps Bennu comes to greet us?"

Their boat was carried into a stone enclosure. A thousand torches lit the walls. It was as wide as the main street—of course, large enough to fit their float—a huge stone chamber with paintings on the walls and columns that were similar to those outside. Another thousand Egyptians in perfect rows surrounded them, shirtless men, many bald with kohl, and a great many women wearing the same thin linen sheaths as the revelers outside. Before a grand altar was a giant painted image of a man with a bird head. And more strange writing along the sides of the image. And large blue ceramic containers lit with fire, twice the height of people.

Their ship-float stopped before the altar, and all the men carrying the barge carefully lowered it. Before them was a golden chair on a dais and a man Sol had already met, outside of the ceremony, when first arriving in Egypt. The pharaoh of Egypt. He sat shirtless, wearing black kohl around his eyes and a double gold crown and holding a gold scepter. Yet his clothes were not much different from those of the spectators. And standing beside him was a group of priests wearing the same leopard skins over their white linen clothes as Sadiki.

"Welcome, Emperor of Atlantis, to Ipet Resyt, the southern sanctuary," said the pharaoh, walking down from his throne. His words echoed in the hall. "Pharaoh Solinair Solinaray, you've traveled far. Your presence is a great honor to me."

Solinair, Cambria, and Cassandra were helped off the barge. They walked toward the throne. Then Solinair embraced the pharaoh. The crowds applauded.

"Peace be with us, Sol," the pharaoh said quietly and less formally. Then he looked at Cassandra and Cambria. He stepped back. Sol figured it was Cassandra's thick blue makeup that surprised him. He smiled and held out a hand for hers. "A vision of Hathor. Welcome, great queen of the Amazons. During your stay, I would very much like to show you private murals in our royal chambers. There are images of a pharaoh with a striking resemblance to you."

The phoenix fluttered on Casey's shoulder, and the pharaoh opened his eyes wider at the bird. "And welcome to you too, friend," he said with a laugh. He gestured to them all. "You are all welcome in the lands of Kemet."

"Aye," said Sol. "I'm in awe of your city. And of your Nile. You live in a wondrous world, Pharaoh."

The pharaoh nodded. Then he leaned forward, close to Sol's ear, losing his smile for a moment, and whispered, "We must talk later over the more unpleasant business at hand."

But then he took Sol's hand and raised it high. He shouted words in Egyptian that Sol did not understand. The people responded with thunderous applause. Then a translator beside him shouted, presumably, the same words in Atalan: "Praise Amun-Ra." He gestured to the hall and the paintings behind him. "Welcome and worship! Pharaohs of the Solinaray family have arrived! Welcome the gods from the north. Extend greetings in love to our family. And behold their new Azure queen. An Ambrosia returns from Aaru after leaving us so many centuries ago!"

People cheered more loudly than ever.

But their applause quieted with Mainax's shriek. The bird made everyone quiet. The phoenix's call echoed through the halls, and all gazed up as he soared above them and flew around the rooftops of the temple.

2

THE HANDSOME RUFFIAN

Casey didn't attend supper with the pharaoh. Her father had made it clear that the private dinner would include talk of war. She wanted nothing to do with that. Such talk reminded her of the battle plans after the death of her beloved uncle. And that war had led to the death of her mother. Cassandra had enough of politics.

She enjoyed resting and bathing in an outdoor pool on the private terrace of her chamber. Her hot bath was prepared by a slave of the palace, and she sank with pleasure into the water.

The patio was lovely. It was surrounded by stone columns, and lines of red and yellow linen served as a roof that opened into the outdoors. She surmised the tenting could be closed completely during heavy rain, but tonight it was open, allowing a vista of beautiful constellations shining through the dark sky.

She closed her eyes and took a deep breath. Peace surrounded her with the sound of crickets and a gentle breeze through the garden leaves around her spa. A pleasant floral smell of water lilies emanated from the surrounding gardens. She could still hear the murmurings of revelers outside the palace walls, but it was faint. The festival was for her and her father, but the sounds were quiet enough to mix with the soothing water to nearly lull her to sleep.

She had been amused to learn that the Egyptians were celebrating not only the visit of her father, the Atalan emperor, but the return of an Ambrosian queen. She'd laughed when the pharaoh had told her his people believed her to be not only a nymph queen visiting Wasset, but Nefertiti herself returning from Duat, the Egyptian underworld.

Tomorrow she would travel along the city roads with her father and Cambria to gaze at the Nile. And in a few days, on their way home, they planned to visit the great pyramids in the lower kingdom, in Kher Neter. A vacation promised by her father, indeed. She looked forward to seeing these pyramids. Once—she had learned—before Cora destroyed it, Mount Ambitus was similar in shape to a pyramid.

But tonight, she would rest. Perhaps sleep…

SHE OPENED her eyes to the sound of stirring in the bushes. A rabbit? A bird? Perhaps Mainax?

She heard it again.

"Gyasi?" Casey asked. Gyasi was the name of her slave, who had prepared her bath. She sat up, the water still covering her chest, and searched the veranda. "Gyasi, is that you?"

No one said a word, but she heard more shuffling.

"Who's there!" she asked sternly. "Come out."

"I beg your pardon," said a male voice.

Casey gasped and splashed in the water, doing her best to cover herself with her hands.

"I assure you," said the voice behind a tree, "I've turned away." He did not have a local Egyptian accent. It sounded Hinterland or Greek.

She leaped out of the pool and grabbed her white linen towel from a nearby table. She tied the towel in a knot by her side and wrung her long dark hair out in her hands. Then she picked up her sword. "Come out so that I can have the pleasure of seeing *you*."

"Are you dressed?"

"Don't you know?"

"My eyes are closed, maiden. Please, I must speak with you."

She glimpsed someone behind tree branches. He was a young man dressed in an elegant tunic. He hardly looked like a brigand, but he didn't look Egyptian either. She walked right up to the tree and put the tip of her sword against his flank.

"You may open your eyes now, degenerate."

He raised his hands in the air as she led him out from behind the tree.

He was around her age, if not a year or two older, with dark hair in curls, fashioned like the Greeks. He had tanned olive skin. And his face was clean-shaven, not like a Hinterland man, but like a man from Hellena. He looked like a nobleman.

"I'm embarrassed," he said. "I came to speak with you, but I thought you'd simply be enjoying the outdoors."

"Why are you here?"

"I'm Greek. You're an Amazon nymph, yes? And since you're not in your isle in the sky, you must be the queen? Yes? Queen Cassandra Ambrosia, Amazon nymph queen of Azure Blue?"

She glowered at him. Then she noticed the fiend's eyes wandering down to her chest. She repositioned the towel and pressed the sharp point of her blade more firmly against his throat.

"My name is Theseus," he said, raising his hand. "I had to speak with you. I gather you're the queen, for you're the only blue girl in Wasset. You know our nations don't get along. The Egyptian guards wouldn't have let me in if I knocked."

"Queen Cassandra," shouted a voice through the door. "Is everything all right?"

"Yes, Gyasi," Cassandra said. Then she narrowed her eyes at Theseus. "Everything's fine."

"Be quick and tell me why I shouldn't stab you, boy," Casey

hissed. He looked down again at the folds of her towel. "And look up here into my eyes."

"I am a Greek prince. I need your help."

"Perhaps you're a spy?"

"No," he said, shaking his head. "I've come in search of a way into the Underworld. In order for me to return to my people, the gods have willed that I must travel through the depths, like you."

"The gods are monsters." She nodded. She permitted a smile at his look of shock at her heresy. "They imprisoned me. If you enter the Underworld, there's no way you'll get out. I had a goddess on my side and a mother willing to sacrifice herself to save me. You have none of those, right?"

"You're the only one I know who survived."

She still had the blade pointing against his throat.

"Let me explain my upbringing and my tale. Then you'll believe that I'm a prince needing your help."

Casey felt her eyebrow rise. He smiled smugly. But she didn't lower her sword.

"My father, King Aegeus of Attica, met my mother, Aethra, in Crete. They fell in love and he asked her to return with him to the Acropolis. She agreed but, according to legend, they met up with Poseidon at sea. Poseidon fell in love with my mother too. Legend says that my birth is of two fathers—King Aegeus and Poseidon."

"A humble upbringing," said Cassandra.

What an arrogant man. If he smirks at me one more time...

"Out of Poseidon's jealousy, he barred my mother and me from ever returning to Hellena by sea. That is why I come here now. I'm left only with your Underworld to regain my crown." He examined Casey's eyes, then he put a finger up. "My mother herself wasn't sure either. After telling me the tale, she led me to a rock. She told me that whosoever lifted the rock and took the contents underneath would be the rightful King of Attica. People all over the villages knew of this legend. You see, Poseidon buried my father's shoes and sword underneath a boulder."

Cassandra shrugged.

"Take a look." He carefully moved the cloth from his chiton and revealed a hidden sword. The hilt was beautifully studded with yellow gems, emeralds and rubies. A priceless xiphos. He carefully removed his belt—for she had her Mandrigelian sword still pointed at his neck—and laid the sword, sheathed, on the ground. "And while you're there, look down at my feet, Amazon Queen." He wore similarly jeweled shoes.

"How did you retrieve it under a boulder?"

"I figured my father is Poseidon. The ground was dry when my mother showed me the rock. So I surmised that the god used water to move the stone. So why not me? It was dry enough to wet and cause the stone to shift. With enough water, I moved it."

"Interesting story. Nice sword and shoes. But how does that make you a prince and not a thief? And what does that have to do with entering a queen's private chamber?"

"Aside from staring at a vision of Aphrodite?"

That did it. Casey felt her eyes bulge. She pushed him against a column. Her sword arm shook as she considered thrusting the point into his neck.

"Wait! Please! That was a very stupid thing to say. If you were from my home, you'd believe me. And look at the rest of my clothes. I'm noble in truth. And I told you. I came here to find out how you entered the Underworld. Please tell me so I can recover my birthright. Then I'll go."

"Why not just sail?"

"I told you. Poseidon's curse."

"Traveling the depths will only lead to your death."

"I didn't ask you what would happen to me. I asked how you did it."

"I fell," she mumbled. "All right?" She stepped back, but she didn't lower the sword.

"What do you mean, *you fell?*"

"I fell ..." The words surprised Casey. "Or, I was pushed." She couldn't believe she still felt shame even after all these years. "Look, you shouldn't even be here."

"Tell me how you *fell*. Please. That's all. Then I'll go."

"What will it matter?" she replied, throwing back her long black hair. "After you're taken to the dungeon for entering a queen's chamber?"

"Please tell me," he implored with a smirk.

"I entered by the base of Mount Ambitus in Napea. There I found the ruins of Hermes's abandoned throne. I was pushed by a creature into the water below. But the gods will not let you fall. If you fall from that height, you'll die. The gods of Olympus wanted me to live. Many of my father's men fell down the hole to their death trying to rescue me. The walls are as slippery as iron."

"Are you certain? You say I can't survive? Is there another way? I've learned of tales that say there's an entrance through the caves of Eleusis, but that's on the Greek side. I need to find a way through your country. Or even Crete."

"No, there's no other way. Sorry."

"You're sure? Perhaps a trail near your River Stratos?"

Cassandra shook her head.

Theseus lowered his head, forlorn. His sadness made him appear vulnerable, and that made her feel bad for him for the first time. He stared, deflated, at the stone floor. Then he nodded slowly. "All right. Hello and goodbye then, beautiful Amazon Queen."

"I'm sorry, Theseus."

He picked up his sword and belt. Then he put it on and bowed before her.

When he straightened, he smirked again. Then he stunned her by moving faster than she thought possible, hitting the dull side of her sword with his palm and knocking it to the ground. He leaped beside her, touching his lips to hers. It was so fast that she couldn't back away. And yet, the kiss was tender. Then, like the animal she thought he was, he scurried up a nearby column, climbing like a monkey up a sheer surface to the top. Above the patio, he looked down. "I tell you, your face and body is a vision bested only by Aphrodite,

Queen Cassandra. I hope it shall be imprinted in my mind forever."

Then he jumped off the outside ledge and fled.

3

——————

THE WAR ROOM

"You have my dearest condolences over the loss of your wife," the pharaoh said. He sat on a central wooden chair, the only raised chair, across from Sol and Cambria in a dark private room. Everyone else in the dimly lit chamber sat on wooden stools. The torchlight flickered over the dark kohl around the eyes of the pharaoh; his chief advisor, Sadiki; and two Egyptian elders. "There were cries of anguish along every road and promenade. You know my people revere and sing songs over our beloved Nefer. Avivae was her great-granddaughter."

On the rug were cups of beer, cheese, olives, and figs, along with maps on rolled scrolls. Sol ate a handful of olives and nodded absentmindedly. Then he thumbed through a papyrus map of ancient Babylon.

Their sympathy only upset him. The visit to Egypt had been a complete failure. The pharaoh and his advisors had agreed to help on land but refused their desperate need for aid by sea.

"Within these private walls, let me tell you more." The pharaoh paused. Then he looked at the other priests and they nodded. "Nefertiti never died. Where she is now is a mystery. Some say she returned to the ground and presides in Duat with Osiris. Others say she left, like the ancients Amun-Ra and Isis, for the stars. And some of my people say she went to a city in the clouds."

Sol furrowed his brow at Cambria. Cambria shook her head.

"Did you know her?" the pharaoh asked Cambria.

"I wasn't born yet, sir. But I was trained by my predecessor, Jaida. Jaida was Nefertiti's best friend, general, and even ruler for a brief time as regent before Dainya ruled. All I ever heard from Jaida was great things about Nefertiti. But Jaida passed after intervening with the Hittites and Assyrians in Colchis."

"Your people were in search of the golden kursa," the pharaoh said with a nod.

"It was the only time we battled outside of Azure under Queen Dainya," Cambria said. "I remained, caring for princess Delia, as my people went to war in the North. Under Queen Dainya, many loyal nymphs died."

"The death of Nefertiti's daughter, Dainya, was mourned along the promenade as well," said Sadiki.

"It was tragic," Cambria said with a nod. "Jaida raised Dainya. Jaida was, in many ways, Dainya's mother. When the Hittites murdered Jaida, it changed our queen. Dainya became full of hate. Striking Colchis was the first time we had raised arms outside of Azure since Harmonia. And our last. It meant Queen Dainya's end. But Dainya would have done anything, including lose her life, for her beloved general and foster mother."

"Humph," Sol said, leaning over his map. "Tragedy indeed, but I don't see how such ancient history has much to do with our grave troubles at hand."

"On the contrary, Emperor," the pharaoh said, shaking his head. "I believe the mystery of Nefertiti and her kin has a great deal to do with recent events, and means a great deal for you. How do you know your wife died?"

Sol raised his eyes from the map.

"I told you Nefertiti never died," the pharaoh said with a rueful smile. "So how do you know your wife died?"

"You've been kind." He felt himself stiffen. Then he shook his head. "But this is something I don't wish to discuss."

"Just one moment," the pharaoh said, raising a finger. "Your wife descended into the chasm in Azure Blue. The hole leads to the entrance into your Underworld. There is a very similar hole in Amarna, near the ancient temple ruins of Akhenaten. Your people's Stygian Hole is exactly the same as our Udat al Mawt."

Sol was going to object again, but the priests gave him a look of disapproval—for, to them, this pharaoh was a god.

"In sacred books that only my family possesses," the pharaoh continued, "I've read that Udat al Mawt was created by Persephone. Our people call Persephone Nephthys. The story is very sad, my friend. They say that the hole was dug by Persephone's hands in desperation to see her Nefertiti. Only, when Persephone finally emerged in Amarna, Nefertiti was gone. She was too late. Some of our people claim to have witnessed Nefertiti rising up into the sky a year before and disappearing. And with it, the bright light in the sky soon disappeared."

"What's the point in this?" Sol asked.

"The hole in Amarna appeared right after the disappearance of Nefertiti," interjected Sadiki with a bow. "That same light, Emperor of Atlantis, reappeared after the loss of your wife."

The pharaoh and the elders infernally nodded.

"In Wasset," the pharaoh continued, "Our Nefer ruled as a female pharaoh after Akhenaten died, ruling Kemet like our revered pharaoh Hatshepsut. But it was only to restore her kingdom. Such was the greatness of Nefertiti that she helped in the destruction of her own legacy. Nefertiti destroyed her capital, Amarna. Many believe Akhenaten was so hated that he was murdered. Nefertiti's only choice to restore order was to erase the history of her husband's power. I have the secret papyrus documenting it if you wish to see it. But so great was Nefer that my people did not forget her. The people may have forgotten Akhenaten, but not Nefertiti. That is why your daughter was approached in the parade." The pharaoh paused and drank from his cup. "Sol, Nefertiti writes of a land of light under the ground.

The walls of the hole at Amarna are too steep for climbers, but we believe they lead to this light in Duat. And some claim to see bright flashes by the hole in Amarna. This is all interesting. As your people well know, your Mount Ambitus on the Isle of Napea was once a pyramid. And underneath it, Nefertiti recounts having traveled the depths."

"I don't understand the meaning of all this?" Sol asked again.

"Many of us believe Nefertiti lives," Sadiki said. "But more important for you, we, and our blessed pharaoh, believe Queen Avivae lives. As I said, right after we received news of Avivae's fall in Azure, the bright light reappeared in the sky over Amarna. We believe it is a beacon for the return of an Ambrosia in Amarna under Udat al Mawt."

"Anna passed," Sol said, shaking his head and rubbing his temples. "She died."

All of the Egyptians in the room infernally shook their heads.

"I saw it, Pharaoh," Cambria said. "King Solinair wasn't there, but I was. Avva died. She leaped off her monokera. No one could have survived that fall."

"Thank you for your concern," Sol rumbled. "If the Greeks attack your people, I will fight them. You have my word." Then he shook his head as if shaking off his thoughts. "But, by the gods, don't give a man false hopes over his deceased wife."

"For my family, our concern is not only with Kemet but with Duat," replied the pharaoh with a smile. "Life and death is one on our black soil. This is our way. I tell you, your wife is alive in the Underworld under Amarna."

The fact that the pharaoh was still talking about this made Sol furious. He rose. Standing before the pharaoh was considered grievously rude, but Sol felt like the pharaoh had slighted him with the same impertinence.

The pharaoh rose, smiled, and nodded. He grasped Sol's hand tightly. "Be in friendship, great emperor," the pharaoh said, patting his back. "May water rise and sprout forth ample harvest for you and your people. You and our lands are one."

"Stay as long as you like," said Sadiki with a smile, rising too. "You have the royal chambers."

***

SOL AND CAMBRIA walked alone together, through the now darkened torchlit halls, into the main royal buildings. Cambria was back to being his guard, her eyes wandering everywhere, scrutinizing their surroundings.

"It was going well until he mentioned Avva," Cambria said quietly. "I'm sorry, Sol."

"Aye."

"They meant well. Your rudeness will be forgiven."

"My rudeness?" Sol glanced at her, taken aback. "I asked that they not speak of her anymore. He went on. And he spoke of freeing my brother, which was also none of his business."

"Torinth is renowned at battle at sea," Cambria continued quietly with a shrug. "They gave us a great deal of intelligence regarding skirmishes we didn't know of, far west in Phoenicia. If the Greeks are now dominating the sea over the Phoenicians, the situation is grave indeed. And, indeed, we need every renowned seafarer we can get. Even if we can't get them."

"Perhaps."

"But you were no less forward when you asked if they have our back in war, Sol. What do you think of his assertion?"

"Nothing has changed. They will side with the ultimate victor."

"I'm not talking about our alliance with Egypt."

Sol fell silent. He realized he didn't want to speak about this with Cambria either.

"The Egyptians are an ancient race," Cambria said quietly as they walked down another corridor. "They understand magic far more than we do. But I..." She flashed a smile at Sol under the torchlight. "I don't know. I so wish it was true of Avva, but I watched her fall from Inghorn. I don't think she lived, Sol. I'm sorry."

"We didn't get the support we desired at sea," replied Sol.

"It's not because they won't give it," Cambria said with a nod. "They simply don't have it. Perhaps they've grown weak from complacency. None of the kingdoms of Nubia seem a threat. The Hittites are controlled since the Battle of Kadesh. The Assyrians stay to themselves. Their borders are sound."

"They are becoming weak," he agreed with a nod. "That is why they are so quick to be our friends."

Cambria stopped by the door to her bedchamber. She surprised him with an embrace. "I think they were just trying to help, Sol," she said with a broken voice. "I miss her so much."

"Aye. Aye. Goodnight, Cambria."

"Goodnight," she said, patting his back. "I shall be at watch if you need me."

He walked alone to his own chamber across the hall.

I shall dream of you tonight, Anna. By the gods in this land, I swear it, if I truly believed you were down in their underworld, or anywhere, I'd go to the farthest reaches of the world and find you. I swear it. I might not speak of you, but I shall think only of you tonight, my love.

4

HASEVALAH

Avva stood leaning against a wooden column on her
outdoor patio. Her hair was wrapped in black cloth in the
fashion of her mother, Delia. This amused her, for she had spent
her whole life refusing to wrap her head in this fashion out of
distaste for her mother. But now she used it to shelter her head
from the cold. Hasevalah was bitingly cold. She wore shoes with
a long black peplos under thick white-and-black animal fur. Cora
had given her the dress and coat. Cora had given her shoes too.
The goddess had given her everything.

She squeezed her arms more tightly around herself and
squinted up. The yellow "sun" was bright.

Then she took a deep breath. Behind her was their one-room
cottage. Avva marveled that Cora had claimed to have built the
entire house by hand.

Avva's eyes fixed on the distant horizon. It was sand dunes as
far as the eye could see. But in one direction, if she gazed hard
enough, she could make out dirt walls rising to the bright sky. But
here, below the porch of her one-room wooden cottage, was only
dead sand.

Only a few insects and occasional black shrubs survived the
land. Otherwise, it was just sand dunes. This was her home now

and the desert landscape was her view, a breathtaking, seemingly endless dry frozen desert. It was all strange because her daughter had told her that the Underworld was dark, but here, through a bright glare, all she could ever see was light. Cold light. There was an evening, but it was far shorter and darker than any night back home.

Beside her desert cottage lay a grove of Myrle berry bushes. Cora had planted a few pomegranate trees, but most of the fruit was dried up. Cora watered them, bringing ampullas full of water by horseback every time she brought Avva food. Avva figured they'd die in a few days without being watered. Just like Avva. Cora kept her pomegranates alive just as she kept Avva alive.

Avva looked down upon her blue palm glistening under the yellow-white light. Then she covered her eyes with them and looked up at the "sky" again. She imagined it was warm, like her sun back home. But a cold breeze blew over her cheeks.

She heard movement. Her heart raced. It must be Cora!

In the far distance, the goddess Persephone was riding fast along the sand with her black-winged konobera, a fire-breathing winged horse. Now the beast's wings were folded. She stopped the black horse by the front of the house.

"Blue," greeted Cora with a smile. "I snuck a special treat from my bastard husband! A sugar tart." Cora giggled. "If we add some of the pomegranate tonight—"

"I don't care," Avva said with a smile. She helped the goddess down from the black beast and hugged her. "I'm just happy to see you. It's been days, Cora." Avva gently pushed her back and smiled. Cora wore the same animal fur over a beautiful red peplos. "You look good."

"I'm happy to be back," Cora said, touching her shoulder. "And I also brought us some meat."

"Meat! What kind?"

"Mutton."

"You're kidding."

"It's from the surface. Hades brought it for me, so I stowed it in the bag. I was kind of hoping that we could sit by the fire tonight and eat while we play spades or dice?"

"Sure, Cora."

"Help me with the bags, won't you?"

Avva untied leather bags from the konobera as Cora brought two into the house. Avva ran her hands over the tarlike black feathers of the horse. She marveled at how ugly this horse was compared with her unicorns back home. Even the feathers felt prickly.

"Any news from the surface?" Avva asked, turning to Cora as she fetched more bags. "Everything well in Azure? My daughter, Casey? And my husband?"

"Everything's well," Cora said, flashing a smile. "Don't worry. It'll be easier if you just forget about them."

"But I still want to know they're all right."

"They're fine. Your daughter is the Azure queen. And your husband is ruler of all of Atlantis."

"Casey, I'm sure, is a better queen than I ever was. She learned from the horrors your family wrought when Zeus brought her down here. It matured her. As horrible as it was, it made her a better person."

"Can't say it made me a better one," Cora said with, indeed, a sly grin. Then she kneeled down and removed meat from a bag. Though it was not cooked, Avva relished the smell. "You believe your daughter's abduction was Zeus's doing now? Not mine?" Cora stopped for a moment and looked up at Avva with her bright blue eyes, seemingly hopeful. "That means a lot to me."

"You've been so kind, Cora."

Cora smiled and handed her the meat. Then she emptied more bags from the konobera.

Avva looked back at the desert. She hid her rage. She would never forgive Cora and her husband for imprisoning her daughter, whether it was her fault or not. She'd never forgive any of the gods.

When Avva was first brought to Hasevalah, she fought constantly with Cora. But she learned quickly to back down when Cora's eyes scorched red. In rage, Cora turned into a monster with so much venom that she could hurt or even kill Avva.

"Night is coming," Cora said by the door. "Why not come inside, Blue?"

The darkness in Hasevalah was short, so Cora and Avva would spend some of the "night" with the shutters and door closed to create more darkness. Somehow, after centuries down in the depths, Cora always knew the time. Avva still didn't.

Throughout their "night," they played spades. A single lantern, the same lantern that Avva had seen when she first met Cora under Azure, was their only source of light. This was enough light for, soon, if Avva looked toward the door, or even the walls, she'd see the bright light of "day" cracking through the wood. She'd sleep under this light later.

After supper, Avva reclined on a fur rug. She yawned and looked at her bed to prepare for sleep. There was bitterness in that. Her life had become akin to her being a pet. She had no purpose other than to eat, sleep, and entertain this goddess. She seemed to simply survive for Cora's amusement. Meat or not, everything was becoming a monotonous routine.

"I don't think I can carry on like this much longer," Avva said, in a tone far bitterer than intended, staring at the fur rug. She was speaking more to herself.

"What do you mean?"

"I can't do this," Avva said, shaking her head. "I'm trying. I'm grateful. But I don't see why you're letting me live, Cora."

"Oh, Avva," Cora said, sorting through cards on the ground beside her. "I'm protecting you. If my family knew you were here, they'd hunt you down and kill you."

Avva lowered her head and cried. It wasn't the first time. Avva cried often. Oddly, it was only when she was in the company of the goddess.

"I'm sorry," Avva said, choking up. "I'm so happy to see you again, Cora."

Cora jumped up and walked to the door. The light was

blinding as she opened it. Then came a frigid, icy breeze. She cocked her head back and said, "I swore to you that the days are worth living. In time, I foresee you'll be happy. You must wait. You have to be patient."

"I won't live forever like you," Avva said between tears. "Not after I left Azure and stepped foot in the Hinterlands. I'm mortal and I don't have forever, like you."

"Try a little meat," Cora said, still holding the door. "Oh, please, give me a little bit of happiness, nymph. Please. Don't talk about it. I'm your friend. Trust me. Just a little longer."

"Why save me to be imprisoned?" Avva said, shaking her head. "It shall drive me mad. I'm going completely mad! One day, I warn you, you'll return from Tartarus to see my body lying in the sand."

That was it. Cora slammed the door behind her. Cora always did that when they fought. Sometimes she'd return, other times she'd be gone for days. When she was gone, Avva would miss her again. But Avva's torment never left her.

5

THE SEA GOD

Theseus's ship landed in Naxos toward evening. Naxos was a small island known for celebration and festival. It was the island of the god Dionysus. Out of all the Greek islands, it was the only one Theseus had visited more often than Knossos in Crete. Perhaps it was because it was the only island close to his homeland that the gods permitted him to sail to. He anchored his ship and set up camp on the beach with his men. In darkness, he couldn't appreciate the beauty of the desolate isle. There wasn't much to see except shadows of hills in the distance and a dark sea. But it was pleasant and a perfect destination to think.

Whenever he fell contemplative, he resigned himself to walking along the shore. So while his men slept, he walked along the sand.

Waves brushed his shoes calmly. He could just make out the dark outline of them moving in the sea under the full moon. He picked up a shell and threw it toward the water. Then he looked down again at his shoes. These were his father's, one of the only possessions he held from King Aegeus.

He would have to return to Azure Blue to try to obtain the cap again. The cap was his only way into the Underworld. And upon landing in Azure Blue, he'd see that wonderful girl, the

Amazon queen, Cassandra, again. She so enchanted him. She was as lovely and dangerous a nymph as the ones myths sang about.

The water rose higher. After it receded, it rose too high, crashing against his knees. The next wave knocked him off his feet. He turned in the shadows and saw something moving toward him in the water. A tall, shirtless man with broad shoulders and a long beard carried a large trident that glimmered in the moonlight. His eyes glowed green in the darkness. And although he had a gray beard and long gray hair, his stomach was rippled with muscles. The water parted as he stood before Theseus.

Theseus did not rise.

"My son," Poseidon said, standing over him. "I heard your prayers."

"Ah father. Such an honor." He bowed low again. "It's been too long."

"Rise, Theseus Aegeus. Come walk with me."

"Yes, Father."

"What troubles you?" Poseidon asked as they walked. "You've made me proud as our champion of justice. Calliope sang of Sinis, the tree bender—great justice you bestowed, indeed, killing a villain who tore his victims apart between trees; then the Crommyonian sow; then Sciron, the wicked, who killed innocent guests when washing their feet; Procrustes, who changed his victims' size with an axe. And Cercyon, who dared wrestle you. All these villains you punished rightly, and Zeus shall reward you."

"When will I be home?"

Poseidon gazed at him with those glowing emerald eyes, so green that they shone under the moonlight. "After the Minotaur. Why ask me this?"

Theseus sighed.

"Soon cometh the climacteric year," continued Poseidon as they walked. They headed back to his ship and tents by the shore. "Such a fight shall be sung about for the ages. Upon this last feat—so says the prophecy of the grain goddess, Kore—your crown will be yours."

"Yes, Father."

"And now, I see your camp. You travel with your friend Pirithous and that pretty Minoan princess, Ariadne?"

"Yes, my companions and the princess travel with me."

"Where do you sail next?"

"Azure Blue. I still must retrieve the cap."

"I will aid you with swift travel."

"Thank you. But it is not the sea that worries me."

"What troubles you? Do not hold doubt of Zeus's will. You only need to slay the Minotaur. Is it that? Or do you fear travel through my brother's lair?"

"The Amazon are strong, Father. I met their queen. She is a very strong woman."

"Did you like her?" he said with an amused smile. "I helped my dryads be beautiful—not far from my sea nereids. Ah, like my lovely wife, Amphitrite. But Cassandra is a wood nymph. A heretic. She's born and bred for Atlantis. So she shall be cursed in Atlantis."

Theseus nodded. The god stopped and scrutinized Theseus curiously.

"I do like her," Theseus said.

"How so, my child?"

"I was struck by her. When I failed in my search for Hades' helm, I found her. I adored her spirit. I've never met a woman like her." He gazed up at Poseidon, but he didn't like his wry smile. "I will have her as my own. Out of all women, she shall be mine."

"You will not," Poseidon said, as if it were common knowledge. "I tell you Zeus and Hera will see to it that you do not. Why did you fail in retrieving the cap?"

"I searched her chamber in Egypt, but couldn't find it. Are you certain she had it with her there?"

"Do not doubt my words."

"Well, I'm betting on it now being in her royal quarters in Azure."

"How will you get it?"

"I hope to search and find it."

"No," Poseidon said, stopping again with a smile. He unfolded a golden fabric carried in the folds of his pants. The fabric shone in the moonlight as he handed it to him. Theseus stared in amazement. "Offer her this."

"How did you come across it?" Theseus's eyes bulged. "I thought it was lost?"

"Do not doubt the power of the gods," Poseidon said, resuming his walk. "Offer her the Golden Fleece. You will not find my brother's helm in the nymph palace. The nymphs are far too clever. Trade the fleece for the cap. Remind the queen of her great-grandmother's sacrifice for it in their Amazon war in the North. This is a treasure that is of unmatched value, particularly for an Amazon. She will give you the cap in return. I'm sure she will."

"Yes, with such a trade, surely." Theseus shook his head. "I don't understand you gods. How is it so easy for you to carry this? If it's this easy, why don't you just go and retrieve the helmet?"

"Do you think I could have evaded the dragon in Colchis? Jason had the help of that witch Medea. Getting it from a castle might have been easy for your friend, but not for us. We are mighty, but we don't have dealings with witches and dragons."

"Medea," Theseus said with a nod, running his fingers along the soft golden hairs of the fleece. "What a bitter tragedy for Jason. I still grieve for him."

"Your stepmother, Medea, is as vile as a wood nymph. When you finally see your father, Aegeus, you may avenge Jason."

"I will."

"Good. Trade the fleece for the cap with the nymph."

"If Cassandra will accept. And even if she does, she insists there's no way into the Underworld. I have another plan, but it's treacherous."

"What is your plan, my son?"

"I can't say."

A flash of red twinkled in Poseidon's green eyes. "Don't hide anything from me."

"Father, if I tell you, it could compromise the quest. You're too close with your brother."

He squinted at Theseus. Then he slowly nodded. "So be it. Get the cap before the first day of the climacteric year. Then comes your great battle with the Minotaur. Then pass Tartarus and claim your birthright."

Poseidon picked up some sand. He sifted through it and took out a small abalone shell with multiple shades of blue.

"Beauty can sometimes be only for the eyes, my son. The Azure queen is a wood nymph. Wood dryads delight in hubris. Cassandra Ambrosia is not a woman you can control. You shall be a great king. This was foreseen by the oracle at Delphi. Your rule will provide order in Hellena. You must find a fine Greek woman, not a Napean nymph."

He cracked the beautiful shell in his hand and inside slithered a black worm. The message was clear enough.

Then, with a powerful arm—Theseus guessed he had the strength of ten men—he patted Theseus on the back. "And now, I ask *you*—when will you claim your throne? Do not ask me. You tell me."

"In Naxos, I am close."

"Yes." Poseidon took a deep breath and nodded, closing his eyes. "We've waited too long for Zeus's kingdom of man. Finally, he and I shall rule over man in Attica, as is our right."

The god gazed at Theseus's camp of tents. Then he gazed at the hero's ship, anchored near the shore. The god frowned.

"Theseus, I must ask one more thing of you. This is something that will be hard."

"Anything, great Poseidon," he said with a bow.

"Perhaps this won't sting so much since you fancy other women." He put his hand on Theseus's shoulder again. "Leave

Ariadne. After you defeat the Minotaur, after the job is done, I ask that you abandon her."

"What!" Theseus forgot about all social qualms with the god. He felt his face blush with rage.

"You must," Poseidon said with a gentle smile. "She is Minoan. You must find a good wife from Hellena. Anyway, the gods have decreed that you shall give your lovely Ariadne to Dionysus."

"Dionysus? Why does he lay claim?"

"You don't love her," Poseidon said. "You just mentioned Cassandra. Your eyes are on another woman. But you can have neither. Dionysus came to your tent tonight. He watched this young girl with great interest. She is very attractive with an adorable spirit."

"Ariadne is with me!" he snapped. "You won't let me take a nymph? Fine. But I planned to take Ariadne to the Acropolis in Attica to be my queen. She is a princess."

Poseidon burst into laughter. "Oh, come on, Theseus, a Minoan? Not for the great hero Theseus Aegeus. I tell you, you shall have a proper Greek wife."

"Ariadne comes with me."

Poseidon squinted his eyes and the gray flashed red again. He lifted a finger. "Careful. I'm very proud of the rock you lifted and your justice as a hero, but you must follow the rule of the gods."

Theseus looked about him frantically. His mind whirled with thoughts on how to change this verdict. Then he glared at Poseidon.

"Father, you're Poseidon, brother of Zeus and Hades. Certainly, you can stop this. Speak with Dionysus. Tell him that you want her to remain with me. If all the gods respect my hero-ism, let me have her."

"I don't understand why you care. Truly, it's best that you love no woman and simply have your way with them."

"I've lured her to kill her brother!" Theseus clenched his fists and gnashed his teeth. "Now you ask me to use her and then abandon her! That is injustice. You say I am about justice. How can I do this? This is unforgivable."

"You will follow the will of the gods and give her to Dionysus."

"All you gods are heartless!"

A wave crashed to their knees again, as if the tide had changed. Then another threw him onto the wet sand. Poseidon didn't move. The god remained standing over him. But his eyes burned fiery red.

"I didn't hear that." Poseidon shook his head violently. "I couldn't have heard those words… Now you shall provide libations. When you take your throne in Attica, you will build temples to me, structures this world has never seen, as an apology for the words you just uttered. Then you will honor Athena and even Dionysus, yes Dionysus, in your future city. Particularly Dionysus. How dare you compete with a god over a woman. Are you an idiot? You risk losing everything. If you do not apologize, such words will not go unpunished. And you may face the same fate as the nymph you so covet. Will you provide these offerings?"

"I will!" Theseus snapped.

"Honor us, King of Attica," the god said more softly. Then he took a deep breath, closed his eyes, and shook his head. "You've upset me. Oh, Theseus, let us not leave like this. Ariadne is lust. This is as foolish as speaking of love for a wood nymph. Don't anger me like this again. We'll provide you a fitting Greek woman. And your name shall be sung for the ages."

Theseus nodded. But a darkness fell over his heart.

"After you get my brother's helm, son, return to Ariadne," Poseidon said, his eyes turning green again. He even smiled under the moonlight. "Have her help you reach the Minotaur on the first day of the climacteric year. Do this last heroic deed and then go to the Underworld. It is so willed by Zeus."

"As you wish, Father." He kneeled before him, but it seemed to take a great effort of will.

"Go swiftly with the speed of Hermes, my son. Take your crown. After you do, I will visit you in your city. We have decided that we will bless your city with a new name. You shall call it Athens after my niece. Together, Athena and I will make Athens a powerful empire for man. A city of justice under the king of justice. And believe me, it will be far more glorious than Egypt or Atlantis, for your people shall respect the gods of Mount Olympus."

Poseidon tapped Theseus's shoulder gently and walked slowly back into the sea. Theseus watched as the god simply walked into the shadows of the waves until his head was submerged.

6

MY ARIADNE

THESEUS GAZED AT THE GORGEOUS TANNED FIGURE OF THE GIRL
sleeping naked beside him, in his tent, under soft yellow flickering
candlelight. Her flowing curly brown hair ran all the way down
her side, tangling around cleavage, mocking modesty. They were
alone. The room was small with only a bed and a long wooden
table. A faint sliver of torchlight shone through two small holes in
the tent.

Ariadne.

He clenched his fists. She was to be his wife. Now Poseidon
demanded he abandon her. That would make him exactly the
fiend Cassandra claimed he was.

Cassandra. She was as beautiful as Ariadne, and she was
fearless and strong. She did not act like a woman, nor like any
girl he had ever known. She acted like his equal. No other
woman had ever acted like that around him.

He could not have either of them.

Now he thirsted for beer, wine, and spirits to forget it all. And
Ariadne.

He stared at the girl's mouth, rhythmically opening and closing, and her shoulders and breasts, covered by strands of long

curly hair, moving in unison. Up and down, a soft calm rhythm, almost hypnotic. Instead of making love to a woman like Cassandra, later, he would make love to this Minoan girl named Ariadne. Not more beautiful than Casey, but more vibrant and, perhaps, just as dangerous.

He turned and looked out through the crack in the tent, but he could see nothing outside in the darkness. He carefully rose from bed. He sat with his head in hands, running fingers through his curly hair. Then he felt a cold hand on his shoulder. Ariadne blinked at him with her lovely large green eyes that seemed to glow in the candlelight. He didn't like her eyes. They reminded him of Poseidon.

"What's the matter?" she asked. "Hmm, Theseus? You look sad. How can anyone be sad when we're together? Hmm?" She kissed his cheek and neck, giggled, and touched him between his legs, but he quickly pushed her away. Then she giggled again, just like a little girl, and said, "Come back to bed with me."

"Go to sleep, Ariadne."

She yawned. "I'm not tired."

"It's late. Go to sleep."

"You're not my father. And I said I'm not tired."

She reached out her arms and gave a great stretch. Her hair fell back behind her and revealed her perky breasts. He knew she did that on purpose.

He rose.

"You're not going back to drink with Pirithous, are you?"

"No. And I wasn't out drinking."

"Well, where are you off to then? Are you going to slay another dragon?" She laughed.

He whirled around, angry. But her smile and the sound of her sweet laughter disarmed him. "Go to bed, my Aphrodite."

"Humph!" She folded her arms and fell back in bed, pouting.

"Well, don't go." She patted the bed. "Lie with me for the rest of the night. I ask that a hero keep this princess warm."

He shook his head, but she snatched his wrist and gently

pulled him back on the soft mattress. Then she leaned over and played with his curly hair.

"Does your father know where you go all these nights?" he asked as she massaged his head.

"No. I tell him I travel to my auntie's. She doesn't live far from the palace, you know. He never knows where or when. I just sneak out." His back was turned to her. She chuckled and pulled at him to turn toward her, but he wouldn't. "Anyway, Father wouldn't mind so much knowing I'm with a hero such as yourself."

She grabbed his forearm, nearly twice the size of her own, and wrapped her naked body around his massive physique. Then she giggled some more as she kissed his arms and back.

"Come on, Theseus. Make love to me again."

"I'm leaving tomorrow."

"What?"

"I have to sail for Napea in Atlantis. It's too dangerous for you to accompany us this time." He finally turned toward her. She looked angry. He shrugged his shoulders. "Sorry."

"Humph!" she exclaimed and jumped up. She walked over and pulled a transparent saffron night peplos over her head. Then she grabbed a brush, leaned on her side on a rug, and ran it through her long dark hair. He came to her and lay a hand on her shoulder, but she swatted it away.

"Don't touch me! You always go somewhere. Naxos. Ogygia. Egypt. Now to stupid Napea." She turned to him and scowled. "Going to have sex with a wood nymph? Huh?"

He laughed. She turned away from him and hammered the rug with her fist.

"Hmm? Is this the last time we shall see each other?"

"Of course not." He touched her cheek. She grabbed his hand and pushed it away. "You are my Ariadne."

"And what is that? Hmm? What is *my Ariadne*? What does that mean? Am I some thing? Some Minoan prostitute?"

"You are a princess. And more beautiful than any other woman in all of Gaia."

"More beautiful then Cassandra Ambrosia?" She cocked her head back and squinted. He furrowed his brow as if he didn't know who that was. "You know," she said, raising her eyebrows as if he were an idiot, "*the queen of Azure?*" She smiled a little. Then she pointed her brush at him as if it were a weapon. "What do you intend to do to their *beautiful* Amazon queen when you see her? Hmm?"

"This!" And he grabbed her and threw her back onto the bed. Then he pulled up her dress, exposing her naked legs. She giggled the whole time.

"Stop!" she said laughing. "Stop it! You'll tear the dress!"

He lay on top of her and kissed her lips hard.

She looked up with hungry eyes in the candlelight. "Theseus, what will you do with this *more beautiful* nymph? Bed her? You can tell *your Ariadne.*"

"I love only you."

And perhaps that was the truth. But that made him more bitter as he remembered Poseidon's command tonight.

She pushed him off. Then flashed a wry smile, still lying with her dress up to her neck, exposing her breasts. She smiled lewdly.

"It's time, princess."

"Time for what?" She smiled, blinking.

"It's been too long. I need you to grant me an audience with your father when I return. It must be done exactly the day of my return."

She looked at him as if considering the request. She pouted again. But then she nodded with a smile.

"Ariadne, you must not tell anyone my name," he said, raising a finger. "Say I am Aejades, if you must. Do not call me Theseus. Just grant me an audience. Can you do it?"

"But why?"

"You'll see soon enough."

"It'd be easier if I tell him you're Theseus, the great hero."

"Don't give him my name."

"All right. Perhaps. Only if you do something for me in return."

"What?"

She giggled, pulled her dress over her head, and embraced him tightly, kissing him passionately.

7

THE AZURE QUEEN

CASSANDRA FOLLOWED HER FATHER DOWN THE ROYAL HALL TO AN indoor lookout. This interior balcony faced three stories of glass. It was her and her mother's favorite spot in the palace, perhaps everybody's, for it showed a vista of the entire blue kingdom. Legend said the indoor balcony was created by Hades for Harmonia. At the base of a spiral stairway always stood two guards at attention in scarlet armor. It was a magnificent lookout, one her mother had showcased to foreigners when they used to visit her in Azure Blue. Of course, her father knew how much Casey loved it too.

This afternoon it was cloudy, but she could still see the brown lands of the Crescent Kingdom on the horizon. And the coastal blue-green forest by the sea. The giant wall of blue, Mount Ambitus, reached to the clouds on her right. And many nymphs were lounging or playing in the purple grass fields below.

Her father leaned over the rails somberly and stared off at the horizon.

"I've gazed upon this ever since I was a boy, Casey," he said. "Ever since your grandfather took me to his summer castle in Crescent Blue. Aye, it's beautiful. The blue is so blue it can burn a man's eyes. And to think..." He turned and smiled at

Cassandra and ran his hand along her bangs. "I've been blessed with being able to touch it."

Mother again. He's not thinking of me, he's thinking of Mother.

"You have me," she said, forcing a smile. It sounded childish, but she didn't mind after a day of queen business.

"Aye," he said, gazing back at the window. "That I do. You inherited your mother's beauty. You even look like her. And I hear you've also inherited her distaste for the crown."

"You noticed?"

"Engel told me," he replied, shaking his head.

"It's boring," she said with a sigh. "But that's okay. I'm getting used to it."

He just nodded and stared at the horizon.

"What's the matter, Father?" She touched his hand. "What did you want to tell me? When are you leaving?"

"What makes you think I'm leaving?" He turned with an amused smile.

"You always look sad when you leave. You're never happy doing it. Only, this time, you're not leaving Mother."

"I'm leaving you," he said, touching her hair again. He turned back to the window and took a deep breath. "I wish you were still a princess."

Because then Mother would still be here.

"I'm proud of you, Casey. You may hate being queen as much as Anna did, but you rule as well as she did, if not better."

It started to rain. But even the rain behind the glass was welcoming in the warm hall.

"I hope this isn't a bad omen for my journey," he said.

"Where are you going?"

"Arbor Dunn."

"Where Uncle passed?"

"Aye. King Philipp ran the town to the ground. As nomads, his men didn't care for buildings. It was not only the land of Henri's death, it was where he was born. So we shall honor it. We shall rebuild it. But there's another reason."

Cassandra turned and her father peered into her eyes for a moment, as if considering whether to tell her more news.

"We've been attacked." He quickly lifted his hand. "Don't worry, it was a small skirmish, more of a test. It was far out to sea, closer to Crete. The villains were Greek bandits coming to torch our new port. But we anticipated it. Azerban is closest to our merchant routes to the West. It's an important port now."

"So it's war, Father?"

"It's been war for a while," he said with a shrug. "We sank one of their ships and captured another."

"Is the harbor safe?"

"Safe enough. Thanks to Torinth's naval ships. And, speaking of your uncle…" He leaned forward and paused, gripping the rail tightly. "I'm freeing him."

"You're freeing the Tiger King?"

"Aye," he said. It was raining hard now, and Casey spotted many nymphs running back up the grassy hills to the palace for shelter. "I need him. Just as I need you—not as a daughter, but as a queen and the protector of my nymphs. In my absence, while I am in the South, I need you to rule Azure Blue."

"I don't want to."

"As I said, neither did your mother," Sol said, chuckling. "But I need you, Casey. Just as I need Torinth right now."

"All right. And go ahead and free a madman while you're at it, Daddy."

"I have. He's coming here."

"What!" She stared at him. He laughed. But as pleasant as it was to finally hear laughter from him, she didn't share his merriment.

"Azure Blue is a direct neighbor of Adelain. Not only am I freeing my brother, I'm allowing him to be regent in Adelain and Crescent Blue. He'll rule and defend your shores while I'm away in the South. But you will protect my greatest treasure—the Isle of Napea."

"Why are you freeing him?"

"He's sulked in prison long enough. Out of all of my brothers, your grandfather, Darius, used Torinth as our chief general in battle before the civil war. He is a fierce warrior. His people love him—well, his army does. And not only that, he's the greatest sea commander in Atala. My brother will die for us because our lands and our way of life are threatened.

"The Greeks remind me of the gods, Casey. They espouse freedom and democracy while, you and I know, they are full of lies and deceit. I tell you, if we are conquered, we shall be enslaved. Like I once was with my mother and father. Man is man. And that…" He winked at her. "That is why you must protect your race from us. Azure must remain unsullied. That's been my wish ever since I met your mother."

"Torinth doesn't hate you?"

"There's no love between us," Sol said with a shrug, looking back at the view. "But he respects me. And though unstable, perhaps mad, he's loyal."

"We don't need his protection. I can defend the isle without him."

"I don't agree. You nymphs can't fight at sea. You need one another. Give Torinth a chance. He'll claw at you. He'll bite. But the tiger has great honor. Show him strength and he'll respect and defend you with his life."

"If you wish it," she said with a sigh.

"I wish it. He'll be arriving shortly after I leave. In one moon."

"One moon! You can't be serious?" Cassandra felt her eyes bulge.

As a little girl, she had heard of the atrocities of the Tiger King. He was an animal. Indeed, a tiger, known to send soldiers, even his own people, to certain death for even minor offenses.

"When we speak of war, we speak of battle in moons, not years," he said with a forlorn smile. "This comes quick. Treat him as a royal guest. Extend all courtesies. He is a part of our family."

"Father, even if you've made amends with him, I haven't. I was told he wanted to burn Azure to the ground. And Mother fought many of his men when they invaded during the Battle of Polis. She froze a great many too. I think Mother would never allow this."

"Take this as your first test as an Azure queen. Be yourself. Unlike your mother, you do not have Imada. But you have Engel. Work with him. We will weather this war together. I ask that you cooperate with your uncle for defense."

"Well, I won't suddenly become his loving niece."

"Just as I'm not his loving brother."

Cassandra hung her head. But she nodded.

"Be the princess who survived the Underworld," he said, lifting up her chin. She looked up and he brushed her hair back. "Goodbye, Casey. Our world is in peril. And it is because of the power of your mother's family. Truly, your mother created this empire. Not me. But I will protect and defend it with my life."

"You have, Daddy."

"I give you, out of everyone I know, my most precious jewel." And he gestured to the vista before them. "You are not only queen. You shall protect Azure Blue. Do you understand how important this is?"

"Yes."

He embraced her. "Without your mother, you are the only one I have left in the world. I have nothing else. Take care of my home. But most importantly, take care of yourself."

8

YOU AGAIN

It rained for days after her father left, flooding parts of her kingdom. Already, even without the problem of war, her people were asking for support with the harvest. And now it was late. After delegating many difficult decisions over property, Cassandra returned, alone and exhausted, to her bedchamber.

Her royal bedroom was the largest in the palace, said to have been built for the great Queen Harmonia. The floor and ceiling were white marble, and each of the lovely columns was embellished with vines made of gold in relief. Scarlet curtains draped the walls. And a bed big enough for three people to sleep in. When Casey was little, she remembered playing on an animal hide next to the bed while her mother and father played spades. She felt it was her father's room, and when he had come home recently, she had actually expected he'd reside there. But it was Queen Cassandra's room now.

It lay on the third floor, facing the east side of the palace. It was sectioned in two by steps. One section had a table where she could take supper or, if desired, conduct business. Down a few steps were the bed and dressers. Like everything created by Harmonia, the table section was likely created for war. There was an additional oak room, through an adjoining narrow hall, full of clothes. She was about her mother's size and Casey wore many of her dresses.

Cassandra untied her rope belt and pulled the fibula from her shoulder, laying it down on a bench. Then she sat by a beauty table, on a stool, removing her earrings before a large mirror. Candlelight flickered off the mirror from candles, all about the room, lit by her attendants.

Oddly, she noticed two unlit candles in a corner of the room. Why were they not lit?

She rose and peered more closely at the darkness. Then she lurched back after seeing a man's shoe in the shadows near her wooden desk. And she recognized his shoe. She shrieked and covered her linen bra.

"Sorry, I tried to leave," said a man's voice. "I didn't mean to catch you unaware, maiden."

That royal jeweled shoe was Theseus's. "Show yourself, Theseus, you degenerate!"

This time she didn't have a sword, but the guards were downstairs not far from her bedchamber. They'd hear her if she screamed.

"I must protest," he said with a chuckle. "I'm a decent man."

"You're a fiend! How? Why are you in my bedchamber?"

"I had to see you," he said. "I mean…" He walked out of the darkness, covering his eyes with a hand. Casey ran to the bench, grabbed her clothes, and threw them back on. "I've been bewitched ever since the first time I saw you in—"

"Enjoying such a view is not complimentary."

"You put a spell on me, Cassandra. I can't stop thinking of you."

She laughed at his bravado.

Now his face was illuminated by the flickering light. He was tanned and clean-shaven with dark, curly hair, perfectly groomed. He wore royal clothes with a pressed chiton. Handsome. But he still stupidly held a hand over his eyes.

"Open your eyes, idiot. This time it's my bedchamber? And…how did you possibly get in?"

"I'm very sneaky," he replied with a wily smile. "Please, don't call your guards. I told you last time, with the current state of affairs, this is the only way I can see you."

"And I told you everything I know about entering the Underworld."

"That may be true, but—"

"Step back! You're getting too close. I haven't forgotten how fast you are and what you did last time."

"I liked that." He smirked but stepped back and bowed. "As you wish, Amazon Queen."

"You came in my chamber to look upon me naked again?"

"No. I came to speak with you again. I have an offer. Let me tell you before you call your guards."

"Speak quickly."

"Hades is known to use his chariot to fly into the Mount in Napea. Right?"

Cassandra nodded.

"He flies by winged konobera, special stallions made by my father, which allow him to travel to the surface and spread his evil throughout Greece and Atlantis."

"Aye. I've seen the chariot."

"Incredible." Theseus's eyes widened. "It's incredible that you *saw* the chariot, woman."

"I am not a woman."

"You're better," he murmured, looking down.

"What?" she asked with a laugh.

"Ah, and that laughter, too," he said, closing his eyes as if in rapture. "It is like the greatest elixir from the gods."

She couldn't suppress another laugh.

"We are cursed in that we can't share more time."

"But we can't. And in another moment, I'm going to scream."

"Before you scream, let me tell you what I will do. I intend to sneak up on the god of the Underworld and hitch a ride."

Cassandra burst into laughter. Then she laughed even more

at his serious expression. Yet, of all men, she thought he was crazy enough to do it.

"What's so funny?"

"You'll be killed on the spot!"

"True. That's true for a normal mortal. But not with your help. Rumor is you have his helm. Give it to me. If you give me the Cap of Hades, he won't see me enter his chariot. I'll hitch a ride. Then I will travel the Underworld and exit Eleusis. From there, I'll emerge, head to Attica, and take my crown. Easy."

"Sure. And if he hears you, he'll still kill you."

"I suppose here in Atlantis you have not heard of the feats of the great Theseus Aegeus." He thumped his chest. "I'm not averse to danger. Witness my presence in an Amazon queen's bedchamber, Cassandra."

"There's only one problem with your plan, degenerate," Casey said, sitting back in her vanity chair. But she watched him cautiously. "Who's to say I have it? And why would I ever give it to you?"

"If you give it to me, I shall offer you something of far greater value."

He lifted a finger. Then he walked back to the shadows where no candles were lit. He brought out something that reflected gold in the candlelight. It was beautiful. He approached Cassandra, took a knee, and offered it to her with both hands. She jumped back in her chair. He gently laid the fleece along the floor under her. The gold shimmered over the white marble.

"This is the Golden Fleece of Colchis. I went with Jason on his journey to take this golden kursa. If you've not heard of my heroism, perhaps you've heard the tale of Jason and his ship, the Argo? I was one of the Argonauts."

"I've heard of it," she said with a nod. Carefully, while still looking at him, she snatched the fleece. Then she laid it on her lap, staring at it.

"You're young," he said as she ran her fingers along the Golden Fleece. "Your mother, the great Queen Avivae, passed only a few moons ago. If you were to show your people this fleece, the fleece that your people fought a war over under your queen Danaë, your rule would be unquestioned. This and your scepter would assure your power in Azure Blue for the rest of your days. Not to mention the sheer worth of the fleece alone."

Cassandra was speechless. Her blue fingers stroked the soft hide. Even the touch was pleasurable. She couldn't even believe she had it on her lap.

She shook her head and offered it back to him. "I can't take this. Not for what you ask for. I can't trust you. I fear you'll use the cap against us."

"So you do have it," he said with a wide grin.

She nodded. "No one should have the power of Hades' Cap. No one but Hades. Truly, if things had been different and he had come to me, I would have just given it to him. But my mother never told me that he had asked for it back. Persephone gave it to me when she cared for me down in Tartarus. It's how I escaped."

"Then you must understand how important it is for my quest. I don't see any other way of traveling the depths and escaping."

"Your quest is suicide. You'll die. I told you in Egypt that Persephone watched over me. And I learned that even Hades protected my life. Without their protection—"

"Legend says your second queen traveled without any such protection."

"She went down to save Persephone."

"To save her," Theseus said with a nod. "Yes. And Nefertiti survived. It can be done, Cassandra. Give me the cap. You have no need for it. But I must travel the depths. It is the only way Olympus will give me my kingdom."

"The gods are so cruel."

"More so than you can imagine."

He gazed in her eyes and flashed a rueful grin. For a second, she felt like he was meeting her gaze to hypnotize her with guile. But he shrugged. Casey couldn't suppress a laugh.

"I tell you what," he said, smiling again. "I will offer you far more even then King Pelias's fleece. Not only do I offer you this Golden Fleece, I offer you my heart. If you give me the helmet, you will aid a man in his quest to go home. And—think this over carefully, Queen Cassandra—I will be ruler of the greatest kingdom in Hellena. And I will be forever in your debt. Do you believe that I would ever raise arms against you after this gesture?" He shook his head hard and fell on his knees again. "No. I swear, I won't. After seeing you, I could never. Not only do I offer you power and riches, I offer you peace. Perhaps that is an even greater reward than the fleece itself?"

"Yes, it is. You swear peace with us?"

"I swear it." And he bowed again. "Peace with you, always, yes."

"Rise, Prince of Attica."

He stood. "You believe I'm one now?"

"That fleece tells me you are. But you're also conceited and a bit of a scoundrel."

"I am a scoundrel," he said with a nod.

Cassandra walked over to her oak dresser. Then she said, "Help me move this."

"You trust me near you, Aphrodite?"

"I would have called the guards if I didn't."

Cassandra showed him where to push the wooden furniture. He placed his hand over her fingers. She turned and looked deeply into his eyes again. Then he broke their gaze and pushed.

She was surprised at his strength. Behind the dresser was a hole in the wall, and deep inside was a silver helmet. Theseus reached in to grab it, but Casey snatched his wrist and shook her head.

"You'll die if you use it. I warn you and beg you not to do this, Theseus. If Hades finds you, he'll kill you on the spot. I know he will. You'll have no protection."

Theseus pulled his hand from her and snatched the helm. He got up and ran his fingers along the shiny silver metal with the same "ah" that Cassandra had exclaimed over his fleece.

He smirked again. Then...he grabbed her. But in his arms, she felt that he hadn't grabbed her to harm her. No. He took her firmly, but tenderly, in his embrace, kissing her. Although fast and sudden, he was so gentle. He held her tight. The kiss in Egypt was a peck. This was passionate. Soon their tongues intertwined, and she felt his fingers brush her bosom and hip. She ran her fingers through the curls on the back of his head.

"Have I erred?" he breathed in her ear.

She shook her head.

"You've bewitched me," he said. "I have never desired a woman more." But he pulled away and sighed. "But I can't ask for more than a kiss. Though your love would be greater. Alas, Amazon, I must go. So that the trade is clear, look at your chair. The Golden Fleece is still there. And now you know my heart. Peace will be ours. And if I am king of Athens, damn be any battle or even the gods that stand in the way of us. I shall be friends with the queen of Atlantis. I swear my life on it."

"Don't do this," she warned, still holding his hand. "You won't survive."

"I hope you're wrong. Then we shall never see each other again."

And with that, he rushed into the darkness toward the door.

"Wait," Cassandra said.

He stopped.

"How will you evade the guards? Even with the helm, there are Amazon guarding every exit to the palace."

"The same way as before."

She walked over and snatched his arm again, this time to turn him so he was facing her. "Don't go. Stay."

He hesitated, looking down.

"Tell me of your lands, Theseus. Tell me of Crete."

He looked into her eyes again and ran his hand slowly down her dark hair. Half of him leaned toward her door, but the other half swayed, undecided, beside her.

"If you go, I'll cry out to the guards." But this time, she laughed. Then he laughed with her.

As quickly as he had pecked her lips in Egypt, he grabbed her once more. And once more, she was lost in his arms.

Had he deceived her? She wondered that as he caressed her.

Perhaps the fleece was a trick, only to fade with the dousing of candlelight in the morning? Perhaps Theseus himself was only an illusion. Yes, perhaps her hero would fade into the night. She was lonely enough to imagine that.

No, he was here.

Soon he was naked in her bed. His strong arms cradled her, caressing her skin and breasts. They lay entwined. He was the first man she had ever lain with—a hero from an enemy country. When the morning came, he would have to leave. The palace intrigue of an Amazon queen loving a Greek at the brink of war would be intolerable. They both knew that. But for now, tonight, they held each other. Now she shared his secret. Now she too would be a scoundrel. And, though this degenerate ruffian was untrustworthy and scheming, a man who had caught her nude and half-dressed, somehow she felt he loved her. And, after all, it was she who had stopped him from leaving. Perhaps she was falling in love with him too?

He kissed her, gripping her legs tightly as if not wanting to ever part.

Perhaps she had wooed him? Just like the legendary Queen Harmonia, who had lured men centuries ago. Whatever the case, being in his grasp was a magical moment that she cherished and desired to never end.

9

THE CLIMACTERIC YEAR

THE PALACE AT KNOSSOS WAS MORE OF A SERIES OF TENTS AND scattered thatched-roof dwellings than a castle. When compared to the palace of the Azures, it looked like a nomadic village. Yet it was the hub of all social life for the Minoans. All dirt roads led to the center of the city, and at the center lay the throne of King Minos.

Theseus wore ragged peasant clothes as two guards greeted him before the entrance. They checked his papers then looked upon his royal seal—a seal given to him by Ariadne the day before. Then they nodded and gestured for him to enter.

There were jugglers and dancers among the inner Court, starting up the path on a slope toward the throne room. The roofing was made of cloth tenting, but it stood almost four stories high. He had to push through many beggars. Then he made his way up some steps and approached another two guards before a main hall.

The throne room was grand. This room was made of stone held by stone columns. It was large enough to hold over forty people. At the center was a wooden stage, and lying on his side was King Minos. He was surrounded by a few advisors in purple robes, sitting or lying on the floor beside him. Many were rustling through parchments. A few maidens in white peploi walked by offering them refreshments. By the right of the king stood another lovely girl in a draping white peplos: Ariadne. Her long white dress was attached by a very large golden pendant over her shoulder. Her face was decorated with thick makeup, making her look older than when she visited him. She was adorned with beautiful gold necklaces, bracelets, and rings. Her hair was tied in a chignon. She was absolutely lovely, the most beautiful woman in the whole kingdom. When she spotted Theseus, her eyes twitched nervously.

King Minos was a large man. He had a long bushy brown beard and bushy eyebrows. In one hand, he held a golden goblet; in the other he made frequent animated gestures to his advisors.

Theseus approached and bowed deeply, but it took a while for the king to notice him.

"Hmm? Yes? What is it? Who are you who bows before me?"

"I am Aejades. Son of Horace and Julia."

"Never heard of you," he said, shaking his head. He squinted at his advisors, and they shrugged. "What do you want?"

"It is the day before the climacteric year. The year of sacrifice."

"Everyone knows that."

"What can be done for it to end, my king?"

King Minos's eyes opened wide, and he sat up straighter. It sounded like a challenge. Ariadne ran to her father and whispered in his ear. King Minos pushed his daughter away and squinted at Theseus.

"Who are you?" asked King Minos. "Who has the nerve to ask a king's business?"

"A thousand pardons, my lord." He bowed again. "Of course, it is only *your* business." Theseus put out a hand in protest. "It's about my son..." Theseus covered his face, then he fell to his knees weeping.

"Do not cry, sir," said the king. "Don't act like a...woman."

"Forgive me." Theseus raised his hand between tears. "I've traveled from Attica. My son was seven. He meant the world to me and my wife, Inathra. But, alas, King Aegeus took him on the ships and sent him to the labyrinths. He was slain. At a very young age."

"It is the fault of King Aegeus."

"No doubt, my king," Theseus said, wiping his eyes.

"What do you want from me? Act a man, sir, or I shall have the guards escort you from the throne room."

"My son is gone. But perhaps another can be spared. It's seven years to the day. Zeus's law is to send seven down the labyrinth to the Minotaur. That law's been fulfilled many times over. I ask, no beg you, my king, that you stop the killing of the Greeks."

"If Aegeus wishes to sacrifice himself, then maybe I'll stop the killing." He looked at his advisors and they burst into laughter. "I have no interest in ending my tribute. My son's hungry. Now off with you! … Guards!" He turned to them. "Take this beggar and throw him on the streets! My eyes are sick of him!"

Ariadne touched the king again, but she lurched back after seeing his bulging eyes.

"My Lord King," Theseus said as the guards grabbed him, "you don't understand. I come, not to ask, but to insist! Ever since the death of my son, I can't sleep. Or live."

"Sard you and your son, beggar!"

"Wait!" Theseus yelled as he struggled in their grip. "Take me! I ask to be one of the seven! Take me to the Minotaur!"

The king stumbled and then stared. He raised his hand and the guards halted. He looked at his advisors. They seemed dumbfounded.

It became silent. Until Ariadne gasped with her hand over her mouth.

"What's this? You wish to die?"

"No, sire. I wish to fight the Minotaur."

The king glared, wide-eyed, at Theseus in astonishment.

Then he burst out laughing. He roared with laughter, nodding his head. Then the whole throne room exploded with merriment.

"All right. All right, poor man! Very well. You may go. Instead of by lot, you can meet my son. But you must know, even if you slay him, you'll never escape the maze."

Theseus bowed low. His success brought a slight grin. Then the king returned to laughing with his advisors. "Never has anyone volunteered. How droll! How droll this is!"

"*No!*" cried Ariadne. "*No!* This man is obviously mad, Father! Leave him alone."

"Why should you care about him?" asked the king, cocking his head to his daughter.

Ariadne hesitated. Then she looked at Theseus. She shook her head at him in desperation, but Theseus smiled.

"Guards!" said the king. "Tomorrow marks the climacteric year. Take this fool as one of the seven. If only I could watch. He's Greek so he will count as tribute." He shook his head and repeated Theseus's words, "*I wish to fight the Minotaur.* What an idiot."

"*Do you intend to kill yourself!*" raged Ariadne, hitting his bare chest with her fists.

Theseus's wrists were bound by metal chains above. He wore only pants. He felt the heat against his chest from the torch she held. And the light flickered over her lovely green eyes.

"No, I intend to kill the Minotaur," he answered with a grin. "Ah, Ariadne. My love, do not worry. I've planned this for years."

"My brother will tear you apart!"

"You think so highly of your hero, princess? I thought I was your hero?"

There was silence. Her gaze wandered around the dungeon in a panic. Her face was drawn and her hair was disheveled, but she still had the lovely makeup of the Royal Court.

"Oh Ariadne," Theseus said, "don't worry."

"Fool!" she said, hitting his chest again. "And what was all that nonsense you fed to my father? I didn't know you to be an actor. Who is Aejades? I thought I knew you, but—"

"How would your father have reacted to Theseus, son of King Aegeus? Do you think he would have permitted a prince to be taken to the labyrinth? He would have killed me before his throne. Perhaps, if I was very fortunate, he would still have sent me, but it is more likely that he would have slain me in this dungeon. Oh, Ariadne, you know me better than anyone, dearest. I have to do this. And you know I will do whatever it takes to accomplish it."

And Theseus leaned over and managed to kiss Ariadne on the lips. For a moment, she seemed to relish the closeness and even came closer, pressing her lips harder against his. But then she started crying, their lips still touching.

"Don't worry," he said. "It is for my people's freedom. I didn't tell you because I feared you'd stop me. No one knows the way of the labyrinth except your father."

"I know it."

"*You do?*" he asked, his eyes wide.

Of course she did. He had known she knew the maze since they met.

"It's a secret." She wiped her tears. "My father made me swear to tell no one. And, anyway, you never asked. You won't even be able to find him. The minute you enter the maze, you'll be lost. But I know the way."

"You do?" he asked, feigning surprise again. This time he cursed himself, because he didn't sound convincing. And she squinted.

"Hold on. Wait a minute. Is this what I've been to you all this time?" She hit him on the chest again, this time very hard. "*My Ariadne?* You met me in order to gain access to my father? All to slay my brother, the Minotaur!"

"Yes." Theseus sighed. "Well, it started that way. But you know it's turned into something far better."

She glowered. Then she surprised him by jumping into his

arms and weeping. "Don't do it, Theseus! He'll kill you! I can help you escape."

"I must. Don't worry, my love."

She shook her head and kept crying. Finally, she ran her face along her sleeve and looked behind her. The door to the cell was ajar. She closed it and spoke quietly, but fast.

"Listen to me, liar. Fiend. I love and hate you so much for what you are."

Theseus nodded.

"If you're stupid enough to still do this, this is the way. Three rights, never left and then all the way straight. I've traveled down to feed my starving brother many times. His head is of a bull, but he has the body of a man. It's said the gods cursed him. But not only is he cursed in looks, he is as strong as a bull. If you must go, take a ball of string. This is what I do in case I take a wrong turn in the darkness. I will hide it in your tunic. Unwind it as you walk. In that way, you can follow it back home if you survive. You will not be able to see in the maze. You must feel for each turn."

"Three rights and straight?"

"Yes," she said with a nod. "When your eyes adjust, you may see a thousand more turns. You take the three right turns and don't turn again. The path ahead will eventually make you think it leads to a wall. Push through it. The wall will move and there he will be. But be quick. My brother, though dumb, knows his home. The people who are sacrificed never find him first. He hunts them. But he always brings them back to his lair. If you go quietly enough, you may surprise him."

"Three turns and then straight," he said again.

She nodded.

"Thank you, Ariadne. I owe you."

"Well, I love you. I will sneak you a short xiphos. When you get it, hide it under your tunic. Not even you can slay him with your bare hands. Then, when it is done, I will no longer have to go there." Her face lit up with a smile. "I shall tell my father of our love. He will overlook your Greek blood over ridding the land of this monster. I know he will. Our people will love you. Such a hero, he will let you live with me. We will marry, Theseus. I just know my father shall want you as his own hero if you slay Minofus. He'll let you stay with me, and we can be together in Knossos the rest of our lives, my love."

She hugged him again and kissed him many times on the cheek. Then she fought back tears again as she pulled from his arms. "Be careful. Oh, by Athena, please be careful, Theseus."

10

HER BROTHER

The whereabouts of the Labyrinth of Crete were unknown. Built by Daedalus under the orders of King Minos, only a select few knew of the location of the secret crypt. It was kept secret to protect outsiders from the Minotaur. It is said that the builders working under Daedalus were blindfolded as they sailed to the cave dwelling. Only three sailors, King Minos, and his direct relatives including, of course, Ariadne, knew how to reach Minofus. Now, Theseus was blindfolded too as he accompanied six other Greeks from Attica to their deaths.

Theseus brooded on the ship. Not only was he fearful of his destination, he could not stop thinking of his plight. As time passed, he realized that his night with Cassandra meant more than a chance encounter. He had liked the Amazon since they'd first met. And after the second encounter in Azure, he couldn't stop thinking of how *she* had liked him. Then there was Ariadne. If he survived the Minotaur, he would betray her. He would have preferred taking her as a bride, for he loved her but, by the will of the gods, he had been ordered to abandon her. He loved two women. He could have neither.

The ship captain went below the deck and removed the blindfolds of all the passengers. Then he cut the rope holding their hands. This final act manifested the true source of his fears: the Minotaur. Love lost or not, the approaching battle brought a feeling of sickness and confusion. Fear.

At sword point, each prisoner walked on a sandy beach. Then the guard bade him enter the caves. It was pitch black, as Ariadne had warned. Theseus went last, behind the others, so he could unwind his string.

At first, he seemed to descend slowly into the depths. He groped along moist and muddy walls. Soon he began shivering from cold. The ball of string ran low after his first turn. He rested against the cold wall for a moment.

His skin crawled as he heard the cries of a boy. There had been one child companion who accompanied them. The sounds of screams mixed with the sound of cracking stone must mean the boy was now slain. The sound was close to Theseus. Then more screams, this time from a man. The echoing cries were mixed with grunting noises. The vocalizations sounded like a bear, but louder and deeper. Then he heard another high-pitched scream followed by a crash, and then a thud.

Three lives gone. Already dead. So fast.

Then silence. No, someone was crying further down in the crypt. What an idiot. It would only help the Minotaur find him.

Theseus's hands trembled. Ariadne had said that her brother usually waited to hunt. Everything seemed to be happening too fast. She also said that the Minotaur returned to his lair. That was his only hope.

Theseus reached into his tunic and touched the hilt of the short sword Ariadne had stowed there. Then he pulled it out and kneeled over it on the ground, whispering a prayer to the great goddess Athena.

"Great Athena, I swear my allegiance. Your name shall be sung in my city. If you permit me success, I will provide libations and sacrifice on this day every year in Athens."

He cut his hand with the tip of the sword and let the blood drip as a sacrifice to the gods. He could only feel, not see, the blood in the darkness.

Go swiftly, great hero of Hellena. Complete this task and you shall win favor and hold claim to your kingdom under my name.

"Who speaks?" Theseus asked the shadows.

I am the goddess Athena. I grant your prayer. Your victory is assured, upon your oath.

"Thank you, blessed Athena. Thank you, goddess of my birthright."

The goddess helped break his hesitation. He felt his way down to the second right turn, then the third. At the end of a long hall, he pushed through a wall of mud. Here the stink of fresh blood and flesh permeated the air. Then, in horror, he heard the beast's breath. The Minotaur had dragged his prey back into his lair, as Ariadne had said he would.

"Minofus!" Theseus cried in the darkness. "Come and meet your end, monster! I fight you for all of my people who you've slaughtered. Come, beast! Fight me!"

There was a roar. Then a dim fire was lit on the ground, revealing a shadow of a huge figure with horns crouching over small burning embers. And nearby the beast were fallen bloody bodies. The only one in the chamber was the Minotaur, who must have lit the small fire. It was still very dark in the chamber.

The monster stood up, two times Theseus's height. Although he had black horns, his face was of a bearded man. He charged Theseus. Theseus flew into the air from the terrible force. The impact was that of a charging bull. Theseus slammed against the wall by the entrance of the cave, and his sword fell from his hand.

Theseus pushed himself up, then he groped in the darkness for the blade. But the Minotaur rammed him again and threw him another twenty feet against the opposite wall of his crypt. Theseus rose, winded, gasping for air. Dizzy and unsteady, Theseus charged the bull. The beast easily caught him by the arms and attempted to squeeze the life out of him. He would have succeeded and crushed the hero's thorax, had not Theseus managed to strike Minofus in the stomach and quickly form a gap with just enough space to slide out of the monster's grasp.

Again, Theseus ran toward the monster, hitting him with both hands like a hammer on his head. Then he heard the sound of metal clang against the stone by his feet.

Theseus fell to the ground and groped desperately for his sword. When he found his blade, he lunged it at the beast. He missed and was picked up and hurled again. He charged, stabbing blindly. Something soft met his sword in the darkness.

The Minotaur let out a high-pitched scream. Theseus dug his sword deep into the monster, turning the blade within. His hands were so close he could feel warm blood trickle over his fingers.

"Why! Ahh…why!"

Theseus was shocked to hear distinct words uttered by the creature. He had been told that Minofus was mute. His words were distorted and twisted, sounding more like grunts, but they were discernible words.

"You kill my people!" Theseus answered. "I smite you to free them!"

"Who?" the Minotaur asked as he fell to the ground. "Who?"

"I am Theseus, king of Athens. I kill you and free my people from your terror!"

"Thes-is," he said, trying to pronounce the word. "I Mino-aur. I Mino-n."

I Minoan?

"You eat man!"

"I…" The monster paused, panting. For a moment, the hero thought he was finished. Then he spoke these last words: "I am man."

The air left the beast.

Theseus collapsed on the ground. His chest and back burned. He felt sick and exhausted. Then, in misery, he considered Mino-fus's strange words: *I Minoan. I am man.* Theseus had expected the beast to be simply dumb. He had thought slaying the Minotaur would be like killing a bull. It wasn't. Minofus could speak.

I am man.

Minofus was a man.

I Minoan.

He was a Minoan prince.

Ariadne's brother, to be exact. Zeus had demanded that Theseus kill him for honor. What sort of honor was there in killing a prince who lived in darkness, only to be forced to kill his father's enemies? Theseus had not slain the Minotaur, he had slain King Minos's weapon against the Greeks—his deformed son. True justice would have been to have slain King Minos.

Poseidon had lied to him. Or worse, this so-called all-knowing god did not know. It bothered him almost as much as his exhaustion and pain.

Theseus emerged from the cave, squinting in the blinding daylight. The guard gazed wide-eyed at him. He easily let him pass.

Theseus took his bloody xiphos and hurled it into the sea. Then he trudged back to the slave ship.

There were no longer blindfolds on the way back. Theseus sailed with the captain back to Knossos, drinking until drunk on the deck of the ship. He passed out and reached Knossos by morning.

***

Ariadne met Theseus alone on the beach. She ran to him still wearing the same pretty white peplos and sandals she had worn in the palace, with her hair neatly tucked behind her head. Then she threw her arms around his neck and wept tears of joy.

"You're alive! Blessed be the gods, you're alive!"

"Yes, Ariadne," he said in her arms. "Thanks to you."

"Did you kill my brother?" she asked with excited eyes.

"Yes."

"You must tell Father personally. He will be overjoyed."

"No, Ariadne."

"Hmm? But why?"

"I'm leaving for Athens."

"Athens?" she asked, stepping back. "What do you mean? What is Athens?"

"My birthright. I must make my way home to Attica. I shall rename the city Athens after the great goddess Athena."

"Theseus, come follow me back to the palace," she said, shaking her head. "Father will offer you riches beyond anything you've ever seen as your reward. You can live here as a prince with me, my love."

"There is no reward. The only thing that pleases me is that no further Greeks will die. If you'd like, you can sail with me, Ariadne. I will take my ship and travel with Elias and Pirithous."

"Of course, I'll sail with you." She dipped her head down. "But…I thought we'd stay here in Crete." Theseus didn't reply. Ariadne sighed, and then she nodded her head. "All right, I'll follow you wherever you wish to take me. You sail tonight?"

"No, we load the ships. Then, as the sun rises tomorrow, I'm off."

"I'll run and get my things!"

He wouldn't see her ever again. He told himself he'd return one day for her. He was simply leaving to protect her from his final crazed quest into the Underworld. Just like he told himself he would see Queen Cassandra in Azure Blue. All of it was a lie. And this time, he wasn't lying to fool his enemy—he was lying to himself.

He would finish his quest and take his crown. Then, somehow, all would turn out all right. Wouldn't it? He was Theseus Aegeus, the great Greek hero, after all.

11

STILL COLD

Avva lay on the ground without the strength to move, scarcely able to bear the icy sand along her bare arms and legs. She hadn't eaten or drunk in days. She shook feverishly. But it was all right because she had given up. When she closed her eyes, she imagined she was back home in the Crystal Palace of Azure Blue with her daughter, Cassandra, and her husband, Sol. She was reunited with them in her dreams, hiking along the Stratos or walking the torchlit walkways of her lovely garden. But when she opened her eyes, all she saw was desert sand.

She felt water enter her throat. She spat it out.

"Leave me alone, Cora! Why don't you just let me go!"

"Stop fighting, stubborn nymph!"

Then Avva felt her pain leave her. But that only upset her more. She had learned Cora had the power to heal. When the goddess laid her hands on her, as she had done before, she felt energy and peace. Her pain was always transferred to the goddess for a moment and then it left both of them. But she didn't want peace now. She wanted to die.

Upon healing Avva, Persephone weakened and collapsed on the sand. This gave Avva enough strength to push herself up and run.

She didn't get very far. The goddess caught up with her and dragged her back toward their house, but Avva didn't stop punching and kicking the whole way back.

It was the third time Avva had run. She believed there must be an end to the sand. All of Cassandra's descriptions of the Underworld had never matched this strange desert. The sand dunes seemed to stretch forever. And once more, Cora found her.

"Let me go!" Avva cried.

"Why? There's nothing but desert for a thousand leagues! I promised you'll be free, but you have to wait!"

"When you leave again, Cora, I won't be here. I'm through, you hear me! I'm done."

Cora heaved Avva's body over her shoulder as Avva hit and kicked the goddess. Cora carried her the rest of the way to their cottage. All the while, Cora's winged konabera—a perverse black fire-breathing version of Avva's lovely Inghorn back home— walked beside them. At the threshold of the cottage, Cora hurled Avva onto the bed. But when Avva made a decision, it was final. She charged for the door again.

"What is the point of this!" exclaimed Cora, snatching her waist. "Stop fighting me! I promised you you'll be free. You have to wait. I waited centuries. I ask for you to wait just a short time!"

"I don't care!" Then tears flowed from Avva's eyes. "Why not let me die? What am I to you? A pet! How are you any different from them?"

Cora's eyes scorched red. Avva regretted it the moment she uttered it. She had learned the extent of Cora's hatred toward her family.

"You don't believe me?" Cora challenged, blocking the door.

"No, I don't trust you!" Avva said, shaking her head violently.

"You don't have a choice."

"You can hold me when you're here. You can block the door. Try to trap me. But the minute you leave, I'll find a way to break free. Then it will be over."

"Then you'll die."

"*So what!*"

Then an odd thing happened. Tears ran from Cora's burning eyes. She shook her head. "I adore this spirit. It's like my mother. But it could be your end. I tell you, Avva, you have to wait just a little longer."

"I've waited long enough!" She ran for the wooden door again. And yet again, Cora held her back with ease.

"If you wait a little while longer, I will promise that you will see your husband. You will reunite with him. *If* you wait."

Avva stepped back. "Is this some sort of trick? I will see my husband? You can arrange that?" It was finally enough for her to stop her charge. "How?"

"When the time is right," she said with a sigh. She leaned against the door, and though things had calmed, Cora's eyes still burned. "He will come. If I fail, then you can go ahead and take your life. You won't have to do it anyway, because if I fail, I'll be imprisoned in chains and you'll starve to death. It's true, I like you, Avva. Especially this wretched willful spirit. You remind me of my beloved mother. But there are many reasons for keeping you in this house. It is not for my amusement, or to hold you like a pet, as you claim. It is to protect you. The other is to reunite you one day with your husband."

"Imprisoned by my mother," she said quietly, more to herself, as she sank onto her bed. "Now imprisoned by you."

"Do you think you're the only one?" snapped Cora. "I've weathered centuries under an abusive brute. I did it for your people, who I love. Your daughter will mark the end of my family's reign. I swear this. I don't know how, but I've foreseen it. Somehow, she will free us from Olympus. Just like I've foreseen you reuniting with your husband. But you have to wait."

Avva panted, exhausted. She turned from Cora and just stared at the ground. Then she heard the goddess breathing heavily too.

Avva nodded.

"I'll return in two days. I'll leave after you eat enough. I can heal you, but not feed you. If you wish, run off again and I'll hunt you throughout the desert by air. You're over a hundred leagues from any settlement. Trust me, you can't survive the trek. I can find and catch you every time."

"But what's happening above? You're acting worried. That worries me. Tell me, Cora. You said I was your friend. Just tell me."

"Your daughter reigns as queen. Your husband is emperor."

"*That's all you ever say!*"

"Because it's true."

"I will see my husband again?" Avva said, more to herself. She stared at the dark stone wall, finally giving up her fight. "Sol again? Oh, if only I could believe that."

"Yes," Cora hissed. Then the goddess did what she always did when they fought. She threw the wooden door open and slammed it shut behind her.

1 2

THE TIGER KING

The first red ships appeared on the horizon of the Strait of Azure by morning. Casey had spotted them from atop the tower stable when caring for her white winged unicorn, Inghorn. Hundreds of blue hoplite soldiers marched past the azure coastal forest and then into the purple fields before the Azure Palace. It was early. And cold. The first snow had fallen a few days before. Still, some of the layered white ice reflected purple from tree trunks in the woods.

The Tiger King's army gathered in single file before the wooden drawbridge. In the center of the lines of hoplites thundered an animated old man, on horseback, wearing a black helm. She instantly recognized her uncle. Mad indeed. He was shouting, threatening some of his own soldiers with his sword, directing the lines into perfect single file. His long white hair flowed over his shoulders, and he had a white beard. As he spat orders, Casey spotted Cambria on her unicorn, trotting across the drawbridge to greet him.

The regiment remained in the fields all morning. Then they waited for an invitation from Queen Cassandra. An invitation she would never give.

Now Queen Cassandra sat on her gilded dais in the company

of her best friend, the blond-haired nymph Lalaina. Lalaina's fingers nervously fidgeted as she sat below Cassandra, wearing a lovely white peplos with a large golden flower fibula. She had repeatedly run to the windows and stared outside. Before the invasion the two of them had planned a pleasant, quiet day practicing falconry in the woods.

The Amazon throne room was a grand hall with rows of elegant chairs leading up to a marble dais. Vines of lush red, blue, and violet flowers grew over large vases and along the rows of chairs. The walls were crystal, framed by Doric columns, overlooking the surrounding lush blue-green gardens. And a glass dome ceiling opened to the sky above. It was beautiful and pleasant. But with an army outside, Casey felt like she was trapped there.

"What are you going to do, Casey?" Lalaina asked her. She rushed over to a column by the window. "There must be thousands of them. How dare he land!"

"Nothing," Casey said, leaning her chin on her hand and sighing. "They weren't invited."

"What should we do, Engel?" Lalaina asked. The Mandrigel dwarf sat on the first step on the throne, as he always did, with his chin leaning on his hand, like Casey. Engel was a dwarf with blue skin, far bluer than Casey's, and thinning white hair. This morning he wore a royal white chiton and sandals. Casey adored him.

"It's not my decision," Engel said with a snort. "It's the queen's. But if it were me, I'd order the monokera down from the tower and shoot them all with arrows."

"I've never seen so many soldiers," Lalaina said. Then she stared outside again. "You can't keep pretending they're not here, Casey. We have to do something. A thousand nymphs are lining the ramparts on Cambria's orders. They might be allies, but they're acting as if they're planning an attack. And Cambria's ready to defend."

"What did your boyfriend say about his father?" Cassandra asked.

"He's not my boyfriend, 'kay?" Lalaina said, rolling her eyes. "Gavin said his father is a brave soldier, but crazy. All the rumors are true. He's absolutely mad. Even Gavin wasn't sure your father should have freed him."

"Tell Gavin to join me for supper. I might need him in case the feral king gets wild."

"You want me there too?" Lalaina asked, smiling ruefully. She walked up the three steps to the top of the dais.

"No," Casey said. She hugged her. "There goes our hunt."

Lalaina shrugged.

"Perhaps we've caught men instead," Casey said with a grin.

"Your Majesty," a nymph said, rushing through the grand double doors. She gave Cassandra a quick bow in her heavy royal blue peplos. It was Casey's "aunt" Hanna, once her mother's best friend. "The Tiger King's insistent. He's threatening Cambria with the intention of marching his soldiers into the palace. Cambria's absolutely refusing. Now she's asking me for orders. What should I tell her?"

"Whatever you do, Hanna, don't let soldiers enter the palace. I agree with Cambria. Make it clear to the animal that if his soldiers so much as touch my walls, we'll shoot them. Launch monokera above and throw warning shots if you have to."

"Gladly." Hanna smiled with a nod. "But what if they scale the wall, my queen?"

"Shoot them down. The edict stands. They've stepped foot on Napea uninvited."

"Yes, my queen," she said with a bow. "I'll tell Cambria immediately."

"Your grandmother would have already attacked," grumbled Engel. "Harmonia would have sunk their ships."

"As for the old man, Hanna, invite him *alone* for supper," continued Cassandra. "Tell him his niece invites him to dine with her, but him alone."

"Yes, Casey." And Hanna ran out.

"What are you saying, Engel?" Cassandra asked. "Hmm? I'm trying to keep the peace."

"Humph. I think this man's already broken it."

"Aye," Casey said with a sigh and a nod. "My father asked that I protect our home. If it means from my own uncle, I will. But let's be civil. Let us act thoughtfully and cautiously, like you said my grandmother, Delia, once did."

Engel nodded but folded his arms and grumbled something to himself.

———

By nightfall, Gavin, Torinth, and Engel sat alone in the dining room. Here not only was the wooden table large enough to accommodate thirty guests, but all the walls, flooring, and ceiling were made of wood. Candles lit up the room, and it was too foggy to see much of the grounds outside the windows.

The guests had been waiting for some time for Cassandra. Cassandra could see them as she made her way down a long hallway. She could also hear her uncle's boisterous laughter echoing among the palace walls.

She walked to the door wearing a trailing azure dress, a black wrap on her head, and thick blue makeup. Then she nodded to Cambria and Falena, the chief guards of the palace, who stood by the door in scarlet Amazon hoplite armor.

Cambria thumped her staff on the ground and cried, "Welcome glorious Queen Cassandra, the Amazon nymph queen of Azure Blue!"

The three men rose.

Casey nodded and sat down near Engel, picked up her utensils, and started eating.

"Nice to finally meet you, niece," Torinth said with a bow, still standing.

"Of course," Cassandra replied with her mouth full. She twirled her fork in the air. "Welcome to Azure Blue."

Torinth furrowed his brow. He turned to his son Gavin. Gavin grinned uncomfortably, but his smile became kind as he looked at Casey. They sat down.

Cassandra noted the similarities between father and son. Both had wild, wandering black eyes. But Torinth's long hair was white and unkempt. His son, Gavin, had dark hair, slicked back formally, with a thin, dark beard. And Casey noticed many scars on Torinth's wrinkled skin along his arms and up to his neck.

Engel was dressed formally in a brown chiton, and it looked a little too cute on such a short man, but his mannerisms weren't funny. He looked as angry as she felt. He seemed to fight showing it, and he even grinned at their guest, but Cassandra knew the dwarf's thoughts well enough.

"I traveled far, Nymph Queen," Torinth continued with a smile as he forked some meat. "Far from my home in Adelain. It took my army over a week to gather and arrive here by the Strait. In fact, I've never been to Azure."

"Not much to it, really," Cassandra said with her mouth full again, shrugging.

"I quite like this room. It reminds me of my galley."

There was no response—only more uncomfortable silence. And the sound of the queen's silverware hitting the plate and echoing off the wooden walls. No one else ate. They seemed to be watching her. Torinth leaned over and murmured something to his son, next to him. Then he picked up his silverware, shrugged, and ate more meat.

"It's not often that I dine with prisoners," Casey said as she wiped her mouth with a white cloth. "Our people believe in freedom, of course, but some outcasts are taken away for the good of the people. Milda..." Cassandra laughed. "Was banished by Father after her attempts to overthrow my mother." She drank some pomegranate wine and raised a finger. "I think she's the only Napean to have ever been banished. Of course, Imada was disbanded after their revolt." She started chuckling. "You should have seen the witch kicking and screaming as she was taken out of my palace and boarded on a ship about to sail across the sea. She feared being damned after landing on Gaia more than my father's banishment, I think."

Torinth stroked his long white beard and nodded pensively.

He gazed at Cassandra, seemingly studying her. Gavin fell quiet. Torinth seemed about to speak, but then he shook his head. He toasted her with a glass of red wine and just gave her a fake grin.

She cut some meat with a knife.

Then she threw the knife down on the metal plate. It clanged in the hall. "Tell me, Uncle, what do you intend to do with the regiment standing outside my castle?"

"Is that why you're being rude?" Torinth asked. "I intend to defend the borders. I believe the foreigners will attack you first as you are closest to Hellena. A base here is sensible, to protect your father's empire."

She finally met his gaze.

"I'm not acting rude, sir. I'm asking a prisoner why he has sent an army into the valley of Azure Blue."

Torinth chuckled.

Cassandra smiled back. "You will order your soldiers to turn around. There never has been, and never will be, an occupation in Azure Blue."

"I beg your pardon, but this is not an occupation, Queen Cassandra," Torinth said, chuckling. "It's my army. They go where I go. We are here for your defense."

"You will order them back to Adelain. If you wish to be here as a guest, Uncle, that is fine, but no soldier will step foot in the palace. If they go with you, as you say, then perhaps you should leave."

Engel dropped his fork on the metal plate. He turned to the Tiger King and stammered an apology. The Tiger King looked at him as if he had never noticed him before.

"What's this?" asked Torinth, pointing at Engel.

"He is Engel, Father," replied Gavin. "He is our chief advisor."

Torinth pounded the table and roared with laughter. "Chief advisor!"

"Father," said Gavin, shaking his head.

"Why, look at him! He's a little blue man. Your chief advisor? May the gods help you and your people, Cassandra." Then he hit the table and guffawed some more with his stupid broken-toothed mouth full of food.

Cassandra stared. Then she jumped up and clapped her hands. Cambria ran into the room and bowed.

"Cambria, escort our guest—"

"Really, niece!" interrupted Torinth, still laughing but raising his hand. "Please, forgive me." Then he gestured to Cambria. "But this is truly droll. You let a little cave dwarf advise you?"

Cambria placed a hand on Torinth. This was enough to knock the mirth out of him. Torinth grabbed her wrist, spun her around, and threw her against the table. Gavin jumped up and pulled Torinth away from Cambria while holding her other hand. Cambria was concealing a knife in that hand, and Gavin held it back from slicing Torinth's throat.

"*You mock my friends and wrestle with my guard!*" cried Cassandra. Then Casey turned to Gavin. "This is the man I'm supposed to trust?"

"Ah…ah…but she grabbed me, Niece!" protested Torinth, rubbing his face.

"Everyone sit down!" shouted Gavin. He pushed Torinth back into his chair. "Sit!" Then he raised a hand, pleading for Cassandra to sit.

It was quiet again. But Torinth was no longer smiling. He was scowling. Cambria and Falena stood in a fighting stance, now facing Torinth. The Tiger King ignored them, grabbed a fork, and started attacking his meal.

Cassandra dismissed the guards.

They all went back to eating in silence.

Torinth regained his smile, shook his head, and chuckled to himself.

"Don't make fun of the queen's counsel," Casey said.

"Umm…" Torinth said, nodding. He grabbed some bread, dipped it in the meat sauce on his plate, and ate more. Then he looked at Engel and just shook his head.

"Sir," said Engel. "If I may ask you: Why did the emperor free you?"

"What?"

Gavin quickly gestured for Engel to shut his mouth.

"What's it to you?" asked Torinth. "Do I not deserve freedom?"

"The timing is peculiar considering—"

"Do you have any idea what it's like to sit and sleep in filth? Always wanting to simply… ride or battle with my sword? Does it really matter, *chief advisor*? Little wise cave dwarf?"

"Just wondering."

Torinth smashed his hand against the table.

"Imbecile!" he cried, gnashing his teeth. He hurled a dish at Engel. It shattered against the wall close to Engel's head and might have contacted him, had not Engel quickly ducked. "Must I be surrounded by fools? Son, is this who protects my border? An inexperienced virgin queen and a dim-witted little infant?"

The doors of the room swung open again. This time Cambria drew her sword and pointed it at him. Torinth jumped from his seat.

"Father!" Gavin exclaimed. "Please. Sit down! King Sol has asked you to get along!"

"She started it!" he said, pointing at the queen. "Not me! Who's ruder, Gavin? Perhaps you should ask what I did to her? How I deserved this welcome?"

"You sent an invading force to my palace!" Casey replied, leaning forward with both her hands on the table.

"Oh come on. You know the men out there are… Well, they're more your father's men than mine. They're no threat to you. Every man out there would die for you, queen. Your whole attitude's been insulting since you came through the door."

Cassandra turned around and grabbed her golden scepter. She had stashed it by her chair. "Imbecile, you say? Who do you think we are?"

As the golden rod lengthened in Casey's hand, Torinth's eyes opened wide and, for the first time, he looked fearful. All knew the terrible power of that weapon, especially Torinth. It was the scepter used by her mother that had turned the tide of the Battle of Polis. It had frozen hundreds of Torinth's own men on the very fields his soldiers now occupied.

At first, he stepped back. But then, if possible, he seemed angrier. Torinth's face reddened and he pounded his fist on the table.

"I am your father's brother!" shouted Torinth. "Your grandfather's eldest son! I don't know the depths of your intelligence, madam! Perhaps you're simply an idiot. But I am a general! I've seen horrors. What have you seen? What makes you think you have the experience to lead this island? That weapon? I come here and you treat me like… Like…"

"*A prisoner!*" Casey shouted back. "Call me a virgin queen? Do you have any idea where I've been, sir? I've seen greater horrors trapped in the depths than you will ever see. And that dwarf over there is wiser than any man in Gaia. You will take your soldiers, turn them around, and sail them back to the Hinterlands. Not one man will spend a night in the palace in my Azure! And if you do not, I'll send my Amazon down from the tower stables to move them!"

Torinth looked at her in astonishment. He breathed heavily and glared at her. Then he turned to Cambria and Falena, who still brandished their swords. He forced himself to sit down.

He grabbed his fork and knife again and forced food down his gullet.

"Disrespectful wench." Then he said quietly, more to himself, "Solinaray, hmm? Your grandfather was Darius. My father. Your father is Sol, my brother. We are family. Whether tainted by nymph blood or not."

"Perhaps you should go, Torinth," Gavin said, rubbing his eyes.

"Ah…" the Tiger said, looking at his son. He nodded, now looking somber. "I see." But Torinth did not leave. Rather, he calmly ate more as everyone stared at him. Cassandra's hand shook, holding her scepter, while she still stood.

Gavin looked over at Casey with a reassuring nod, but she quickly looked away.

"This is very good," said Torinth, raising his fork to them. "Really good. I haven't had food like this since… since Castle Cove. Wonderful wine." He drank some from a crystal glass. "Umm. It is from your legendary Myrle berry, is it not? And the meat is very tender and fresh. I wonder…" he said, staring at the meat on his fork with his mouth full. "If it was blue."

Then he burst into a guffaw again. His laugh seemed jovial, which was unsettling in the midst of all the tension in the room.

"You will withdraw your forces," Cassandra repeated.

"But of course, Your Majesty," Torinth said, waving his hand and nodding. He aped a bow in his chair, still between laughs. "Sit with your uncle and enjoy our meal. Sit. Absolutely delicious. Though I'm not so fond of the company, I am quite earnest about the taste of this *blue* meat."

He looked up at her and burst into more laughter. Everyone at the table stared at him. Finally, as he stopped his own sick merriment, he said, "Take a look at this." He brandished his two-pronged silver fork. "Look." He even showed the utensil to Engel. "See this? This simple thing. Did you know that Atalans are the only people who don't eat with their hands? The filthy bastards approaching your shores do. Did you know there are Greek triremes anchored on the other side of Mount Ambitus, Niece? Hmm? They hide behind your Mount so you can't see them. But they are here. Did Imada tell you? Ah, but as you said, you disbanded your Imada. Unfortunate. Their intelligence was greater than any other."

She didn't answer. She rubbed her forehead, still standing.

"Are you aware of the number of regiments intending to overthrow your castle?" he asked, staring at her. "Hmm? Many of them are cargo ships. Do you know what kind of cargo they're carrying? Men. Men, Cassandra. They store men. Soldiers. Do you know of King Agragon, Minos, Aegeus, and Castoro? Do you know of your father's skirmishes in the East with the Assyrians? Or the continued unrest in the Fox Kingdom? Lanius may have been slain, but they are not a people that can be governed. Or how about the coup stopped in Teleria? Or the pirates threatening my harbor from the Euxine Sea?"

Cassandra had no idea. Indeed, she had ruled for many moons in Azure, but it was all local business.

Torinth lifted a finger. "Ah." Then he nodded, eating more meat. "Of course, you haven't a clue. That is why I was offended by your little blue man's question. It reeked of ignorance. This *prisoner* before you has sworn allegiance to your father. I will die for him. But if I think your borders are weak, I get angry." He ripped apart some bread from his plate. Then looked up at Cassandra again with a fake smile. "So ..." Then he looked at Engel. "As for you, strange little blue man, the king freed me because we are at war. And I wouldn't be surprised if he cages me afterward. That is well, for I live and breathe to fight. I love sending people to the ferryman. But now, let us all be friends. Hmm?"

He shook his head and turned from them, laughing again.

"As one happy family, I'll tell you a secret." Then he cupped his mouth and spoke to Cassandra almost in a whisper. "Your father enjoys killing too." He nodded and tore more meat with his bare hands. "Hmm? And if you were such a wise *chief advisor*, my blue fool, you should have been able to figure all this out yourself. And you should have informed her of business around her borders. That is why I call you, Cassandra Solinaray, a virgin. I know not whether you are a virgin in sarding. I don't really give a sarding ass. But I do know that you haven't the slightest idea what's going on around your kingdom. Am I right?"

She didn't answer.

"Ah. You upset me. But I know, niece, that you are merely trying to poke at me. I know it is not that you lack brains over the empire's affairs. You simply don't care."

No one said a word. But Cassandra propped her scepter against the wall and slowly sank back into her chair.

"I hate women," Torinth murmured to himself as he forked more meat. "Dreadful little wenches. Especially Amazon nymphs. They seem to think power is turning their back on the sword." Then he raised his glass in a toast to the queen with a fake smile. "Umm. To your kingdom. I'm honored to be in the presence of a descendent of Queen Harmonia, truly the greatest general…nearly as good as…the greatest man." Then he thumped his chest. "Me."

Then he burst out guffawing louder than ever, hammering the table again.

"You will remove your soldiers from Azure," Cassandra said.

"Of course, Your Majesty." He nodded between guffaws. Then he lifted his hand as if to apologize. "Oh, Casey," he said, roaring with laughter, "please don't hurt me, blue witch! Save me from your woman guards and your little Mandrigel!"

Torinth would not stop laughing, whether they joined his mirth or not.

"You've insulted me enough!" Cassandra cried, jumping up again.

But before she could grab her scepter again, Torinth turned to Gavin and said, "She's a queen, son. I like her. Her rudeness shows heart. She has Solinair's blood. Ah, I hate both of them. We shall work well together. Tell your father I no longer have any doubt. Tell him…" He started laughing again. "If the enemy sails to her shores, why, she'll claw them with her fingernails."

He got up and limped to her side. "Welcome, Cassandra Solinaray, to war." She backed up, furious. He simply tapped her shoulder quickly with a finger. "I'll be off. If you need my services, there will be an entire regiment across the Strait waiting for your orders, Azure Queen."

"You're mad," Cassandra said, looking at him oddly.

"Am I?" He stared into her eyes.

Then he turned to Gavin. "Goodbye, Son."

"Goodbye, Father," Gavin said and nodded to him.

Torinth looked at Cassandra one last time. "I wish we could have had a real family dinner. But, then again…" He smiled wide and lifted his brow. "This was much more fun. I do enjoy a good fight!"

Torinth limped out, laughing even more. He nodded to

Cambria and Falena, who stood on either side of the door. Then his mad laughter was heard, even after the guards closed the doors, as he limped down the hallway. When his laughter was finally gone, Cassandra whirled around. She stared angrily at Gavin.

"He's insane!" Cassandra exclaimed. "He's out of his mind!"

"Casey, he's a general. If you understand that, you won't hate him so."

"He made my guards rush in and pull their swords! Then he insulted me as a *virgin queen* and called Engel a little cave dwarf."

"Casey, he's a soldier," Gavin repeated.

"Was this a test?"

"Everything is a test for him. Torinth probably figured if you were weak, he'd step over you. But if you were strong, he'd know your loyalty and intentions. You succeeded in convincing him. He's leaving."

"Was it Father's idea?"

"Humph, Sol would never have agreed to an army being stationed in the Azures, Casey," said Engel, shaking his head. Then Engel turned to Gavin. "Do you think your father will return his army to our shores in a few moons?"

"My father is King Solinair, sir," Gavin corrected him. "As for Torinth, he's under Sol's command. I don't see him returning to Napea unless Casey allows it."

"Casey," Gavin said sternly. It creeped her out when he stared at her with those dark eyes, so much like Torinth's. "You might not like him, but if you're fighting to the death, wouldn't you want him on your side?"

"Goodnight Gavin." She shook her head and leaned it against her hand.

"I'm sorry."

She smiled sadly and nodded. "It's... No, I'm sorry. He's revolting."

Gavin rose and nodded.

"Goodnight, Casey." He walked over and kissed her on the cheek.

This left the queen with Engel in the wooden room.

"They're so irritating," she said.

"You mean Torinth?" asked Engel.

"I mean Torinth and Gavin. They're the same."

"No, your brother Gavin was raised by Sol," Engel said. "Gavin is a good man. That old man is a beast."

"Well, I'm sorry he insulted you. Few people know how special you are."

"I don't mind," he said, shrugging. "I'm too old to be bothered."

"Seems you enjoyed provoking him."

"Yes, he upset me. But I'm much more worried about you. How are you doing, Casey?"

She looked through the windows at the trees. The fog was lifting, but it was still thick enough to see only shadows.

"I'm scared, Engel. I'm afraid for Azure. Not just Napea, but for all of Atala. Have things become so bad that father has to enlist the help of a man like him?"

"Seems so." Engel nodded. "We can't control the fates. All we can do, Casey, is care for one another. Love one another. I left my home to do that. And I've cared for every Ambrosia since."

"No, you're an Ambrosia, Engel." She smiled. "It's your family." She got up, leaned down, and kissed his cheek.

"And you, Cassandra Ambrosia, are better than any queen," he said, taking her hand. "You are the best queen Azure has ever had. I mean it. I'm so proud of you. If this was a test, you passed beyond any expectations."

She patted his head and quietly left the room.

Casey stood alone, leaning on the rail by the spiral steps, the rest of the night. She stared through the three-story window of her palace, just as she had done with her father only two moons before. She watched her uncle's men march, by torchlight, toward the sea. They headed back to the coastal forest.

She stood so long by the rail that when the guards by the steps below relieved each other in the morning, they glanced up. She had never seen those guards avert their gaze from the windows before. Only at this time—in the very early morning, when they exchanged places—did they look up at their queen.

Casey dug her head into her hands, on the rail, and ran her fingers through her long hair. The green sun would rise shortly. She hadn't slept all night.

Torinth was a test—perverse, but a test nonetheless. Her uncle had cleverly staged an invasion. But he had also told her ships were anchored behind the wall of Mount Ambitus. A real enemy was mobilizing, and the tiger wanted to see what she would do. They would be here soon, and Torinth knew it. How much longer? And what would she do when they really arrived?

13

MEDEA

THESEUS LAY ON HIS SIDE ON A SOFT FUR RUG WITH HIS BEST friends, Pirithous and Elias, in the grand outdoor plaza of Attica. The plaza, an outdoor courtyard on the palace grounds, sat on a field of grass, high enough to see the seashore. The fur rugs lay on a granite floor. Sections of the floor that weren't illuminated by torchlight reflected white under the moonlight. White columns spread out in rows along the plaza. And young girls in lovely white peploi walked beside rows of people, lying on their sides on fur rugs, on the plaza or the surrounding grass, offering olives, cherries, and dates, or filling goblets with red wine.

At the furthest end—across the grassy field, before the castle entrance—sat the royal couple. They sat on a pair of gilded chairs on the dais. Two slaves fanned them while Theseus's father, King Aegeus, sampled grapes from a silver tray a slave girl held on her knee. Theseus was proud of his successes in the Underworld and was now overjoyed by the sight of his father. But he had not revealed his identity to the king yet.

His tall father was animated, laughing heartily at everything around him. He wore a gold band around his thin blond and white hair and a red and white tunic that mostly covered his broad shoulders and waist, leaving his chest bare. But beside his jovial father sat the vile queen.

Theseus had really never known Medea. But he remembered seeing her when aboard the Argo. Queen Medea's face was still beautiful, but she had aged. Now her long wavy black hair had lines of gray. It had been this demon witch who, in sick revenge, killed Jason and her own children. Then she ran from Jason. King Aegeus was, no doubt, oblivious to her infamous identity.

The witch seemed to be scrutinizing everything when she wasn't attending her prized son. Like a mother bird, she fawned over the tall lanky boy, Prince Medus, helping him arrange his plate of food and directing him whom to converse with, how to speak, and how to act. This was odd as the prince wasn't much younger than Theseus.

"What are you thinking of, sire?" asked Pirithous with a smile. He ran his fingers along the bangs of his short curly blond hair. "You're not drinking. Are you unhappy? Why? After everything you've accomplished, what's wrong? Why aren't you enjoying the festival?"

"She stares."

"Who?"

"The witch." He gestured to the royal couple.

"Shouldn't we be celebrating at this festival?"

Theseus took his silver wine goblet and studied the drink with disdain. "Water," he said, shaking his head.

"It's not to your liking?" asked his other companion. He was his wise elder advisor, Elias. The old man was bald and had a thin gray beard. "Perhaps you can show your subjects otherwise."

"Yes, when will you reveal your identity?" Pirithous asked in a whisper, gesturing to the royal couple down the grassy knoll.

"Your hesitation could lead to what you fear," Elias said quietly, also staring at them. "If you take your crown now, it's possible you could sway the king *not* to strike Atlantis. But if you do nothing, he is bound to attack."

"Whether by my hand, or my children's, there will be a great war between us, Elias."

"But you can change that. You can assure this war will not be waged with the Amazon queen you spoke so fondly of."

"I'm surprised at you, old man," said Theseus, finally tearing his eyes from her. "We've waited so long. Why can't we wait another day?"

"One day might be too late."

"She watches," Theseus said. And, in fact, the witch was looking right at them.

"Perhaps she honors Aejades," Pirithous said with a shrug.

"Perhaps she remembers Jason," cautioned Elias. "And the young Argonaut who traveled with him?"

Theseus raised his cup to her in greeting. Medea quickly turned back to her son.

"I will kill her," Theseus said to Elias.

"I think you just need some fun," said Pirithous, shaking his head.

And with that, his drunken best friend, Pirithous, grabbed the wrist of a maiden walking by and threw her down on the rug beside them. The lovely-haired maiden giggled and fell into his arms with her cup of wine spilling on the ground.

"There was a time you would have joined him, my lord," Elias said, laughing.

"Stop! Please! Stop it!" yelled the young girl, laughing and hitting Pirithous.

"I'll take you to my chamber," said Pirithous in her ear, but loudly enough for everyone to hear. "Here there are too many watching us, says my master. But in my chamber, I promise you wonders you've never seen."

"Wonders?" she asked, struggling in his arms but still giggling. "What sort of wonders?"

"The wonders under my cloth."

One of the lady's older friends ran to her rescue. She wore a yellow dress and her brown hair was tied in a long ponytail. Pirithous simply scooped both of them into his thick arms.

"Hey!" cried the older woman.

"Come!" Pirithous said. "The both of you, then!"

Pirithous looked down at Theseus. Theseus nodded and dismissed him.

All the while, at the far end of the plaza, Medea still watched.

"She knows, Elias. You're right. She recognizes me. She could ruin everything." Theseus turned and looked toward the sea. He could make out the shore on the horizon. "Curse our luck. I've traveled the Underworld. Now this old crow stops me?"

"Would you like another drink?" asked a pretty blond girl, with a big smirk, holding a cup over him. But she was not a server. She was another beautiful maiden with perfect olive skin and bright blue eyes. Her eyes reminded Theseus of Cassandra.

He shook his head.

"Are you certain, hero?" she asked with a big smile. "Aren't you Aejades, the brave man who slew the Minotaur?"

"Away with you."

She furrowed her brow, shrugged, and walked off.

"That wasn't nice," said Elias with a chuckle. "They're the daughters of Trajan. Trajan is a wealthy merchant who owns property in these parts. Remember what Poseidon said. You need to find a proper Greek woman. Trajan's family is probably looking for husbands, and his daughters would make nice wives for you."

"Let Pirithous play. You and I must strategize the situation at hand."

"The strategy is simple. Walk down to the king and queen and announce your identity."

"That simple, eh?" asked Theseus, amused.

"Yes." Elias nodded.

As if Medea had heard, she whispered something in a male servant's ear. The servant was a lanky man with very short hair, wearing a flower garland. He was clean-shaven and spoke using big gestures with his arms. He wore a white tunic, hanging from one shoulder, that was ornamented with multicolored flowers like a jester's. The jester nodded and made his way slowly up the grassy hill, swerving through the drunken crowd.

"Sir Aejades," the jester said when close enough. "Sir Aejades." His voice was high like a woman's. "I am Orpistos." And he bowed. "Queen Medea invites the man who killed the Minotaur to join her and the royal family to watch the festival. You are the man who killed the Minotaur?"

Theseus nodded.

"What an honor," replied Elias, opening his eyes wide.

Theseus and Elias followed Orpistos as he swayed his hips through the field. Orpistos whispered in Theseus's ear, "She's in a terrible mood. I think it has something to do with a tantrum from her son."

"I'll be on my best behavior."

Orpistos nodded. Then he opened his eyes wider, staring at the hero's broad shoulders.

"Aejades!" said King Aegeus, rising from his dais. "Aejades! The festivities of Dionysus will continue late into the evening. Come join us. What great fun, isn't it?"

He and Elias sat beside the royal company, on a rug under their gilded chairs, on the raised stage.

"You give great honor, my king," Theseus said with a bow.

Aegeus searched around him. "Yes. But where, where is your spirited young friend Pirithous? I so enjoy him. It's not often that the Court has such young heroes."

Medea finally turned as if noticing him for the first time. "Medus, dear, come see who is visiting us, my son. This is the hero who slew the Minotaur."

"Yes, yes!" shouted Aegeus. "You've freed us, Aejades!"

"Ae-jades, is it?" Medea asked. "I've never heard of you. Seems strange that such a great hero had not made a name for himself until now."

"I travel by sea most days."

"I have been watching you and your strong friends with great interest," Medea said. She sipped some wine. "Not only do I invite you to sit with us during the festival, but I had hoped that you could tell us and the rest of the Atticans the tale of how you slew the beast. This festival would be a great time, don't you think?"

"A great honor, my queen," Theseus said, bowing to her.

"Oh, how fun, Mother," Medus said, clapping.

Theseus nodded and rose. And as he rose, Medea looked down at his shoes. Then she quickly turned to her husband with an incredulous stare.

Men in bronze hoplite armor, standing by the sides of the throne, blew horns. And all the guests—those who were not drunk—listened.

"Atticans," Theseus said loudly. "Atticans. I've been asked by his and her highness to tell the tale of my battle with the Minotaur. Would you like to hear it?"

The crowds raged. When they quieted, he began, "It was the first day of the climacteric year when I descended narrow and steep steps into the dark cave. Already entering, I heard screams. With barely any light, I heard the crunching of bones." The crowd gasped. "Then…nothing. Not a sound. I braced myself. I prayed to blessed Athena."

"Blessed be," interrupted King Aejades, again raising a golden goblet of wine. "Our great Athena! Of course, a great goddess of Olympus indeed."

"Blessed be," cried many in the audience.

"I crept forward. Inside my coat, I had hidden a short xiphos."

"Clever Aejades!" cried King Aegeus, again laughing and nodding to Medea. "Clever! Isn't he?"

"When I got close enough, I pulled out my sword. The creature charged me like a bull." Theseus moved about the stage, pantomiming the fight. "I would have been finished, had I not taken a lucky roll and fallen to the creature's side." Medea's stupid son clapped. "Now I glimpsed the terrible monster. He was no man. He had the head of a bull with two horns. His eyes were flames. His body was three times the breadth of mine." Again, many in the audience cried out, afraid. "My heart beat fast. I charged. I came so close to him that I could see the fresh blood and sinew of his victims still on his lips. And those eyes, those red eyes... I was petrified. But, somehow, I swung madly at the beast. He charged again. I parried, then thrust like mad once more." He pantomimed again. "It seemed like a hopeless struggle. I kept being thrown about the labyrinth."

Theseus paused. The servers and slaves held their food and wine, waiting for his next word. Even his good friend Elias, who knew the tale, waited in anticipation below on the rug.

He did not tell them what had haunted his soul. He did not tell the audience that prince Minofus was simply a deformed man and that he felt like he should never have slain him.

"But in darkness I managed to meet the tip of my blade with his flesh. A thrust. Then a thrust again. Until finally the beast lay dead at my feet!"

The crowd went wild. Theseus bowed.

"It was terrible," said Theseus, turning back to King Aegeus. "Terrible. I was so glad when it was all over."

"Well done, Aejades!" shouted Aegeus, clapping. "Well done! But tell me, how did you make it out of the maze? Not only was fighting the beast terrible, but finding your way through the labyrinth must have been equally hard."

"Not only did I stow a sword, I stowed a long ball of string."

"Brilliant!" cried Aegeus. "Brilliant, Aejades!" He slapped his knee. Then the king turned to Medea. "An incredible young man, don't you think?"

"It must have been terrifying," the witch said. "I can't imagine such a hideous creature."

There was more applause and Theseus bowed again.

"But there's one thing I don't understand," Medea said. Everyone quieted. She put a finger to her chin. "Why? Why did you do it, Ae-jades?"

"What do you mean?"

"Why risk your life with this horrible creature and then the danger of being stuck inside a labyrinth? Why volunteer?" Then she smiled a gaping grin. "Was it for fame? Areté?"

The silence from the five hundred on the fields before the palace was deafening. All eyes were on Theseus.

"It was for the justice, my lady," Theseus replied.

"Justice?" Medea cocked her head. Then she laughed.

The cackle of that old witch in the silent plaza before hundreds of his people was humiliating. But not only that, it tore at his heart. Somehow, she knew. Could the witch read his mind? She knew the doubt he felt deep inside. That laughter was the same rebuke he felt within. But for her to bring it out in the open before the whole kingdom enraged him.

He despised this woman. He wanted to run to her and choke her to death. He imagined grabbing and wringing her neck until she fell lifeless to the floor. He found himself clutching his fists so tightly that his fingernails stuck in his skin.

"Yes," Aegeus said, nodding and gazing at his wife suspiciously. "Well, wife, it was for the freedom of our people."

Medea grabbed her goblet of wine from the ground and toasted Theseus, still snickering. Then, under her breath, she said to herself, "Risking death from a bull or being buried to free seven Greek lives every seven years? Hmm? Areté?" She toasted him again. "Yes, areté indeed, it would seem."

"Your brave acts, Aejades," said the king, gesturing with his arms wide, "shall be sung for a thousand generations, my son."

Theseus bowed deeply and the crowd erupted in cheers once more. Then the words "my son" wiped the smile from Medea's face.

"Tell me," Medea spoke again. "What other acts of *justice* have you done? Surely such a hero must have done many miraculous things. We've heard tales of Pirithous, your young companion. And...I vaguely recall great acts of valor by his best friend. His friend's name was...*Theseus*. Theseus was a great young hero too, if I recall. With his club, he dealt his foes the same sentences they inflicted on their victims—he threw Sciron off his cliff, wrestled Cercyon to the death, and amputated the limbs of wicked Procrustes."

"I've heard such tales," said Theseus.

"Yes," said the king, "but even Theseus can't match a man killing the Minotaur, Medea."

"You really think your son can't match this man?" Medea asked.

There was no question now that the witch knew who he was. The question was, what was she scheming in her wicked head?

Now that his story was over, spectators in the field resumed their drunken revelry. A space was made for dancers. Three of them balanced on each other. Others did handstands. Then others spun about in front of and behind the climbers. Theseus thought that at least the people weren't watching the old crow challenge him anymore.

But then she did, in fact, open her loathsome mouth, "Aejades, your cup is empty. Allow me to fill it." She reached behind her for a concealed gilded goblet. "Such an honor to have such a hero in our presence."

Theseus took the golden cup from her, but then he handed it back.

"I've had enough to drink this evening, my queen," he said with a smile, "but thank you."

"You refuse a toast from me?" she asked, pushing it at him again. "Here. Please. Have a little more. This wine is from the vineyard in the South. It is like the nectar of Dionysus."

Theseus struggled with rage at the god's name. Dionysus. The god that had taken his Ariadne away from him.

"I don't care for watered-down wine, madam!" he snapped. Then he regained control and quickly tried to cover his hatred with a bow. "No, thank you."

Medea smiled wider. Many bystanders near the stage turned toward his outburst.

"We've traveled far," Elias stumbled. "We just arrived late. We are very tired."

"Watered down?" she asked curiously. "Watered-down wine? Interesting. I recall hearing of the custom of the barbarians. Barbarians drink their wine straight."

"Indeed. Like the barbarians of Colchis," said Elias with a nod.

Medea shot a glance of fury at Elias.

Perhaps King Aegeus had had too much wine, for he'd missed everything. He just laughed.

"Husband," Medea said, grinning again. "Ae-jades seems to enjoy travel. Why don't you tell him of your plans to attack the outsiders."

The king looked around. Everyone was either drinking or watching the dancers. "This plaza is public, Wife."

"No one can hear," objected Medea, shaking her head. "Only my son, your hero, and his servant. Certainly, you trust them? And there's not much that can be done about it anymore anyway."

The king hesitated. He looked Theseus over. Then he turned to the servants fanning him, gesturing for them to leave.

When the royal party was left alone, the king leaned over and whispered, "I'm pulling men to Piraeus, Aejades: from distant northern Thebes, to the East Isles, down to your friend Minos of Minoa." He put a finger to his lips. Then he started chuckling. "Shh." He finished his cup of wine. "All together to finally bring war to the king of Atlantis. What do you think of that?"

Too late. Elias was right. He was too late.

"Something the matter, Ae-jades?" asked Medea with a smirk.

Could this witch really have read his mind and known his care for Azurea? Was it simply his slip regarding the wine? Or could she know what troubled him, and how he ached, over Cassandra?

"This is secret," the king continued, "so, I trust you will guard the news with your life, of course. I trust you, Aejades. Just as my wife says. Anyone who slayed the Minotaur is our best friend, and Hellena owes you. You've traveled to Crete, Aejades. Tell me, what do you know of the outsiders? What do you think of my plan? My advisors think the continent of Atlantis is becoming weak."

"Surely you recall the battle of Azerban?" Elias chimed in.

Aegeus looked disturbed. No Greek could forget the death of thousands in those terrible battles with the Atlantean King.

"Yes, but that was long ago, when King Solinair was young." Then he squinted at Elias and said to Medea, with a big smile, wagging an unsteady finger at Elias, "This old man is no mere slave, Medea."

She nodded slowly, studying Elias now.

"Solinair is a mighty warrior," Theseus chimed in. "Trintz was but a year ago."

"But is he a good sailor?" Aegeus asked. "No, the soldiers of Atlantis do not know how to fight at sea. That is our strength. That is why we are sending an invading fleet to their shores. We can take their land in pieces. Certainly, perhaps, a full land invasion may not be wise, but picking them off in parts will bring the whole continent down to its knees."

"The time is right," said Medea, nodding. She patted the head of her son, and her son stupidly nodded as if he were her dog. "We must strike now."

"I don't think he intends to strike," Theseus said. "I would advise seeking peace first."

"Aejades," said the king, "Have you seen their ways? They're building a navy. If we don't strike, they will."

Just then, a large group of dancers ran in with torches, and Medea's son clapped again. It lit the grassy field brightly. They danced and hurtled over each other in flips and somersaults.

"Why not meet with the emperor first?" Theseus whispered to Aegeus. "Perhaps talk is better than violence with all the tension?"

Aegeus turned from the dancers.

"Hmm? Yes, well, no one wants to *meet* him, Aejades. We want to *kill* him."

"How far east have you traveled?" asked Medea.

Elias coughed at her hypocrisy, nearly choking on a fig.

"I've been to Knossos. That is all."

"Ah, but Minoans drink watered-down wine too," Medea

said, shaking her head. "Haven't you been to Azurea? Or did you go by the north in Illyria?"

"No," Theseus said, lying. "I heard about the eastern lands when I was in Crete."

"Interesting," Medea said, smiling slyly, knowing he was lying. "Come. Let us toast to your victory with the Minotaur." She pushed her gold cup toward him again. "Enjoy some more of our *watered-down* wine."

But before Theseus could take it, Aegeus snatched the wine with a laugh and an unsteady hand. The king toasted to Theseus. He tipped it to his mouth, but Medea jumped up and knocked the cup away from his lips. Half the contents spilled over Aegeus's chest.

"You stupid woman!" stormed the king, jumping up and brushing the wine from his now-drenched chest. "What's the matter with you!"

The witch shook and gave her husband a wide-eyed expression Theseus had never seen from this sorceress—fear.

Theseus looked at Elias. Elias nodded. The poisoned wine had been meant for Theseus.

"That cup was for our guest, husband," Medea snapped.

"So? Then you spill it on me!"

"Is there something wrong with the wine you offered my master, my queen?" Elias asked.

"It's for our guest," she stammered. "Not the king."

Aegeus flicked more red wine off his chest. But he still held the goblet.

Now was the time.

"She didn't mean to poison you, *Father*," Theseus said, jumping up and pointing at Medea. "She meant to poison me."

"Hmm?" Aegeus said, furrowing his brow. "What? What do you mean, poison you? What do you mean *father*?"

"Silence!" cried Medea, standing too. "*Watered wine? From Crete?* Don't you see, this man is a spy. He probably lied about the Minotaur. He talks highly of Atlantis. He's probably more loyal to King Solinair than to you. He's been deceiving us since he landed."

"And who are you loyal to, witch?" Elias said, jumping up. "Your father's land in Colchis or your former husband, Jason of Iolcus?"

The dancers stopped dancing. And everyone around the plaza stared at the stage.

"What are you saying, slave?" shouted Medea. "How dare you even speak to me. I'm loyal to my husband, our king."

"You just tried to kill the king's son," answered Theseus.

"I didn't!" she shouted back. "I..." Medea squinted at Theseus. Because his secret was out. Twice now.

"Witch," said Theseus. "You tried to poison me!"

"*Silence!*" shouted Aegeus. "*Silence!* All of you!"

Theseus bowed deeply. Medea glared at Theseus with challenging eyes, but she did not speak.

"Come here, server," said the king. A slave in a white peplos, who carried a pitcher, walked to the stage. Aegeus handed her the cup. "Finish my wine."

The server drank it. Then she returned to her duties in the field, even though everyone in the plaza still stared at the royal family.

The server collapsed on the grass.

"Poison is the way of cowards!" thundered the king to Medea. "You could have told me your thoughts about Aejades."

"He is not A-JA-DES, you imbecilic twit!" shouted Medea. "He is The-se-us, Aegeus! Any fool can see! Look down! He wears your shoes! He carries your sword! He is Aethra's son. How can you be the ruler of Attica but be so drunkenly blind!"

"My son?"

"Father," said Theseus with another deep bow.

Aegeus looked around him in confusion. "Theseus?" Then he turned to his wife. "Then... What was wrong with that cup? Did you try to poison me, Medea?"

Aegeus nodded to a group of guards, and they grabbed Medea from behind.

"I should have let you drink it!" Medea said. "You're a buffoon. You don't have a clue what's going on in your own Court!"

The king looked at Medea in astonishment.

"I am Theseus Aegeus, father." And he brandished his sword. "Witness your blade. I am the slayer of the Minotaur. And I am your rightful heir. Forgive me, I've been away too long. But I am your prince."

The crowd in the hall broke out in pandemonium. They murmured and shouted. Some screamed. But Theseus's noble stance was brief, for holding aloft his sword made the guards grab him.

"Unhand him!" Aegeus said to the guards. "Release my son. You are the slayer of the Minotaur? You? You are Theseus?"

"Yes, Father." Theseus said.

"Blessed be the gods!" Aegeus said, clasping his hands in wonder. "My son. My son has returned!" Then he narrowed his eyes at Medea. "But you! You, tried to poison him?" He shook his head. "Take her," he said to the guards. "Take her away... take her to the dungeon."

"Aegeus!" she said, in tears. "Aegeus! But I did it for you! Don't you see? Son or not, he is a traitor. Didn't you hear of his reverence for your enemies? I didn't want to hurt you. I just tried to get information from him. When I saw he was a spy, I tried to get rid of him for you."

The transformation of Medea from wicked and cruel to a victim seemed so fake it was almost laughable. And yet Theseus could see his father's anguish over sentencing his wife.

"Medea is the murderer of Jason the Argonaut's children," cried Elias, pointing. "She is a serpent that belongs in the Underworld."

Medea hissed at him.

"Take her to the dungeon," repeated Aegeus somberly, looking down.

The guards lifted Medea and dragged her from the Court.

Medus, her son, looked at the king. Then he looked at Theseus. Then he ran after his mother.

"Theseus?" Aegeus embraced him again.

"At long last, Father."

<hr>

THE PRINCE and king met in a royal courtyard outdoors the next day. The patio had three walls with the fourth side looking out over a calm stream. They were far from any passersby. And yet they could look out beyond the trees and water and down the hills of his kingdom. In the valley below, the sun shone over granite columns holding a myriad of buildings in their sprawling new city. And the sun shone gently on the two of them as they lay on their sides, by a table, eating soup. The prince and king wore plain gray tunics and pants—unintentionally, but ironically, very similar to each other.

Theseus's head ached. He hadn't lied to Medea when he had told her he'd had enough. He had drunk his share of wine during the festival. The king had drunk far more. Aegeus kept clutching his head.

"I can't believe how quickly everything has changed, Theseus," Aegeus said somberly.

Aegeus had a sadness about him. This was such a rapid change. Theseus had seen a boisterous, happy king when he'd first come to the palace. Or perhaps now this was simply his father sober?

"I'm sorry, Father. Things should have turned out better."

"The harpy's already escaped. I should have known. Medea was right, you know." He laughed bitterly. "I am a fool. How could I not see her evil ways? And how could I not notice you?"

"I'm glad you finally do."

"Yes, I had dreamed of your return. Ah, I wish it had been with your mother, Aethra."

Theseus dipped a piece of bread in his soup bowl. He looked down the hillside again. It was a magnificent kingdom that he could finally call his own. But he didn't eat. All he could think about was Cassandra and the planned invasion of Azure.

"Father, I need you to tell me more of this attack. Where are our ships? When will they strike? We must stop it."

"Was the queen right?" he asked with a rueful smile. "Are you a spy?"

"Actually, Father, some of the things she said *are* true. I have been to Atlantis. The Amazon nymphs are a good race. They are not what you've heard." Aegeus lifted a brow. "I once traveled through Azurea in order to find my way here. Azure Blue is near Mount Olympus. I took a terrible detour through the Underworld to find my way home. I've done all this, by the will of the gods, to find you."

The king nodded, staring back at his kingdom.

"Father, those travels led me through the depths of the Underworld. I then met my friends through Epidaurus."

Aegeus turned with amusement. He made a superstitious sign with his hands.

"I was trapped for a long time," Theseus continued. "I was able to get here only because of a girl. A nymph from Azure. Her name was Cassandra. She is their Amazon queen."

The king nodded, but he seemed to be losing interest. He was probably thinking of Medea again.

"It's hard to believe you traveled to the Underworld, my son."

"I have. And Azure Blue. That's why I need to speak with you. You have no idea what you're up against. Solinair is a great warrior."

"I spoke of this at the festival. It is because of his strength that we must act now. But they are not good at sea. Surely it is a great empire, but their threat is too great to not attack."

Theseus shook his head. "Cassandra gave me the Helm of Hades," Theseus said. "It was this cap that rendered me invisible. The Amazon queen saved my life, Father. I wouldn't be here without her."

Aegeus now had a bigger smile. Because he probably didn't believe him.

"There's more. I fell in love with this girl from Azure Blue. I was taken by her beauty and her spirit. Cassandra Ambrosia. She and her father are good, strong people."

Aegeus raised an eyebrow but still gazed at the view.

"Father..." Theseus took a deep breath. "Cassandra Ambrosia is the queen of Azure Blue. She is the daughter of Avivae Ambrosia...and we fell in love."

Theseus stopped, for it didn't seem like Aegeus was listening.

Theseus got up and leaned his weary, dizzy body against a white column of the atrium.

"I see," Aegeus said finally.

"Where is the naval fleet now, Father?"

Aegeus turned to Theseus. He attempted a smile.

"You're too late. I see how important this is to you, but there's no way to stop it. The ships will arrive in Atlantis in a matter of a day. They will meet with triremes already docked on the other side of the Mount and attack."

"I must warn them, then," Theseus snapped.

"Impossible." Aegeus shook his head. "There's no way you'll get there in time."

"Father, you don't know them. Where did you order this attack?"

"I've scouted the lands," the king said matter-of-factly. "I saw very few defenses in Azurea. King Solinair has built a threatening naval fleet, but we see none of it on the northern Napean isle. Only women that we can subdue. It is the perfect area to start our invasion. And, anyway, their emperor doesn't seem to take much interest in Azurea. There are very few bases stationed there."

"Father! The emperor will give his life for that island! It's their custom for no man to step foot there. But if you fight there, he'll pour everything into fighting back!"

"Seems he'll have to," he said, shaking his head. Then with careful words, "Theseus, our lives are... difficult. So much has changed. But, alas, I finally have you. And, why, what a wonderful surprise—you're the perfect informant about our enemy's empire." He chuckled. "Stay. Don't leave here now."

"You don't know the king of Atlantis. He'll stop at nothing to destroy you if you invade that island."

Aegeus gave him a blank expression.

"Goodbye, Father," Theseus said with a bow. "I will return. I need to travel to Azure and stop our fleet."

"You'll only see destruction," Aegeus objected, shaking his head. "You won't be able to stop it. I told you, you can't arrive in time. There's no chance, Theseus. This emperor of yours is a threat to all of Hellena. We can't allow him to continue to expand his empire. Let this go."

"I have to try. If I can reach the ships in time, will you allow me to stop the fleet as your son, the prince?"

The king ran his fingers along his chin. Then he nodded solemnly. "I don't know about this talk of the Underworld, but I believe you've traveled. Indeed, you probably are more versed in foreign lands than my own advisors. Yes, you may have my royal seal—if you can get there in time. But you won't. I'd much prefer you remain with me. Don't let me lose everything, my son. I can't lose you now that I've lost my wife. Why not stay?"

Theseus shook his head.

"I see how much this means to you," he said with a sigh. "Ah, tragedy has really struck me. On one hand, I've lost my wife, on the other, the gods have bequeathed to me my glorious son—one who now wants to leave me."

"I'll return, Father. I promise. I'm destined to be here by the grace of Athena."

14

THEY COME

CASSANDRA AWAKENED TO BANGING ON THE WOODEN DOOR OF her bedchamber. She heard the rush of footsteps and shouting. Looking out her window, she saw that the green sun had not risen yet and it was still dark. When she opened the door Hanna, in red hoplite armor, and Lalaina, still in a nightgown like Casey, were standing by the door. Behind them was the sound of nymphs rushing down the palace passageways.

"Their ships are battling ours on the Strait," said Hanna. "Get dressed and I'll accompany you to the throne room. There you'll have our protection."

"I'll go to the stable towers," Casey said, shaking her head. "I must meet them by sea and not allow them to land on our shore. But is there even still time to keep them away?"

"Yes, Casey." Then she surprised her with a tight embrace. "Just be careful. Cambria thought as much. Your mother didn't want to hide in the throne room during battle either. Cambria said that when you're ready, she'd meet you with the cavalry in the sky above the ships."

"You two stay back," Casey said with a nod. "Okay?"

They shook their heads.

"Stay back. I need you to guard the palace. If they breach

the shore, you'll still have plenty of opportunity to fight." Then she asked Lalaina what she didn't really want to know. "Did Cambria tell you how bad it is?"

"Mother said the sea is covered with Greek ships," Lalaina said. "They already captured our patrols west of the Mount. Their numbers are very large, Casey. Some of Torinth's scout ships are fighting them now, but most of his navy is still anchored. Cambria thinks that if they breach our defenses, they'll come ashore by early afternoon. She's sent messengers to your uncle, but there's no way he'll arrive in time."

"You two are in charge of gathering our sisters," Casey said with a nod. "Have everyone take up arms. March into the fields and meet them if I can't stop them by sea. No defense. Organize in a phalanx—like Queen Harmonia, in the old days—along the fields, and push them back if they arrive."

"Like your mother, we might have to," Hanna said wearily, shaking her head. "We might not have time to stop them."

"Well, like her, auntie," Cassandra said with a smile, "I'll take the scepter."

"Casey, maybe we should let them come ashore and fight them in the purple fields," Lalaina said. "Even if they take the palace, your father will come and push them back."

Cassandra shook her head. "No Amazon queen has ever let a foreigner step foot through our castle walls—certainly not occupy it. I won't be a part of such a disgrace."

Then Casey darted to her dressing room to put on her scarlet armor and get her things.

<hr>

THROUGH HER ROYAL RED HELM, Cassandra saw so many Greek ships below that it appeared as if the sea was not water, but one moving ship. The enemy was close enough to Napea that the sun's rays above them were now green. They had tried to evade detection by arriving during the night, but she was told they had been slowed down by her father's patrol ships.

Mainax cooed on Cassandra's shoulder. She petted him.

Some Greeks tried to shoot arrows at her from below, but she was too far in the clouds. Behind Cassandra, a hundred other nymphs in scarlet hoplite armor hovered on monokera, their wings flapping. Torinth's navy was forming far off on the horizon, but there wasn't enough time. Indeed, the Greeks were nearly on the beaches.

"Oh, Mother," Cassandra said aloud to herself, gazing down at the fighting. She squinted up at the green sun. "I know you'd fight them with me today if you were alive. Give me your strength to fight like you once did. Let me battle with the courage you showed Father when they surrounded the palace."

Mainax cooed again on her shoulder.

Cassandra permitted a chuckle and petted the bird. "Mainax. You know where Mom is, don't you? And Dad? He must be a hundred leagues away. If only he were here too."

With the thought of her father, she reached into a pocket in her armor and brought out a compass. It was a gift he had once given her. It was worn, with dents along the edges and a discolored lens. She ran her blue fingers along the dents and clutched it tightly in her hand. She kissed it.

Then it began.

Ships that had been docked along the beaches of Napea rammed triremes. Wood splintered and cracked, and men in brass armor were thrown into the raging water. She was surprised at the speed of the violence. Many blue-armored Atalans and scarlet-armored Amazons landed on the invading vessels and began sword fighting the enemy. Casey considered very bitterly that every nymph that landed on the ship, whether they died or not, was giving their immortality in defense of Azure. For the Amazon, this battle was not only gambling with death. For according to the edict of Hades: *any outworlder who steps foot on Gaia will come to me.* A ship's deck was part of the outer world too.

She heard cries of pain from mutilation. She witnessed stomachs being fileted. The speed of the violence shocked her. She had never witnessed battle. So many died so quickly.

The first ship fell. It was burned by her people. The smoke mixed with the smell of iron and excrement, nauseating Cassandra.

Then the sea turned rough. Was it interference by the infernal gods? It must be, for waves three times higher than normal began crashing on the hulls. Not only was there the edict of Hades, but a prior edict from Harmonia and Poseidon, which forbid any nymph to travel by sea. No doubt Olympus watched as nymphs now disobeyed two edicts. In the torrential surf, men and nymphs were killed not only by blade, they were tossed overboard.

Cambria, who flew close to Casey, shot her a stern glance. The general held a fiery look of rage mixed with hatred for these invaders, only to seethe at the sight of Poseidon's waves. The general raised her hand, and the flying cavalry took quivers hanging on their backs and armed their bows.

Then a cold wind came. Not only the sea, but the air started storming. The gods were attacking the nymphs in the sky too. Wind blew a torrential rain against her flying cavalry. Casey had to grab Inghorn's head tightly to not be thrown. Lightning crackled above. And the sound of thunder made Casey shake. She watched a couple of nymphs further out, she couldn't make out who, fall in the wind and plummet into the water—perhaps far enough to not survive the fall.

That was enough. Cassandra forced Inghorn against the wind in front of the hundreds and faced them. She raised the Scepter of Azure high and it lengthened. Then she shouted, "Fight!" Many would not hear, but she knew they'd see her. "Fight and honor your queen! They invade our lands! Protect Azure and our people!"

The Amazon cheered.

"Defend Napea! Hold allegiance to Emperor Solinair, my father! We fight to defend our world. The Greeks approach. *Show them why we are feared as Amazon!*"

The nymphs thundered. And the salpinx was heard—this time from the air.

Cassandra looked back at her island homeland. She could not see her palace, but the shine of green, purple, and blue of Azure Blue could be seen like a jewel off on the horizon. They were getting so close that a crazed sailor might try to reach the purple sands by swimming, if the rapids weren't so rough.

Her people, no doubt, could not see her body shaking. She struggled to stay aloft on Inghorn, not merely because of the winds but from her fear. She had survived the Underworld. But her uncle was right. She had never fought in war.

Cambria nodded to her in encouragement. Then Casey stowed her scepter in her baldric and armed her bow.

She dived with Inghorn toward the closest ship. As she fell, she aimed her bow. She had practiced, as a girl, how to shoot arrows atop flying unicorns, but never in real battle. For the first time, she watched her arrows hit real men, not targets, instantly killing them. Arrows passed through helms or cut at the sailors' bare legs. Soon all the arrows of the hundreds of her sisters around her rained over the invading triremes.

In an instant, Inghorn was over a ship. The unicorn skipped her hooves over a wooden deck, fast enough to nearly throw Cassandra overboard. Cassandra used the momentum to launch herself over her unicorn and land in her Amazon stance. She straightened her red helm over her sweaty hair and looked about her.

A huge Greek soldier charged her. Casey pulled out her Mandrigelian sword and blocked his thrust. She parried another thrust. Then, before he could hack back, Cambria fell on the man from above and struck him in the back, killing him.

Back to back, Cambria and the queen now battled. As they thrust and parried, further Azure hoplites fell from the sky to join the melee. And the arrows still rained down on the enemy as nymphs strafed them from the sky. Casey drew her blade across the neck of a toothless bald sailor. Yet as she cut, another managed to guide his sword along her lower right leg.

The searing pain stopped everything. Cassandra closed her eyes and fell to the ground. She felt Cambria grab her but then let her go with the clash of a sword against another blade.

The fall gave her a moment to catch her breath. She opened her eyes. She wished she hadn't. The air smelled of a foul odor of blood and sweat mixed with salty brine. She fought back nausea that only worsened at the sight of a Greek losing an eye to an arrow.

"Can you stand, Casey?" yelled Cambria, cocking her head back and reaching for her.

She nodded. But she wasn't sure. The pain was sharp, and blood trickled down her lower right leg.

Cambria was about to comment, but then another bronze hoplite jumped her. Cassandra turned Cambria to the side and managed to thrust her own sword into the charging sailor. The Greek fell, lifeless, against the wooden bridge.

The fighting was everywhere now. More reinforcements fell from the sky, but many Greeks, who had been under the deck rowing, ran up to the deck to give aid.

"Can you walk?" Cambria repeated, helping her up.

Cassandra nodded. Then they were both thrown from the deck as a wave hit the opposite side of the ship. Casey grabbed on to a wooden ledge for her life. She watched four other fighters, one an Amazon, get thrown overboard.

The strangest thing was what she heard from the captain below. "Row! Row! Almost beached! Row!" The Greeks were doing everything they could, in the midst of battle and a raging storm, to land the ship on Napea.

"Get back to the sky, Casey!" Cambria said, brushing the rain from her face as she grabbed Inghorn and pulled the drenched white unicorn to the queen. "You're hurt. You've got to go back."

Everyone on board was knocked off their feet again, including Inghorn, by another swell.

Cambria rose next to Cassandra, winded. Cambria whistled for Inghorn. The fierce rain and wind drowned her call. She whistled more frantically.

Finally, the queen's flying unicorn flapped its wings against the wind above the two of them. Cambria helped Casey limp toward her, but as she approached, Inghorn was hit in the neck by a javelin.

"Inghorn!"

The unicorn looked badly hurt. It was enough to throw Inghorn off the ship. She was injured, but not killed. Cassandra saw three Azure soldiers swoop down and help the royal unicorn head back to the beach.

"Inghorn!" cried Casey.

"She's hurt like you," Cambria cried. "Let her return to the towers, Casey."

Cassandra nodded.

"We need to get you up in the air."

Another group of hoplites in bronze ran at them with xiphos drawn. Cambria fell behind her queen again. The two readied themselves as the overwhelming enemy charge approached them. It seemed hopeless. Then more arrows overhead came down for support.

Another crash threw Casey and Cambria against the deck. This time, it wasn't a wave, it was a red Atalan galley—perhaps one of the ships finally arriving from Adelain? A whole army of blue hoplites boarded and fought back bronze-clad Greek sailors. Then the hull below was breached, and the men oaring the ship were attacked.

The trireme was swiftly claimed by the Amazon. The fight on this ship was over.

Cassandra removed her helm and brushed her wet black hair back. The view of another trireme sailing alongside her was strange. It wasn't seaworthy. Half of the ship was on fire, and the other half was sinking.

Icy rain fell. Then it turned to hail. As if the fight weren't enough, the gods were interfering with the weather again. She rubbed the pelting ice from her eyes in order to see. Meanwhile it continued to thunder and flash lightning.

Far out on the waters, many Greek triremes began retreating. And with this, the Atalans and Amazons cheered.

"The Greeks are running, Casey!" cried Cambria.

"We've won!" shouted Vayla. Vayla was a young Amazon. Now she raised her sword and shouted to Casey. "We've won, my queen! We've won! They're running!"

"Aye, Vayla," Cassandra said in exhaustion. "Gather the army, Cambria. We can fly back home."

"I've been trying," Cambria said wearily with a nod. "At least this ship is secure."Cambria ran back to the bow of the ship. She whistled and waved toward the cavalry to try, yet again, to get a unicorn to land.

Cassandra held on to a wooden pole as the ship swayed, bucked, and fell a few feet, in the roughest waters she had ever witnessed. The bodies of the dead rolled around the ship, their blood sloshing back and forth on the wooden deck in the turbulence. Cassandra was sea sick; beyond sea sick, battle sick. She was so dizzy from the stench of rotting meat and burning ash.

She limped over to the edge and vomited.

She tried to balance herself. Then she heard cheers from more of her Amazon. As bad as she felt, they were winning. Many Amazon above, who had been strafing their enemy, waved their fists in triumph.

Cassandra let out a great sigh. They were free and she had achieved what her father and that infernal uncle had asked her to do. She had protected Azure Blue.

Ironically, and very late, she caught many of her uncle's ships, with yellow and black flags, now arriving.

But then someone screamed. And then another. The screams were not of victory, but of horror. And many cries came from the sky.

Cambria was still at the bow. She was trying to help get a unicorn aboard, from the air, when she froze, looking out at the sea. She turned and cried out to Cassandra, but the noise of the waves and the screams around her were too loud to hear her. Cassandra limped along the deck. There in the distance she saw a huge swell, larger than she thought possible, approaching. Cambria cried out again to Casey, gesturing at the pole she held, but Casey still couldn't hear her. But she understood. Cambria jumped down closer to the base of the hull and grabbed the pole as tightly as she could. This wave was so great that it made a clean breach over the ship. The water pounded over Casey, and she found herself horizontal in the water for a moment, struggling to hold on. She knew that if she let go, she'd likely drown. Eventually, she couldn't hold on any longer, and she was launched, but somehow caught by the wooden wall of the ship.

She kneeled and coughed out salty water, gasping for air. As she looked around, she realized, in horror, that many of her sisters that she had seen before the wave had disappeared. Vayla was gone. Cambria was still there. The general ran to Casey and grabbed her, helping her up.

"The waves are too strong," shouted Cambria.

Cassandra nodded.

Then... All became still. Completely motionless. Cambria stared wide-eyed at Cassandra. With Cambria's support, Casey hobbled over to the side of the ship. The water was receding. The icy rain still limited their visibility but, on the opposite side of the ship, Cassandra could see over twenty Atalan galleys and recently acquired Greek triremes, no doubt full of Amazon and Atalan sailors, desperately trying to get back to shore. Ironically, her own people now were as desperate as the Greeks to beach their ships.

Cassandra turned back and spotted something, under the red firelight and smoke, beside the receding wave. She squinted under the cold rain and shook her head because she couldn't believe her eyes. A bare-chested gray-bearded man was walking on the ocean floor toward her ship. He moved his arms and huge waves parted before him. As he parted the water, waves crashed all around him and pushed toward her ship.

"Poseidon!" cried Cambria.

Cassandra did not have time to respond. A dark wall of water, larger than the last, crashed upon the hull. Cassandra was completely submerged again. Then, as soon as it fell, the ship shot out from under them and the hull smacked into her body hard, throwing her against the floor. For a moment, all turned dark… Serene.

She awoke sick, coughing and gasping. She retched out salty water. Cambria lay beside her with eyes closed. Then the general's eyes bulged, and she fell to her side, coughing up water too.

Then came another wave.

Somehow Cassandra managed to hold on to another pole, but it jettisoned Cambria right off the ship. Cassandra crawled to the side of the ship and forced herself up. Poseidon still directed waves with his arms, forcing the rapids toward her. Behind her, the ships were almost home. She could hear the cries of her people from the ships and from the flying unicorns above, trying to do everything to rescue her. Many shouted her name. And, thank the gods, she saw Cambria clutching a board in the water, being helped by other Amazon.

Cassandra struggled to stand starboard.

"Poseidon!" Cassandra raged through the pouring rain, limping across the ship. "Poseidon! Why fight me? We were once your people!"

The white-haired god turned and seemed to actually hear her, even though he seemed half a league away. His eyes shone red, glowing over his wet bare chest. Then her ship rapidly moved closer to him as the water receded.

Once more, it was oddly calm. But Poseidon was gathering more and more water. He moved his arms, forming vortices around and around, as if stirring a cauldron, to form a swell as large as possible. Then, finally, he sent the water barreling toward her. This one seemed a couple of hundred feet high. It was the largest wave yet, a wave that would not only submerge her and the fleet, it would bury her. It was so large that it might even bury the Isle of Napea and Azure Blue.

She would not make it to shore. Her Atalan ships and the triremes captured by her people would be destroyed. Thousands would die. Then the water would make its way to the palace and kill all of her people.

Thunder and lightning raged in a darkened sky. And hail turned to sleet.

Cassandra searched her baldric, with drenched fingers, for her scepter. Then she climbed to the highest point on the ship.

She would die. There would be no way that she could survive this. And yet, because she was queen, many of her soldiers still hovered over her, begging her to take their hands and try to escape. Escape where? This wave was going to destroy everything.

Much farther along the beach now, she could make out a regiment of blue hoplites forming lines and guarding her home world. Her father's men had arrived, likely from Torinth's reinforcements. Perhaps Torinth himself stood on horseback now defending the isle. But if Casey didn't do something, he and all the rest of these reinforcements would be run down by this tidal wave and drown.

Cassandra lifted her scepter and, as loudly as she could utter, she screamed the words:

"*Eneich Aneu Loriaan!*"

Ice flew from the staff. A blizzard of freezing air before her formed an ice wall.

"*Eneich Aneu Loriaan!*"

"*Eneich Aneu Loriaan!*"

She repeated the words again and again, until all the air left her chest, building more ice to buttress her wall from the ship.

"*Eneich Aneu Loriaan!*"

A wall of ice as thick as a house and half the height of the incoming tidal wave formed before her. She had not known exactly what the great staff would do, but she had willed this barrier. Then she dug into the wooden rampart of the ship with her staff as it continued to grow blocks of ice to block the wave.

"*Eneich Aneu Loriaan!*"

She repeated it over and over. And although she no longer

held the scepter, the staff continued to obey, thickening the wall with more and more frozen ice.

She finally turned to a unicorn above her, trying to grab the hands of her sisters. As Casey was taken aboard a monokera by an Amazon, the water crashed against her ice wall. Water burst up and around the shield of ice. It held.

But then the ice developed cracks. The pressure caused it to bulge. Water poured over it and the ice wall shattered. The force of ice and water hurled Cassandra and her companion into the water. She was submerged with her arms out straight. The force pushed her down so fast that she raced straight to the bottom of a dark chasm. Her ears popped. She was forced to breathe in water, choking. She couldn't breathe. More water poured into her mouth. She couldn't breathe. She couldn't…

15

THE AMAZON KING

Emperor Solinair wore a heavy fur coat, sitting in a wooden chair in the chilly air. The clouds had not cleared, but the ice had stopped falling. He sat, during most of the speeches, in the front row, in the violet fields of Azure Blue before the palace. During most of the ceremony, he buried his head in his hands and brooded. He greeted no one. Many nymphs spoke of Cassandra. Lalaina, her best friend, and Hanna gave speeches. It was heartbreaking.

There was an ominous sense of unease. Not only sorrow, but unease. Sol believed the nymphs were afraid. They had no ruler. Not only were they imprisoned on the island; now they had been broken by the Mount that towered over them. The last of all Ambrosias had passed. Unlike all those before her, Cassandra had left no heir.

When the trireme Casey had stood on to face Poseidon had fallen under the wave, it had not completely capsized. The staff she had used to save Azure had been thrust into the wood and remained in the wreckage. So now Cambria raised their scepter and crown before the crowd with more ceremony than she normally would have at a coronation. That was heart-wrenching for Sol too. Because no one rose to claim it.

For a moment, Sol figured Cambria would simply put the crown on herself and keep the scepter. When she didn't, and sat back down, Sol jumped up. He surprised himself. He approached Cambria and gestured for the scepter and crown. Cambria gave them to him. Then the king stared at the gold in his hand as he stood before a thousand Amazon and Atalan soldiers on the purple fields before the palace.

"My daughter sacrificed herself for you," Sol said. Many wept. And yet it was quiet. Though thousands sat in the purple fields before the palace to pay respects, no one said a word. Sol coughed and straightened. "With the courage of an Ambrosia, she fought a god. If only my eyes could have witnessed that. Her courage ended a wave that, I assure you, would have sunk a hundred ships and crashed down on this field and the palace itself. This was the greatest and last test of your queen…" He turned from them and looked toward the Strait. "Aye, such a queen she was. The best of them. Too young to be queen and too young to be killed." He paused. Many nymphs cried more. That only made him angrier. "She survived the Underworld because of the spirit of her mother. Then, with that same Ambrosia spirit, she faced Poseidon. I know of no other mortal so cursed by the gods with such a hard life. No matter how brave, she was dealt the hardest cards." He looked down again at the scepter in his hand. "It is unfair to have your daughter pass before you." He paused for a moment, tightening his grip. "I've battled to protect your lands. An Atalan kingdom formed, not for conquest, but for safety. For you. No longer are our people threatened from within, but now from outside, by Hellena. My daughter would have saved us from the Greeks and triumphed, had it not been for the cursed Sea God. She won the battle, but Poseidon, in a cowardly act, intervened. I've never had to fight the gods. But now, like my daughter, if given a chance, I surely will."

Many of his soldiers stood and cheered. Some Amazon rose as well.

"For this burial, I order that no one pour libations. Not even to your god, Persephone. Do not sacrifice food or livestock. Not for my daughter, not for anything or anyone. No just god would allow such a tragedy. As your emperor and king, I ask you all to obey only Anna's last law—disobey the edict of Hades. I tell you, whether you land outside the Strait or not, they aim to destroy us anyway. We are not their slaves. And, judging by the acts of the Sea God, we are not their friends."

He placed the small thin gilded crown on his own head. Many gasped at the display of a king crowning himself an Amazon. Others were likely in shock over his blasphemy.

Sol had learned that when his wife had spoken such blasphemy by the Stygian Hole, Zeus had thundered in the sky. Not this time. Perhaps the gods knew that they had gone too far.

At first, only Cambria and Falena, the queen's guards, stood up and took a knee before Sol. But then followed nymphs from every row bowing before him. And yet, from their expressions, it did not seem to Sol that they felt pride, only his festering rage.

The ceremony ended. Sol reluctantly did his duty and met with many of the guests. Some of them had come all the way from Egypt.

In time, it was nightfall. It was cold. Most had finally left the fields. It was as bright at night as during the day with a clear sky and full moon. That provided a light that made it seem almost like a dim afternoon.

Torinth, who had sat near the king but had not said a word, hobbled over to him in the deserted grass fields before the palace. Torinth was using a wooden cane tonight for his weak leg, injured in battle so many years before. He wore polished blue hoplite armor, unlike Sol's black chiton of mourning.

"I am sorry, brother," said the Tiger King. Torinth gently placed a hand on his shoulder.

Sol nodded.

"A horrible thing. I'm so sorry."

"We did what we could to defend the island."

"Aye, Sol. We did. I tell you, it was the interference of the gods that took your daughter, not the Greeks. Her victory, our victory, over their ships was glorious. And your daughter fought bravely. I witnessed the fight myself. Not only was she a nymph, she was Darius's granddaughter. A Solinaray. And I am proud to have been her uncle."

Sol nodded.

"When I met her, I was impressed," Torinth said, smiling cautiously. "Did I tell you that? She was as stubborn and willful as you. The same feistiness. In fact, she threw me out of her kingdom."

"I see."

"I've always hated Napean nymphs, you know, ever since Father was bewitched by Queen Delia. And yet, after what I've witnessed, I now understand your father's love. They are strong women. I admire strength, brother."

Solinair nodded again. The two watched as a handful of nymphs who were still in the fields spoke to one another. But most stragglers were taking the chairs and heading back to the palace.

"Of course, the gods heard your hubris," said the Tiger King.

"I don't care."

"It was a foolish thing to do. Very much like your words toward me and our brothers at Queen Delia's funeral. You don't need to tell everyone who you hate publicly at funerals."

"I tell you, I don't care."

"Aye," Torinth said, smiling but still staring at the others. "I know it…but, sometimes, Sol, you lack proper tact."

"I was told once I am not personable," Sol said with a nod. "I am a warrior like you."

"You're personable enough. More than me. You're just not political."

They walked for a while, in silence, back toward the palace.

"An incredible land," Torinth added. "Though now the night seems to cover some of its magic. It doesn't look much different from home at night. I don't know if you know this, but I had never been in Azure until you sent me to meet your daughter."

"What is it, Torinth?" Sol said, suddenly halting. "What do you want? We were never friends and we aren't now."

"Emperor," he offered a short bow and chuckled. "And you never were one to not get to the point, even as a boy. I think it is time. Time to move forward with our plans. I know why you freed me. The threat is greater than ever. And now, with our victory, despite the gods, we have the Greeks on the run."

"We've given them a heavy blow."

"It's not enough to protect the border. You know it. So… I'm asking: Do I have the order, brother?"

Solinair looked down. He sat down on one of the remaining wooden chairs in the field. He leaned his chin on his hand for a moment. Torinth seemed uncomfortable standing over him. The old man leaned on an empty chair. He seemed to be expecting a quick "yes."

"I do not thirst for war like you."

"Really?" Torinth laughed. "I think that's a lie, Sol. Your conquests in your lifetime have now been far beyond my own."

"If I give you consent, we will be embroiled in a fight that will never end."

"Our forces are stronger," he said, shaking his head. "Our ships are sturdier, and our will is of iron. Your men are fiercely loyal. We can win. And at the risk of not being modest, I'd say that you and I are the greatest generals in the world. There are no Morteuses or Philipps left to fight. The Greeks had a navy, now decimated. And they are not known to fight the way we do on land. We can conquer them."

"I just started a war with the gods. Now you ask me to fight the Greeks?"

"The Greeks started the war."

"We provoked them with our ships."

"Perhaps we should speak later," Torinth said, suddenly losing his smile. His mood had turned sour at that comment.

Then one of Torinth's commanders, in hoplite armor, ran to him for news, but Torinth quickly gestured the man away.

Torinth reluctantly sat beside the king, but he didn't seem to have any interest in keeping Sol company.

"Who will defend the South?" asked Sol after some silence.

"Egypt will leave us alone. You've told me that yourself. I wouldn't worry about them. Besides, surely you care little for the Hinterlands even if they choose to invade. Everything you've said tonight is truth. You care for this wonderland over all else."

"I was born in Kitheria."

"It seems you're bent on quarreling," said Torinth, suddenly angry. "Perhaps we should speak later."

"I just lost my daughter."

Torinth said nothing. He looked out toward the sea. Yet Solinair did not rise. He watched his brother writhe next to him, struggling with his madness while trying to be respectful. What a strange man.

"There is no casket!" Torinth suddenly blurted out between his teeth, gnashing them in anger. The comment infuriated Sol. "The lovely maidens just walked with the crown and scepter, empty handed—"

"*Enough, Torinth!*" shouted Sol.

"Brother," he said, lightly touching Solinair's arm, "we are born to fight. I do not have the stomach for doing nothing. Perhaps I'd rather fight with you than do nothing. The bastards may not have won the battle, but their allegiance to Poseidon led to the death of your daughter. That is truth, Atalan Emperor. Now allow me to do what you wanted me to do when you freed me. Allow me to teach them a lesson."

The Tiger King, indeed, was a wild animal. And now he was banging his cage. As kind a heart as Sol had, Torinth had none. If let loose, Torinth would destroy and burn any who survived. He would be ruthless and cruel. He would unleash the pain in a way that Solinair could not. It was why he had hesitated in freeing him. But now, as he considered his daughter, Sol realized that this madman who lusted for war was the perfect instrument for his revenge.

"You will move your men to Knossos in Minoa," Sol said.

"Take King Minos's castle as our first buffer. With the castle, Crete will fall. That will protect the lands I so covet, so you've said. Then wait with your army there. You will go no farther than Crete. I will move onto the Greek Isles with you, but not you alone."

"As you wish, my king." Torinth's rage vanished instantly and a large grin appeared. He nodded.

"You will not travel beyond Crete. Do you understand? I warn you, if you do, I shall imprison you again."

Torinth shrugged. "If you wish. But if the momentum is right, you should allow me."

"You will take the Minoans. If you do well, I shall give you Crete."

"My king! A wondrous gift!"

"Spare their temples and altars, for they do not worship our enemy on Olympus. But take King Minos and ensure he submits to my rule. Then build bases around the island to form a northern buffer for Azure. We will ensure Azure is never invaded again."

"As you wish."

"I will meet you in three moons. I shall sail the rest of the fleet to Phalasarna. Then we will look over our remaining forces and decide when the time is right to strike. It is my hope that we shall be ready then."

"Three moons," Torinth said, opening his eyes wide. "That is a tall order, Brother, for a land a third the size of Atala."

"If this is to work, we must move fast. If we dawdle, Attica will obtain help from Sparta and Thebes and rebuild their ships."

Torinth nodded and bowed. "Of course, Sol. Wise as always."

"When we fight Attica, you will destroy every temple of their worship. Burn them to the ground. Zeus and Poseidon will regret taking sides against me."

Even in Torinth's lust for battle, he furrowed his brow over that order. He was certainly not a pious man, but not a blasphemous one either. Nevertheless, he nodded.

"We will torch their remaining ships and surround Attica. Then I will have King Aegeus's life. I will. You will not move before me. I wish the honor of killing Aegeus personally."

"The sea will still be wrought with danger from the sea beast. I worry about our fleet under Poseidon's wrath."

"That is why, brother, you must move swiftly. Try to avoid any fight along the sea. Our advantage is our superior numbers and superior methods on land. Fight as we always have. Attack Minoa swiftly *on land*, not by sea. Use the cavalry like Father and the army like Henri."

"What of their ships, Sol?"

"Torch the Minoan ships by Phalasarna. We've already damaged many of them. But act fast. Do not wait. As far as the Greek fleets, they will be useless if they have nothing to attack. Use our fleets for swift travel, not battle. In time, hopefully, we will have smooth sailing around that bastard Sea God."

"I am ready, Sol."

"Then move. Move now."

"I shall sail tomorrow."

Solinair shook his head. "Now."

Torinth was beaming. "Very well," he said, standing up and bowing.

"Aegeus is Morteus. Go."

"As you wish, my king," he said with a bow.

"I wish it. Go!"

The Tiger King turned and looked toward the beautiful emerald palace. The green shone along the white snow. "I'm… sorry, Sol."

"Don't lie to me."

"I will have Crete within a week. Truly, it was an honor to have met your daughter before she passed."

"Avenge the death of your niece. The Minoans are old and weak. Destroy them and make their neighbors fear us. Then I will follow and trample on the altars of the Greek gods."

"As you wish," he said with a low bow again.

"As *I* wish."

16

NEPHREA'S DAUGHTER

SOL SAT ON THE GILDED AZURE THRONE IN DARKNESS. AFTER THE funeral, he had emptied his Amazon throne and preferred it dark and empty. Outside, the afternoon rain and clouds masked the beauty of his blue world. Today, the rain was ceaseless, pouring harder than Sol remembered on the Isle of Napea. Normally there was a lovely green glow from the sun shining through the glass dome during the day. Now, even in the midst of the lovely flowery vines flowing over the seats from the large vases in the hall, everything was drab and colorless, with only a handful of torches lit.

He did not host or entertain. He did not even allow Cambria to stand guard inside the throne room. He wanted no one around him.

His eyes grew heavy.

With his eyes closed, he ran his fingers along the golden staff: Anna and Cassandra's staff, the Scepter of Azure. He had no right to it. Grabbing it during the ceremony had been a fitful move. But who would rule? Cambria? Hanna? He couldn't stand the nymphs searching around the field for a new queen. But he was not their ruler. The Amazon nymphs would never accept rule by a man.

When he was nearly asleep, he jumped. He heard the two great wooden doors creak open. From the entrance emerged a figure wearing a black cloak and a hood. It reminded him of a pallbearer. Then he stiffened. Not a pallbearer, this looked like the Dark Lord. Hades.

The figure walked slowly down the dark hall. For a moment, Sol wasn't sure if he was simply asleep, dreaming. He instinctively checked his side for his sword—he had left it in the armory. Before the dais, the hood was removed, unveiling beautiful flowing blond hair. She was a woman with pretty features. Pale skin with a red dress under the cloak. But her prettiness ended with her eyes. They were burning red.

"King of Atlantis," said the woman with a nod. She looked about the hall. She walked, no glided, to a window. She touched the glass window with a finger. With broken words, she said, "Cold. The glass is so cold."

"Who are you?" Sol snapped, standing up before his throne.

"My name is Cora," she said, still looking outside at the pouring rain.

"Cora? Cora? The goddess Persephone?"

Could it be Kore? How? Henri told me Persephone was imprisoned, like my daughter was, in the Underworld.

"I am Persephone," she said, cocking her head back to Sol. "You have something of mine. It was my husband's staff before it was Harmonia's. And now that my dear Casey was murdered, it belongs to the rightful heir of Azure. That would be me."

"Your kingdom lies underground."

"I am Nephrea's daughter. This palace belongs to me. You, sir, aren't a nymph. If anyone should be sitting on that throne, it should be me. I am the only Ambrosia nymph queen left." Her voice broke when she said that. Then she violently turned back to the window. "The death of your daughter left no heir."

He hadn't been able to stop thinking that. But a goddess claiming to be the heir was madness.

Then Cora walked over to the front row and sat down on one

of the wooden chairs. She covered her face by placing her hood back over her head. But those red eyes continued to glow.

"Give it to me. You have no need for it. I'm not asking for permission. Queen Harmonia used it to conquer Atlantis. I used it to destroy the pyramid. Your wife used it to empower your empire. And your daughter used it to save Azure Blue. Now the scepter is mine. Give me my scepter, and I will do what must be done to finally right what was wronged."

"What will you do?"

"I loved your daughter. I will make things right."

"You imprisoned her."

She shook her head. "Zeus did."

"You abandoned her on the Mount."

"I was tricked by my husband."

"And you wish to return the scepter to him? No." Then he rushed down the steps and shouted at her. "Get out of here!"

"I will not return the scepter to Hades until after the deed is done," she said, undeterred. "Now I claim it for myself."

"You're not a nymph, you're an infernal god like all the rest—"

A bolt of lightning crossed the dome. Then the room was shaken by a crash of thunder. Cora did not rise, but she looked up at Sol with burning eyes. The flame glowed over her face. Then the rain pounded hard against the glass dome above. But the goddess didn't move. Only her hands, gripped in tight fists, shook.

Another bolt of lightning and thunder crashed down.

Cambria and Falena, wearing their scarlet armor, charged into the chamber. Sol lifted his hand warning them to stay back.

"Give me what is mine," Cora said, standing up before him. "I am the rightful queen of Azure Blue. Give me the scepter and this goddess will sacrifice. A goddess shall sacrifice for you, mortal. I will avenge what has happened. Your daughter's death shall not be in vain."

Another four guards ran to the door of the throne room as rain poured outside.

"Cora?" It was Engel's voice. That was enough for the goddess to finally turn her head toward the door. Sol was surprised to see tears running down her cheeks.

"I failed, Engel," Cora said. "I failed her."

Cora straightened and took a deep breath. The guards rushed closer to the throne but stepped back as Cora looked at them.

"What will you do with it?" Sol asked.

"Hurt them."

"This scepter is the symbol of the nymphs' power," Sol said. "I can't give it to you. It would mean the end of Azure Blue."

"Azure Blue ended when your daughter drowned. Give me the scepter and I swear I will avenge her death."

Sol shook his head.

"Give it to me and I will reunite you with your wife."

"What?" Sol asked, opening his eyes wide. "How? In death? Elysium?"

Cora shook her head. She put her hand out for the scepter, waiting.

All the guards now stood behind the goddess. When Sol still would not offer it, she moved faster than he had ever seen and snatched it from his hand. The guards, thinking that she intended to strike their king, advanced, but then Cora swung the golden scepter in a circle, forcing Sol and the guards back. She stood in an Amazon stance.

Then she looked up to the dome and whistled. A winged konobera, breathing fire, shattered the glass dome. Shards fell on all the aisle seats. Then the torrential rain fell upon everything in the throne room.

Cora mounted the winged demon beast as water poured over her. Then, all of a sudden, the rain stopped. As she rose into the air, the sky cleared. And a green light shone over her through the now-broken glass dome in the throne room.

"Your blasphemous words were heard on the Mount, Amazon king," Cora said, hovering above on her konobera, flapping its black wings. "War is declared. But fear not, I'm the one god on your side. I stand by you. You were my husband's instrument, I shall be yours. Witness my sacrifice as I destroy every one of them."

The konobera breathed fire out of its mouth like a dragon. Then Cora raised her scepter above her head, crying out the ancient Amazon battle cry, as she launched out through the dome and away from the palace.

17

RISE KHEPRI

CORA RODE HARD, CARRYING A LARGE LEATHER BAG OVER HER shoulder, traveling over shards of volcanic rock and ash atop a giant black demon horse. The eyes of her steed shone the same fiery red as her own. Smoke flowed from the stallion's nostrils and mouth. Her red dress and long flowing blond hair contrasted sharply with the horse, the black ash, and the broken soil, though her hair was getting peppered with the kicked-up dust. At times, the horse jumped and wailed in pain as its leg dug into a sharp edge of cracked ground or a stream of flowing red lava. These beasts were made for the terrain, yet Cora would not relent, pushing him beyond his limits and as fast as he could move. She raced to protect her last beloved nymph queen. Avva would not survive if Cora could not complete this final task in time.

Soon a red glow and the large stone fortress and Dark Tower of Tartarus could be seen in the distance. Then she rode over the steep cliff and over the moat of fire. The guards at the main entrance fell to their knees as the queen of the Underworld rode through the gates.

As empty as it was outside, inside bustled with ghosts and devils. Some turned, licking their lips at the sight of a girl. But upon recognizing their queen, they cowered from her.

She rushed up a steep incline and into the winding stone street of the city. She nearly knocked down merchants in carts and on horseback standing in line waiting to enter the black glass tower. A drunken man in tatters walked up to her charging horse, but he was quickly whisked away by an old hag. Then she dodged a child beggar, then a prostitute.

She reached the courtyard. That pained her. She came so infrequently now to the palace that the courtyard simply brought up memories of Cassandra.

The girl had been kept in a cell there many years ago. Perhaps this was where they had grown attached to each other. The girl wrote poems and talked of her homeland and, through it all, the lifeless dead trees and black spikey brush didn't seem to tarnish her innocence. Cora loved her laughter the most. It reminded her of her mother, Nephrea. Even Avva had that wonderful laugh. No, even Casey's thoughtfulness, kindness, and sophisticated air reminded her of Nephrea—so grand a royal demeanor that she didn't even seem affected by living in the dirt and shit of the Underworld. For Cassandra, like Avva, was an Ambrosia.

Cora jumped from her horse near the entrance to the Dark Tower. Then she swatted the butt of the fire-breathing beast. It took off into the air.

She walked to the line and cut in front of a mother in rags holding a little girl's hand. Some men behind her shouted at the break in the line, but they quickly looked down after seeing who she was. Two Eruboi in black armor by the threshold fell to their knees.

The entrance was a huge open chamber. In the past, Cora had avoided this busy plaza, preferring the quieter entrance through a broken gate in the courtyard. But she didn't have time.

Black columns rose from a dirty, tarnished, cracked marble floor. A large field of black ivy lay in the center with a gigantic gilded white marble statue of her bastard husband. The statue of Hades leaned on an elbow before a great central fountain. The fountain was broken and full of mosquitos. It was large enough to accommodate ten to twenty people and, indeed, now a party of just that many, some naked, squatted in the shallow water, splashing, before the mighty monument. Around the fountain, lying on their sides on animal fur, were many more. But everyone who saw the goddess fell on their knees as Cora rushed to the central stairs.

The walls of the tower were made of glass like the Crystal Palace of Azure, but this glass, looking upon the volcanic lands, reflected black. When she reached the middle of the great hall, Cora could see floors above, where men in chitons and women in more elaborate peploi traipsed along walkways. She saw some transparent ghosts too. Some couples were powerful dignitaries who had petitioned her husband to live with their dead spouses. It didn't matter if they were dead. Nor did it matter that the price was servitude to Hades. But all of them, including nobles, stared listlessly at the floor. For everyone, even the nobles, was destitute in this broken land.

Cora made her way along a broken stone path that meandered into vast fields of indoor ivy. Merchants lined these walkways but, again, gave her distance.

The Underworld throne room did not lie at the top of the tower, like her bedchamber, but at the very bottom. She took a walkway that slanted downward until she headed below the plaza. Then, after turning a few more corridors, she approached giant double doors where two burly guards, Eruboi in black armor, towered over her. They were standing at attention. Then they bowed before her.

"Is he here?" Cora asked, moving her bag to her other shoulder.

"He asks not to be disturbed," a beardless man said. The man removed his helm and bowed again.

"Even by his wife?"

"Especially by his wife," said the other, trying to suppress a laugh. "Pardon me, Your Majesty." He quickly lost his smile and bowed again nervously. "Forgive me, my queen, but even you are not allowed to enter. Not now."

Cora rolled her eyes and pushed them aside. She walked through a stone hallway, lit only by torches, that led to stairs descending far down into their throne room.

The throne room door was cracked open.

Usually it was an empty torch-lit earthen room with only a throne and a few chairs. Not tonight.

Cora saw why the guards had tried to stop her. The room was full of scantily dressed men and women, many naked, embracing each other and writhing on the rugs like snakes. All drank. Some sang stupidly, raising silver goblets in drunken stupors. Many were fornicating. It was a great orgy. Her husband had joined too, lying by his throne, roaring with laughter, with three naked women. Music from a band could be heard but not seen. And many ate meat and cakes as they partook in the sinful indulgence of their neighbors.

Persephone looked away. Even after centuries of this filth, the view disgusted her. Then she shook her head violently and cried, *"Out! GET OUT!"*

When some did not hear, she screamed so loudly that it hurt their ears.

"OUT! EVERYONE OUT!"

Looking at her, many got up and bolted to the open double doors. They rushed out so fast that few bothered to dress themselves.

Soon the entire cave was vacant—except one. A giant bald-headed man, seven feet tall, with a goatee. He leaned his elbow on the ground in the same fashion as his stupid marble statue. He nodded at her with a smile.

"Cora." He rose to his knees before her, naked. "What a surprise." Then he jumped up, walked to a table, and poured himself a glass of wine, turning his ass to her.

"You should get some clothes on, Husband."

"Oh, it's nothing you haven't seen—a very long time ago, anyway. What can I do for you?"

"You have no shame."

"I am Hades, lord of the Underworld." But then he reached

for a white robe and clothed himself. He raised his silver cup of wine and snickered stupidly as he drank.

Cora didn't speak. She approached the dais.

To her right was Pan. The satyr sat on a carpet squinting curiously at her. And to the left were two black-armored Eruboi guards, the only ones dressed other than Cora.

"I… " stammered Hades, drinking from his glass. "I know you don't approve of it when I indulge myself, but, well…is there something I can do for you?"

She said nothing. But her eyes shone so brightly that it created a scarlet glow before her face.

"It's good to see you," he said, turning toward the small table with the flask of wine. "It's been a long time. Care for some wine? You don't come here often anymore. Coincidentally, this wine is from Argos. They say the grapes were chosen near your home by Dionysus himself. It tastes delightful."

"I've accepted everything from you," Cora replied. "I've lived this wretched life. I've turned away from filth and dung and called it home. I've ignored it all, all to feign love for you. Perhaps—"

"I'm really sorry for this festival," he said with his hand up. "But, as I said, you haven't been here in a very long time."

"*I don't care about sex, you idiot!*"

He furrowed his brow. Two more guards walked into the room. They stood by the door and bowed before the Dark Lord, checking to see if their services were needed.

"*Out!*" she raged. "*Leave us!*" Then she turned to the two guards still standing to the left of the throne. "*Get out!*"

The two guards looked over at Hades. One was visibly shaking. Hades nodded.

"What is it, Kore? Is something wrong?"

"As if you didn't know."

"I don't," he said, shrugging. "Truly."

"Cassandra's dead!"

Hades actually chuckled. But he quickly put his hand over his mouth. "She's a nymph."

"She's Casey!"

"She's a wood nymph."

"A Napean nymph! An Amazon. Nephrea's!"

Hades' eyes squinted. He walked beside her and wagged his finger. "Be careful."

"What kind of justice was there in taking her life! She won the battle. Your bastard brother intervened. He intervened with mortals and drowned her! I can't revive her from the bottom of the sea. I won't ever find her and, if I do, it'll be too late. Her body will not be salvageable. Poseidon knew that. And my father and mother knew it too. And you knew it. She was just a little girl! An innocent girl. Why take her!"

"If anyone should be angry, it's me. You said Cassandra was going to free me."

Cora slapped him. The impact was so fierce that it threw his head to the side and cut his lip. Pan jumped up. A few Eruboans rushed into the room again, but they stepped back at her fiery gaze.

The edge of his face dripped with blood. He brushed the blood on his hand. Then he licked it.

"I hope for your sake that this is a new fashion craze of sadistic coition," Hades said.

"You coward! You did nothing! You loved them. You loved Harmonia more than me. And you let our family kill her!"

He flicked his hand in her direction and a magic force threw her a few feet. Then he growled at her like an animal as she lay on the ground.

She was beside the small wooden table with the wine decanter and crystal wine glasses. She grabbed the whole pitcher. Hades opened his eyes wide and put up a hand to object, but he was too late. With two hands, she splashed the red wine all over his face. As he fell to the ground with his hands up, impotently trying to block more liquid spilling over his head, she drained every last drop on him.

"Isn't this what my mother did to you!" cried Cora.

Two Eruboi grabbed for her. She snatched one guard's wrist

and twisted it until it snapped in half. Then she took the bag still hanging on her shoulder and swung it at the other guard's head, knocking him across the room. Hades jumped up and shoved her back on the floor.

"*You dog!*" Now his eyes burned red, standing over her. "I could never tame you! That's why I left. Who do you think you are?"

"*I left you,* you turd!" She got up on her side. "I'm the only clean thing left in this dung heap."

"You're a rotten whore who sticks her nose in our business. You're a spoiled brat as dumb as the nymphs you so covet! You care more for these nymph pets than for me!"

"*She was my daughter!*"

And she fell to the ground, covering her face with her hands, and wept. "Damn you! You knew that. You did nothing! Just like you hurt my mother. Call me a nymph? That is an honor. I hold more honor as an Amazon nymph than I'd ever hold as a god."

"Cry. Go ahead. Cry." He ran to the table and lifted a glass of wine. The crystal wine glass was empty, so he threw it at her while she lay on the ground crying. "That's better. Cry, cry, cry about the world. You think I'm happy? Yeah, you left me. That's right. You preferred a desert. And don't think for a moment I don't know who you're hiding there. Perhaps if I'm as bad as you think, I'd have snitched and told Zeus and Hera about that. Imada's searched. Too arrogant to go to your foster mother's homeland. Your *foster* mother, Kore. But I know your stupid sentimentalities. Your real mother, by the way, is Sara, the goddess Demeter."

She didn't stop crying.

"*Curd!*" he shouted.

But his shout was not meant as a slur for Persephone. He was calling for his servant.

"Curd! Damn it! Where is that little sarding bastard?"

A disheveled old bald man wearing rags ran barefoot to his master. He bowed deeply.

"Get me more wine! The bitch broke the crystal decanter!

That was Mandrigelian. Very valuable. I give you my jewels and gold, but it's never enough, is it?"

"Don't bow, get me wine!" Hades gave his slave a swift kick. "More wine, you idiot!"

"How could you let this happen?" Cora asked, not lifting her head.

"I don't want to talk about it… Not until I have more wine."

"I once loved you."

"Oh, shut up. You love whatever you use. You're a demon, and you know it. You don't even know what love is."

Curd ran back with a tray with another crystal decanter and two glasses. Hades lifted the decanter and examined it. Then he smiled and toasted his wife. He drank the wine directly from the decanter with two hands. Some of the red wine dripped from his lips, mixing with the blood from his cut lip. Then he took a deep breath and, with a dreamy expression, smiled toward his wife. "Ah, lovely, Curd. Lovely wine. Just like my lovely sick wife." Then he handed it back to his servant and walked up the steps to his throne and sat down. He shook his wrists and brushed spilled wine off his bare chest. Then he glared at her.

"Where were we?" he asked.

"You killed Cassandra."

"Why would I do that? After all I did to help her leave."

"You are the god of the Underworld. Her death is on you. You doing nothing killed her."

"Yeah? What did you do? We all know you're the goddess of prophecy. Hardly Sara. Why didn't you foresee it? You told me that this queen would free us. You're obviously wrong."

Persephone got up and brushed her wet eyes with the back of her wrist.

Pan slowly sank down on his hairy legs. Then the satyr cautiously took some grapes with a shaking hand.

"Frankly, I really don't get it," said Hades, running a hand along his bald head. "You told me that if I let Casey go, she'd free us. I've been waiting." He gestured and looked around the room. "Where? Where is my freedom? If she's dead…" He jumped up again and thundered, *"Does that mean I'm prophesied to stay down here forever!"*

She stared at the ground.

"Hmm?" He smiled, sitting back down. "Speak. Why come here, witch wife? You didn't come here for a cry. For all I know, that was for show. Oh, I love your guile. Tell me what stirs in your head. You wish to cry in my throne room? I'm sure you've done enough of that in the cold sand dunes of Hasevalah with your dear special friend. Or…" He paused and leaned over. "Did you not tell her yet?" He laughed and brushed blood or wine from his lips. "I'm sure you'll be pals when she finds out about it. Well, there's no one who schemes more than you, Apate. Tell me what's on your mind, Kore. Go ahead. I adore it. It is the one thing, aside from your inimitable beauty, that excites me. Why storm? I didn't kill your wood nymph."

"Your passivity did."

"Frankly, I think the girl had it coming to her. I protected them until Avivae. Perhaps the death is on her. Now you were supposed to—"

"I will chain Zeus."

"Such rebellion is blasphemy. I warn you."

"I will chain him. And I will chain Poseidon. I came to see if you wish to help me."

He squinted at her and shook his head. "I won't. But I'm listening."

One of the Eruboans ran up to the throne and fell to a knee. "Thoris is hurt badly, sire," he said with a bow. "They snapped his sword-wielding hand."

"He was protecting me. She'll mend it."

"I won't," Cora said, standing up.

"You're such a baby." Hades took a deep breath and shook his head. Then he gestured to the guards. "Leave the Court. Leave now."

The Eruboi bowed and left. Only Pan and Hades remained in the chamber.

"Go on," Hades said. "You have my attention."

"When you took me from Gaia and brought me down to the pit, I wanted revenge. I wanted to hurt you. And I did. All the comforts of Gaia, brought here by the fires, could be removed if I froze them. The only way I could do that was by plotting with you to bring back my nymph friend, Nephrea, from the depths."

"You needn't rehash old tales of misery, wifey."

"I got my hands on the scepter. I doused the flames and turned our home darker." She met his gaze with her eyes blazing so red that it caused a red glow to flood her vision.

"Yes," he said, grinding his teeth, "indeed you did, louse."

"You're a puppet. You've done nothing to right this misery that your brother brings us. You couldn't even stop me from freezing your realm. You're weak."

He leaned back in his throne and scratched his groin. He gestured for her to continue.

"I'm really not mad at you. Of course, I hate you, but I learned over the centuries that you suffer as much as I do. I'm disgusted with *us*. Now, just as I caused you pain, I can hurt them. I will punish them. Do not doubt my rage. Consider me now a god of my mother's people. Witness Khepri. I have survived your shit. Now I shall be reborn in scarab dung. You may side with me if you wish, but if you don't, don't you dare try to stop me. Or I will chain you too." She removed a golden rod under the cloth of her red peplos and laughed as his eyes widened. "Behold! A scepter materializes before your blind eyes! You hold no control over your own house. I have your rod."

"Where'd you get that?" he asked, jumping up again.

"It is my right as the daughter of Nephrea."

"*You are not the daughter of Nephrea!*" he thundered, pointing at her. "You confused, stupid girl! You're the daughter of the King of the Gods and Demeter."

He rushed down the steps.

"I will battle him," she said, challenging him with her glare. "I will take your staff and destroy Poseidon and Zeus. Cassandra, a woman worthier of life than any of us, did not die for nothing. I will use her sacrifice for war. You may watch, as you so enjoy doing, but I will avenge her, or perish. Help me or not, I will hurt them."

"You're mad," he said, violently shaking his head. "You're completely mad. Even with my scepter, Kore, you can't fight them. Give it to me," he said, reaching out. "Give me the scepter."

"It's not yours," she said, laughing and stepping back. "It belongs to the queen of the nymphs. That's now me. But you can have it after I'm done."

"What will you do with it? I won't protect you. They'll chain you like Kronos."

"If I fail. Otherwise, I will chain them."

"But how will you not fail?"

"With your help. We read the prophecy wrong, husband. We can be free. Indeed, freeing Cassandra set the fates. It is now our fate. Because her death has made me no longer care whether I am imprisoned in chains before the fires. Watch me rise from this dung heap like Egypt's scarab, like Khepri, and fight. And if I'm brought back down to filth again, so be it. But since I no longer care, I will fulfill the prophecy."

"Don't do this, Kore. He's too powerful. You read Cassandra's fate wrong, now you'll be shackled forever if you attempt this. Ares and I tried. Why do you think I was banished to Tartarus in the first place?"

"You know I never left you. I waited thinking the Amazon would free us. That it'd be my mother, Nephrea who'd free me—after even Avivae and her daughter. Now all is evident. Our family thinks that by destroying the Amazon they have destroyed us. No. They've unleashed Khepri. Khepri will destroy them."

Hades squinted at her. His red eyes faded to blue. He nodded solemnly and said quietly, "How, Kore?"

She walked over to her leather bag and untied the rope. Inside lay a shiny silver helm. His cap. She took it out and laid it by Hades' feet. Then she looked up at him with burning eyes, so bright that the red shone over his face once more.

"You've had the power all along, you simply never used it.

Allow me to show you how." She placed the helm on her head. "Accompany me or leave me alone. Either way, I will have revenge."

"Pan," Hades said, cocking his head back. Pan was standing up. "Did you hear or see any of this?"

"Hear what, sire? See what?" But, indeed, Pan's eyes were bulging. "I wonder, my king, when your wife will return from the sands and give us the pleasure of visiting us again?"

"Indeed. Leave me alone for a while, won't you? Apparently, I need to talk with myself some more."

"As you wish, Hades," Pan said.

After Pan left the chamber, his hooves clopping on the stone floor, Hades said, "Are you still here, Kore?"

"Yes, bastard. But not for long."

"Tell me your plan."

18

A GREEK HERO'S RESCUE

Theseus sailed alone, without his friends Elias and Pirithous, as fast as his ship could move to Azure Blue. He had come aboard one of the swiftest royal galleys, made lighter by a small crew. He shouted at his crew, ignoring the tides and the weather, even a terrible storm that limited visibility while passing Arcaseia in Karpathos. Soon he spotted Mount Olympus high in the sky. Here his ship sailed beside the first broken, charred trireme.

It was more of a floating barge of wood than an actual seaworthy vessel. The crew was sick and starving. He brought all on board and spoke with their captain, Timolos, a young naval officer less than twenty years of age. Theseus met the blond-haired captain in his cabin.

Timolos told Theseus of the struggle with the Atlanteans. He said the Amazon queen herself dove onto a nearby ship by flying unicorn and fought his men.

"What happened to her?"

He shook his head. He told Theseus a tale of how the Amazons broke many ships. Then they burned the rest. At first, Amazons were far outnumbered, but with reinforcements from the air and, later, the sea—from Adelain Port in the east—the tide of the sea battle turned against the Greeks. Then…

Timolos became strangely silent.

"What? What is it, Timolos?"

He shook his head.

"Captain, what happened next?"

"I've been at sea all my life, my prince, but never have I seen such a thing. Poseidon's waves started crashing down everywhere. They were the worst waves I've seen in my life. At first our men cheered, for it seemed to be aimed at the nymphs. But it was so rough that it even took the lives of many of our own. Then…" He stared wide-eyed at the floor.

"What?"

"I saw a man." He shook his head violently. "I couldn't believe my eyes, Prince Aegeus. The wave formed around a single shirtless man. He had strong, rippling muscles, but was old with long white wavy hair and a white beard. It was Poseidon. It must have been. I couldn't believe my eyes. He stood there in the middle of the water. My men cheered, for his wrath was thrown at the Atlanteans, but then something terrible happened. The Sea God formed a swell larger than all others. Some say the crest was so high that it seemed to be as tall as Mount Olympus itself. It crashed down over the nymphs' shores and ran toward their wondrous palace. We hadn't made it far enough on their shores to attack, but Poseidon did. I had never seen such a wave. I had never seen anything like it in my whole life."

"Did it destroy Azure Blue?"

"I don't know. We fled. We were happy to make it out alive."

The young man's hand shook as he tipped a silver cup of wine to his lips. Then a wave hit Theseus's ship and made him spill some of it on his white shirt.

"Damn!" He forced a smile. "I've never seen such a thing. No, I've never seen such a thing."

"Here," Theseus said, handing him a white cloth. "You don't know what happened to the queen that fought? Or the others?"

"No. Of course, we were happy to be blessed by Poseidon's

revenge. You know the nymphs aren't permitted to sail the sea. I figured the god was punishing them. I'm sure even landing on our vessels counted as an offense of their edict."

Theseus nodded, leaning his head on his fist. "Timolos, just rest."

The fear left Timolos's face. He smiled. "I am so grateful for your aid, Prince Aegeus."

He wasn't grateful for long. Shortly after that, Theseus's vessel encountered another ship. Then a group of ships. An entire armada. And this navy was not Greek. They were painted scarlet and flew blue flags with a central yellow sun. Their ships were similar to Greek triremes, but larger and newer. He had never seen ships so new. And they sailed swiftly just as Theseus had. But they were heading the opposite direction. Theseus's small ship was quickly surrounded.

Theseus surrendered. His hands were tied behind his back at sword point. He and his crew were gathered and transported onto the largest ship in the fleet. From the deck, he could see thousands of soldiers in blue hoplite armor.

He was taken alone to the hull of a dark brig. His cell had only a single wooden table, nailed to the ship. Here he sat and waited in silence. Then, after some time, the large wooden door swung open.

Theseus had been stripped down to a simple white chiton and boots. He greatly contrasted with the man who hobbled into the room. This old man used a wooden cane and wore a ridiculously multicolored chiton with rows of gold necklaces. He was tall and had a silvery beard with broken teeth.

"Prince Theseus Aegeus?"

"Who are you, sir?" asked Theseus bitterly. He stood up from the wooden floor with hands still tied.

"I am King Torinth Solinaray from the kingdom of Adelain.

I've come to destroy you and your people." Torinth gave him a broad grin showing his ugly teeth again.

Theseus stepped back as the Tiger King hobbled forward.

"I…" stammered our hero, "I came to see the Azure queen. To warn her."

"Warn her of what?"

"The invasion. Seems…I was too late."

"Aye. You were that." Then Torinth shoved Theseus against the floor. Torinth stood over him. Then, bizarrely, he smiled and hummed. And it was all very odd, for there was no sound except the creaking of the ship and the humming from this vile man. "You might want to call your butcher of a Sea God," Torinth finally said. "There is little that is staying my hand from casting you to sea, but I fear the beast would rescue you. Call on him. Only you cowards need gods to rescue you in battle."

Torinth spat on him. Then he stood him up. He hit him with both hands across his face, seemingly as hard as he could. Theseus, a large man, was still stunned by the force of the old man. He reeled back and fell to the floor, only to be kicked in the stomach.

"I will tell you a little secret, eh," Torinth said, kicking him again. "I did not build my navy for defense. I built it to rape you. To pillage you and your people. To rape your women and children." He kicked him again. "I will hang and crucify your fathers. I will tear the flesh from your mothers and cut off the very breasts that suckle your children. I will burn every Greek temple and city of Hellena to the ground. Then I will burn your crops and salt your fields. Do you know why? Because we shall be free of you and your gods. My naval defense was merely a platform. When your army greets me, you will fear me. While I best you cowards at sea, my brother will trample over your villages. You will feel the pain you've dealt us." And he kicked him again. And again. "I swear it! I swear it!"

"Now, Theseus Aegeus of Attica, tell me why you travel here? That was so very amusing." And Torinth put his hand to his ear and leaned over.

"I came to warn the Amazon queen," he said quietly.

"Ah. Well, the Amazon queen is dead. Solinair's daughter, the queen of Azure, drowned before your Greek fleet by the hands of Poseidon. I watched it myself. But unlike you, who hides behind the dresses of Athena, my niece stood before him. She blocked the Sea God's wave with her scepter. She is the bravest woman I've ever known. But now the Amazon queen lies at the bottom of the sea. With that, you've taken our heart, our honor, and all that my brother, the emperor of Atala, ever cherished in this world. And for that, prince, be assured that Sol and I will butcher your people.

"But I am not a savage. I will give your people a little time to rebuild. Unlike Greeks, I prefer a fair fight. We sail first to Minoa. In another moon, we shall use the island as a base to then sail up your ass. Then you will see truly why you all fear Atlantis."

"The Amazon queen died in the fight?" Torinth asked, in disbelief, cocking his head up. The Tiger King spat on him again as an answer.

"I'll spare you for now," Torinth said. Then he laughed. "I'd rather give you to my brother and let him break your neck with his bare hands."

19

AMPHITRITE

Four winged konabera were used to fly Hades' chariot but only a few of the beasts were known to fly in the Underworld. Most konabera were wingless. It was said that when a battle was waged, if a dark red glow came from the enemy at night, the army should run, for it meant Eruboi were charging atop their demon cavalry.

Well, Cora stole one.

She flew atop her konobera, with a leather bag strapped to her shoulder, up through the Flume of Thyra and above her beloved Azure Blue. She could see the Crystal Palace radiating blue-green and purple far in the distance. And the coastal woods, damaged by the waves. Wood was splintered along the coast. And as she looked down, in a moment of madness, she considered combing the sea. But it had been too long. She couldn't revive Casey properly even if she found her. A rotten and decayed body was unsalvageable. And she suspected, as she had told her husband, that this had been planned by her infernal family all along.

Hugging close to the Mount, she flew northward toward Crete. Then some time later, she approached the island of Evia.

There she landed on open yellow fields. The black steed labored, panting, as he landed in the empty field.

"Lazy oaf!" said Cora, slapping the horse. "Why, Antilus flew further and hardly complained."

He snorted.

The sun soon set as Cora walked. Her stupid horse followed by her side.

But as the light dropped below a thick grove of maple trees, Cora dismissed him and walked alone in the fields doing what she had once adored: touching the wheat with her fingertips. She headed to a field of trees to rest for the night. As she walked, she closed her eyes.

She was surprised to hear a voice. It was her mother. It had been centuries since Cora had tread on any wheat field. She had forgotten her mother Sara, the goddess Demeter, could commune with her this way.

I see you are free, Persephone. I am so overjoyed.

Cora laughed bitterly.

Come to Olympus, dear. We will deliberate over recent events. We all know of your attachment to the nymphs. Your brothers and sisters grieve for you. All of us would like to speak about the terrible battle on the Strait and provide libations in memory of Cassandra.

Her stupid horse appeared again, treading through the fields to her. Something about the beast trampling the wheat really bothered her. Then the konobera made it worse by opening his scarlet eyes wide, shaking his head, and whinnying. He coughed flames from his mouth as he limped. What an idiotic, monstrous thing. But then Cora thought: not much different than herself.

"Away with you!" cried Cora to the konabera again. "I said, go! Get out of here, you idiot! Return to your hole."

Finally, the konabera trotted away from her.

Cora skimmed her fingers along the wheat again.

Oh, I cannot wait to see you, Mother. No doubt, we shall meet very soon in the clouds.

She lifted her hands and opened her eyes before she said the other things raging in her heart.

She came to a tree trunk. There she fell against it. She hadn't slept in days.

She soon awoke, and it was dark. She could not sleep, for her eyes still burned red.

BY MORNING, farmers and gypsies passed her in the fields. But the strangers were sparse in this region, and all fled when looking at her eyes. By late afternoon, under a hot yellow sun, she arrived on the beaches. The white and yellow sandy shore of Evia was empty. Only the gentle waves could be heard.

She looked up at the blue sky then kneeled, speaking quietly, as if in prayer. "Oh Nephrea, if you hear me, please give me strength. I don't know if I can do this. But it has to be done, Mother. Poseidon flooded your people. He ended your line. If you were alive, you'd cry with me. He must be stopped. He, we… Oh, Nephrea, *I* must be stopped." She looked down, running her fingers through the sand. For a moment, she wished more than ever that her pale skin were blue. "You should have seen your granddaughter. You would have been so proud. She sacrificed for your people. Just like you would have done. Exactly like you. I hope you were right. You said once there is only one God. I hope there is a God up there somewhere looking down on me. A God who will forgive me for what I am about to do."

She stood up.

"I don't think you will approve of this, but…" She surprised herself with a laugh. "You never did. You cared for me, Nephree. Just as I cared for my daughter, Cassandra. Let the will of your God come down upon me. And let the world see what this tragedy has done to your poor Persephone, mother."

She undid the rope tied to the bag that she carried on her shoulder. Then she donned the Cap of Hades, and her hands vanished before her. She called out:

Eilis Defien Amphritite

She took out the scepter and walked toward the water.

Eilis Defien Amphritite

A great wind picked up along the waves. She had to shield her eyes from the sand as it blew into her eyes. Then water from the crashing waves began to collect and recede. She repeated again and again her enchanted words:

Eilis Defien Amphritite

Finally, the waves began to break and form a tunnel, parting the ocean down the middle. The tunnel was only a few feet in width, but large enough for someone to walk along the ocean floor to the depths.

Then she lengthened the Scepter of Azure and cried:

Eneich Aneu Loriaan

The parted waves froze into walls of ice. They formed an ice tunnel, stilling the moving water as it descended into the sea.

Persephone entered. As she walked through the tunnel, she had to step around coral reefs and avoid stray fish that had fallen from the water.

She could not help marveling at the sight as she descended. She had never peered inside the ocean before. When over a hundred feet of water was on both sides, she saw amazing things. Far in the distance, she saw a giant fish, or perhaps a legendary whale, moving its fins slowly while swimming away from her. Then a school of fish appeared on her left.

Eilis Defien Amphritite

Eneich Aneu Loriaan

As she walked farther, the ice behind her began to crack and the water closed upon her, but the magic kept the water from hitting her. She continued repeating her words.

Then she shivered. Although mostly dry, it became cold the farther she descended. And as she kept sinking deeper and deeper, there loomed the constant threat of water collapsing around her. Then, indeed, the water began to flow over her, only held back by magic. But it did not crash down.

She continued repeating the words:

Eilis Defien Amphritite

She began to see a faint glow in the distance, a beautiful

shimmering yellow light. It was turning evening in the sky far above. Moonlight lit her tunnel from above, but most of the light was now from inside the sea, as her water tunnel was over a thousand feet high. Soon, Cora recognized this shining gold: Amphitrite, the palace of Poseidon.

Amphitrite had been named after Poseidon's water nymph wife (though it was well known that the Sea King rarely accompanied only one woman). The golden palace was a giant city, nearly as large as Tartarus. Persephone's tunnel, by magic, led toward the entrance.

Persephone watched as a number of nereids, or water nymphs, swam from the castle. Unlike her, they went by way of water outside the gates. Some, wearing turquoise hoplite armor, mounted dolphins and rushed around her tunnel, likely in shock as they had never witnessed such a thing. Large fishes and sharks congregated around the bright city gates too.

The city was within a giant air bubble. Cora's tunnel stopped at the edge of the water and led toward the main gates. More nereids in turquoise armor stood beside the entrance of her tunnel, staring in amazement. But they could not see Cora as she still wore the helm.

Persephone stopped near the gates inside the open air. Ice cracked and all the water caved in behind her. Some of the water splashed over the guards. Some were knocked down by the pressure of the water, stunned, but soon stirred and swam back to the city.

Cora leaned against a grand silver Doric column. The giant metallic columns seemed to hold the gates of the city. The magic of fighting back the water had exhausted her. Her dress and her ponytail were sopping wet, and drops of salty water kept dripping over her face. She had to wipe her eyes with a white cloth from inside her peplos—which was futile as it was wet too. The salt burned her eyes. Everywhere it was cold and wet and smelled of the sea—like her uncle, Poseidon, whom she detested. And, as she walked in the air bubble, drops of water still fell everywhere.

In fact, it seemed like there was a constant rain falling throughout the city.

The city of Amphitrite was a golden pyramid that stretched from the surface all the way up into the dark watery abyss above. It had a vast base and stretched upward a league or more to an unseen tip. The giant structure leaned against a large sea wall. Persephone mused that this wall may lead to a shore line somewhere, but she could not see far up enough, through the vast elevation and darkness, to see the Overworld.

As she walked within the yellow-gold walls, she found they were so bright that those within the city could not see the dark sea world outside. Cora surmised that anyone within the walls of the city who had never ventured outside would not know about the surrounding ocean at all. Roads and cottages lined streets that meandered up in swirls toward the narrow top far above. This reminded her of her home in Tartarus, only in the sea kingdom, unlike the black shard in the Underworld, the central tower of Poseidon was gilded and shone bright yellow and white. The "sky" above could not be seen in the distance.

Apart from these incredible things, Amphitrite seemed like a normal everyday town. Perhaps this was weirder. Mud and brick cottages lined dirty streets, and a long dirt road, stretching for as far as Persephone could see, was lined with chariots and horses. And the constant rain collected in flowing gutters that angled down to the edges of the city, returning the rain water to the ocean.

There were horses everywhere. After all, Poseidon was the god of horses, having created the konobera and monokera. Here in the sea kingdom, everyone rode horses, particularly mermen, who had fins instead of legs. They could not travel without a steed or a long wooden cane.

Cora jumped as, all of a sudden, a giant fish fell into the air bubble from the surrounding water. It reminded her of the whale she had seen. Then the large fish transformed into a woman before her eyes.

The woman was naked, with scales all over her skin—blue-tinged skin like an Amazon, but bluer—and she had glowing emerald eyes. This nereid was very attractive, except for her hair. Her blond hair was rubbery, resembling kelp. It was so long that it covered her bare breasts and scaly hips. She had legs, but also a long tail.

The fish-woman walked to a man in green hoplite armor, with black hair and a beard, holding a spear, who guarded the entrance. She lewdly touched his shoulder. This *man* wasn't human either. He was a merman, with gills along his neck and skin of blue-green scales. The guards had fins instead of legs and used their spears, not only to guard, but to balance themselves on the ground before the doorway.

"Tell His Majesty that we suspect a god trespasses," said the siren. Her voice was as sweet as honey. But then she lost her sweetness, narrowing her eyes. "I believe it's the demon Olympian goddess from the Underworld. Take Hawdwee and Nivwah and search the city. This enchantment is very concerning."

"Send a dispatch to His Majesty," said the merman, nodding to another. The other merman nodded, jumped atop a horse, and rode up the main stone thoroughfare.

Cora looked behind her. Her tunnel was still causing quite a flurry of movement. Although the tunnel had collapsed, mermen were swimming about the area where Cora had walked, searching. It made Cora walk into the city, for if she dawdled and they followed her footprints, they'd discover her.

Cora walked quickly up the stone road, keeping her helmet on and remaining invisible. She passed rich mermen decorated with fine gold and jewels around their necks and waists. They used the horses to travel, with their fins draped along the sides. There were humans from the Overworld atop horseback too. And she even spotted wood nymphs. But these wood nymphs splashed around streams and waterfalls, acting dim-witted and stupid compared with her beloved Amazon. Then there were Amphiuma. These were the worst putrid monsters. Like in her kingdom, they slithered like giant snakes along the shadows.

Their leathery skin was dark red and black, and they had fangs and long bright red hair. Many Amphiuma were led in chains by mermen or dragged behind the mermen's horses.

There were more sirens too, or "mermaids" as they were called by seafarers. Beautiful women, like the powerful one by the gate, with glowing emerald eyes and perfect form. Was the one by the gate Amphitrite? That siren certainly seemed powerful enough. Cora did not know. She had never met her aunt, nor ever cared to.

Cora saw blacksmiths, bakeries, even pubs. It was a mirror of human life. And the central golden tower shone as bright as the yellow sun. As she walked up the spiral road toward the light at the center of the city, she had to avert her eyes.

The golden tower stood nearly the same height as her Dark Tower back home. But this one was grander, reminding her more of Azure Palace with brilliant gold and diamond spires. As she got closer, the light of the tower lit the outer boundary of the surrounding sea. No longer was it dark above and, through the upper dome, she could now make out shadows of sea creatures, small, or perhaps large, floating above in the "sky."

It was getting hot. She surmised the glow from the golden tower heated the entire sea kingdom like the sun above. It was a welcoming warmth in her thin red peplos.

She walked by a group of guards by the tower entrance unseen.

Then she followed three young merman guards up stone stairs. They leaned on a pole, dragging their giant tails in order to ascend. The stairs were mainly ramps with few steps, likely making travel easier for the mermen. Torches on sconces lit the path up higher in the tower. These were handsome beardless mermen, broad shouldered, shirtless, with rippled chests. They had the same green eyes as the sirens.

By the top, she entered a multitude of dark corridors, wandering through mazes in search of the right stairway to ascend farther. She had never been to Amphitrite, but she knew Poseidon resided at the very top of his palace.

She cursed to herself as the guards split off. She had hoped they would lead her to the throne room. She wandered on her own through more torchlit stone corridors, looking for more stairs to ascend.

At last she found two great wooden doors. She presumed this was it, as it reminded her of the throne room at home and the one at Azure. The doors were adorned with a relief of golden sea horses.

She opened the great doors and entered the hall. The ceiling had a small glass dome opening into the sea. She had ascended so far that waves were sloshing along the glass above. And it was dawn. She could make out the sky, with a red-yellow hue, between the splashing of water. But there were no windows along the walls. Torches lit the hall and reflected off large plaques of gold. The ceiling and floor were made of white marble. A giant marble dais sat at the far end. Cora had to squint again as all the gold made the throne room as bright as broad daylight.

The distant throne was empty.

Cora cursed.

She was so loud that one of the guards by the door rushed into the room to look for the intruder. Cora was losing patience. Amphitrite had already sent word to Poseidon. Invisible or not, if she didn't hurry, she could be discovered.

She rushed the merman guard and pinned him against the wall. It was easy to tackle him once she removed his cane. Then she cupped her hand over his mouth.

He was a giant well-built merman with a long bushy beard. She removed her helmet with her opposite hand. This caused the guard to fight even more from fright. Cora's eyes glowed red over his face.

"Quiet!" she snapped, looking back at the entrance. "Where's your king? Where is Poseidon? Hmm? Talk quickly if you want to live."

He nodded.

"But talk quietly or I'll snap your neck," she added with a smile.

He nodded again. His eyes were wide in fear.

She removed her hand slowly. Then she grinned at him wickedly.

"Who are you? You must be a god or nymph with those eyes."

"Shut up and tell me where your king is."

He hesitated for a moment. "In his chamber."

"Where?" hissed Persephone quietly. "Take me to him. I shall be invisible again. But don't forget who walks beside you. I am a goddess and one suspicious move and it's your end."

He nodded as sweat dripped down his ropy wet hair.

"Take me to him."

"He'd be in his bedchamber. It's night."

"How can you even tell?" she asked in disgust. She didn't wait for an answer. She snatched his arm and pushed him toward the double doors.

After countless turns and some descending stairs through the labyrinth, he led her up, with his cane, to a private stone stairway. There was another guard before a majestic gilded door. He pulled back from this final hallway.

"He's there," he said in a whisper. "Now, may I leave? If Lord Poseidon sees me, he'll kill me."

Cora struck the guard in the head so hard that the guard's body spun until he fell to the ground. When the guard's eyes closed, Cora sped to the front door. She moved fast enough that the other guard only had time to lean forward and squint toward the commotion. Invisible, Cora grabbed the other guard's neck and quickly twisted it.

Cora tugged at a leather strap to open the golden door, but it was locked. She pulled hard, but it wouldn't budge.

She wanted to surprise her uncle. She did not want to mess with the lock and make him aware of her presence. So she backed up and then heaved with all her might, shoving her body into the wooden door. The force shattered the door into pieces.

The room had a strange dark red glow. At first, she thought it was her own eyes, but the light came from the walls. There was a dark mist with the strong scent of incense. On the ceiling was another glass dome opening to water above, but deeper, and Cora could not make out the sky from this dome. But the room, no doubt, was close to the ocean surface too.

The bedroom encompassed three adjoining rooms. Everything was fashioned with gems, rubies, and gold. It was decorated with the finest wood furnishings. Elaborate tapestries depicted battles, some with Amazon against Mandrigel—the Napean War. Others showing the Amazon war, with nymphs against man. Silvery metallic columns surrounded the three main rooms, holding the great structure.

Toward the center of the rooms was one giant bed. And sitting up on the mattress, clutching a white sheet over their chests and staring at the entrance, were two mermaids. Very beautiful women, but with that strange ropy hair. The Sea God lurched forward beside them, staring. He was naked too having been, apparently, making love to the sirens. The sight hardly surprised her. Her uncle was known for his perversions.

"Poseidon!" Cora cried. She removed her helm. Her eyes glowed so scarlet that, indeed, it made the room look redder. "I come for revenge. Seems you were involved in a fight with my family in Azure. Perhaps you should have had the nerve to fight me instead."

The sirens fell off the bed, tripped, and ran, quickly wriggling their fins along the floor to the door. One passed Persephone staring at her.

"What's this!" Poseidon thundered. He ran his hand over his long white hair and beard. "Who barges into my chamber?"

"Persephone, daughter of Zeus and wife of Hades, Uncle."

He grabbed the sheet from the bed and tied it over his waist. Then he leaped off the bed and ran to her. His gray eyes turned red too.

"You come here, Niece? Under the sea!" He squinted, struggling to control his rage. He was a giant of a man, and he towered over Cora.

It seemed as if he thought he could speak to her. Talking had never been her intention. With both hands, she hit him as hard as she could across the face. When she had struck her husband, it had been with anger but it had been controlled. This was with all her strength. A god's strength, and the skill of an Amazon soldier. Poseidon was thrown across his room.

"You coward!" cried Cora. "You turned your back on your nymphs in Azure to placate Father. Where were you when Hades took me down into the earth? Where were you for your wood nymphs when you drowned their queen! You disgust me! All of you disgust me!"

"Come here," he said, pulling himself up by a chair. "Woman or not, I'm going to hurt you. I swear I'll—"

She rammed him as she had rammed the door. She charged like a bull, knocking him down, and sliding with his body along the marble floor until they both crashed into a large wooden dresser. The dresser splintered under the violence. Then she slammed her fist into his head. She beat him and would have hit him until he fell unconscious if it weren't for his belated response. One swing from his huge arm was enough to toss her.

"*Get out!*" he thundered. "*So help me, Niece, I'll tear you to pieces!*"

Cora got up, winded. She stood in an Amazon stance.

"You face me?" Poseidon asked. "You face me still? Very well. You will see, grain goddess, what the King of the Gods can do to you. I don't fear you. I fear your husband for what I am about to do to you."

"You murdered your own people."

"I killed the Amazon because they had become too powerful. If I had let her win, she and Atlantis would have struck at your father's realm. I held them off for your father by stopping Cassandra."

She answered him by digging into the cloth of her dress and taking out her scepter. She lengthened the golden rod before him and held the scepter like a sword above her head in a fighting stance, prepared for battle.

"*You face me with Hades' Scepter!* Did you steal it, or is he against me too?"

"This is not Hades' Scepter. This is the Scepter of Azure. My mother was Queen Nephratee. Come fight me. I fight for Nephrea's people. And Poseidon, now that you drowned the last nymph, I am their Amazon queen."

He squinted at her comment in confusion. Then he said, "Fight me, goddess, and Zeus will bind you."

She responded by swinging the scepter like a sword at his bare chest. The tip of the staff cut him like a knife, slashing the god's skin and splattering blood. Poseidon was in shock at the attack. At first, he seemed too surprised to defend himself. But then his eyes narrowed again.

He didn't run from her; he ran for a wooden chest. He threw it open and grabbed a scepter of his own: his long silver trident. But by the time the Sea God was ready for a counterattack, Cora put on the helm again and vanished.

"You wily witch! Come out! Come into my embrace, Niece! I'm not done with you!"

Neither was she. She struck his chest again, cutting open his rippled skin. The scepter repeatedly drew blood. He kicked and raged in pain like a pinned wild boar. Then she shouted words through the air:

Eneich Aneu Loriaan!

He laughed. "A god cannot be hurt by the magic from the Scepter of Hades, woman!"

"Look above, imbecile. It's not for you."

Ice shot up toward the ceiling. It coated the glass. Then she hurled the staff like a javelin straight up through the dome. The glass burst open and water crashed into the room. The weight of the water threw Cora to the floor.

"You use my brother's own weapons against me!" she heard him cry.

The room filled with water fast. Cora snatched the staff underwater and swung it again at the Sea God. Merman guards finally swam into the room. Yet as Cora continued to battle him and the water rose, they could do little to join the fight.

Cora was now completely submerged in water. She felt her

feet touch the marble floor. She pushed up as hard as she could toward an air pocket near the ceiling.

"*I hate you!*" Cora said, gasping for air by the ceiling, even if Poseidon couldn't hear her words. "*You, my husband, my mother, my father! All of you! So help me, I'll take you from this world until your hold on us is no more!*"

He started hammering his trident in all directions, crashing it down into the stone and breaking apart the floor of his own chamber. A wave hurled Cora from him into the wall. The force was so great that she closed her eyes and lost awareness for a moment. All the while, Poseidon kept hitting the ground, aiming in all directions, trying to make contact with anything he could and causing waves to storm all around Cora. Her invisibility seemed to make him rage even more. But she still wore the helm.

She choked and struggled in the water by the ceiling. She was drowning. But she couldn't drown, for if she lost consciousness, he'd take her. Desperately, she swam for the dome of light. The current pushed against her, still flooding the room. Her lungs were full of water now. She coughed into the water, only gulping more of the salty sea.

She closed her eyes.

She thought of Cassandra. This was how Casey must have felt when she tried to stop his tidal wave. He killed her. This god killed her. He created a similar wave that towered over Cassandra and drowned her. Her Cassandra. If Nephrea was her mother, Casey was her daughter. And her uncle killed her. This beast!

But he couldn't kill Casey's mother.

She caught another air pocket. Then she removed her helm. She wanted him to see her. She wanted to taunt him. And as the helm was removed, her red eyes glowed like a beacon. She felt a wall or the ground again, she wasn't sure. But whatever it was, she pressed her feet against it as hard as she could and shot upward like an arrow toward the broken dome. She looked behind her and saw Poseidon swimming like a hungry shark toward her. She could not evade this master of the sea.

She grabbed the helmet and threw it over her head once

more—just in time. She felt Poseidon's hand pass by her by a few inches. It ran so close that she felt a wave brush her.

She swam as hard as she could for the sea above.

She was in the open sea. She glanced down and saw the Sea God thrashing about the roof searching for her. Sea creatures swam to her. First a large manta ray then two reef sharks rushed toward her. Helmet or not, they could smell her. When Poseidon looked up and saw the fish, he too darted in her direction from the dome. His speed was great, and it took little time for him to approach.

But Cora had made it to the shore, for the summit of the Sea Kingdom was close to the beach.

She coughed and struggled for air by the shoreline. Poseidon believed he had finally caught his fish, but his fury was no match for her guile. As the waves parted for the approaching god behind her, dark clouds formed in a clear sky above. Cora quickly stood on the sand facing him. She removed her helmet and raised her hands.

Thunder and rain stormed from the sky. Lightning struck the water surrounding Poseidon. Poseidon looked around him, surprised. Wide-eyed, he seemed to understand his predicament. He was too late. The sea was his element, the sky was Cora's. Storms fought against the torrential waves.

Poseidon responded, with fiery red eyes, by striking his trident upon the ground, shaking off the raging winds. The strike was so great that it threw Cora to the ground. Poseidon got on a knee and hammered the sand again.

Cora waved the Scepter before the shallow waters and shouted:

Eneich Aneu Loriaan!
Eneich Aneu Loriaan!
Eneich Aneu Loriaan!

A fury of ice came from her staff and moved along the waves. The effect was to freeze all the water surrounding the Sea God. Then came flurries from the sky above. Poseidon raged, but the ice continued to engulf him.

Persephone raised her hands again. The water rose higher and higher under spinning wind. Cora formed a cyclone rising like a tower within the water. The funnel moved toward the Sea God and lifted him a hundred feet into the sky. Then she dragged him by wind over the shore. When he was as far above the ground as she could raise him, she dropped her arms.

The winds stopped. Poseidon plummeted to the sand, unconscious. Cora ran to finish him. She stood above the Sea God with the intent of shoving her scepter through his naked body. She would filet him. She'd use the Scepter of Azure as a spike to pin him to the ground and leave him on this beach forever. She raised the scepter over him, but then…

A blinding light crashed down a few feet from Cora. Then a burst of thunder exploded in her ears. After the great thunderbolt, her ears rang and she lost her hearing for a moment. Below her, Poseidon blinked his red eyes—they did not seem full of rage, but of fear. She raised her scepter again over him. Once more, lightning burst around her, this time throwing her from him. She got up, dazed, on her knees. She expected Poseidon to charge her, but his eyes closed. He was too weak. The fall had knocked him unconscious.

Then she stood up staring toward the sky.

She narrowed her eyes and cried, "Stop my hand, Father? Why now! Where were you when your brother raped me? Where were you when your brother took me from the fields of Azure? You never stopped your other brothers from taking a little girl!"

She raged, in the shallow water and ice, shouting some unintelligible things in madness. Then she gazed at Poseidon, who still lay unconscious on the sand. She lifted his naked body to the clouds as if to present her prize. Then she dragged him along the sand while gesturing, her fist to the air.

"*Take me Father!*" she cried, gazing up to the sky. "*Take me now! Go ahead! Strike me down! I have witnessed your justice.*" She laughed. "For centuries, I have witnessed your justice! Don't be kind to your daughter. Strike me down. Take me now!" Then she started laughing, dropping Poseidon's body on the sand. "Why should I care? You never cared about me." She bowed in mockery of him. "Strike me down! Better to be turned to ash than live another day under you!"

The sky lit up with a fury of thunder and lightning. More bolts rained down around her, splitting trees and burning nearby bushes along the shore. But Persephone did not run. Each bolt that cracked made her laugh more. She kneeled as icy waves crashed over her legs. She laughed at him. She could not stop laughing. Her hope was that all Olympus who saw her would watch her mockery. He would destroy her, somehow, take her immortal life. But his disgrace was worth it.

When the clouds settled, she stood. Eyes burning red in fury, she addressed the clouds once more: "Behold, I will make you cry tears of longing, beasts of Ida! Longing for lies you so covet that feed you. Man and nymph would have done better if you had been feasted on by Kronos! You best take and devour me now if you want peace! For I cometh to destroy you and all those who are under your power, false gods of this world!"

But the storm settled. The clouds dispersed. All quieted.

She kneeled on the sand and her laughter became tears. She wept near Poseidon's body as he lay unconscious by the waves.

Her tears were interrupted by the sound of light footsteps in the sand behind her. Cora cocked her head and a shirtless man, glowing yellow light, approached her on the beach. He wore feathered wings for shoes.

"I come for you, Kore. You must go with me."

She turned to the horizon. For a moment, she cherished her memory of doing this so often as a girl. She had adored the view of the sea in Argos. Curse her family and the demons who took that peace from her.

"Uncle lives," she said with her back still turned to Hermes. "Thanks to our bastard father. Have you come to take me to meet the ferryman? Ah, but you can't do that, can you? I am immortal and can't die. Why, I'm a god and a member of our illustrious family. So tell me, Brother..." She turned to him, and he stepped back. "Where are you taking me?"

"Lord Zeus summons you to the Mount. Your mother will fly you by chariot to Olympus to await your trial. But surely for this act, you will be chained in the depths."

"I see." Then she finally turned to him and smiled. "But Hermes, If you can take me home…" Her eyes caused his face to glow with red light. "Why didn't you do that before when Hades raped me in Azure Blue?"

"Will you come quietly, Persephone?"

She looked down at the sand and nodded. Then she whispered, more to herself, "Shhh."

2 0

———————————

WAR

Sol traveled slowly, in a thick brown fur coat, by horseback, with his small elite regiment through the difficult rocky terrain of Crete. General Kaios and another thirty thousand remained mobilized in the western harbor town of Phalasarna, boarding ships and preparing for the great invasion. Crete was a large island spanning over thirty leagues. Sol knew he had to conquer the entire island before moving on to Hellena. The last thing he wanted was a counterattack on Azure shores.

He rode beside Engel, who looked rather odd on a brown horse. The horse looked huge with such a small rider, though the steed was the same size as Sol's. Like his men, the dwarf wore blue hoplite armor under a thick fur coat.

They rode a narrow route as the northern open valley was still Minoan territory and had not been secured. But the mountain was treacherous with large rocks and mud, particularly in the heavy rain. A few of his soldiers lost their footing and fell off the trail and over the ledges.

Soon they arrived at vast grasslands. Some were quite beautiful, and Sol thought that if the sky were clear, it would have been pleasant. But the clouds were gray and stormy.

As trees cleared into more open fields, they encountered their first Minoan village. It had been burned to the ground. The attack was recent as smoke still rose from broken stone walls. Parts of the grass along the dirt road were even charred. Thatched roofs were caved in.

They passed a woman in torn rags with a grimy face and a ghostly expression. One of the soldiers jumped from his horse to stop her from approaching the king. He ordered that she show them a package she was carrying. She was carrying a lifeless child that looked more like a doll under the pouring rain. Then they passed a house where a group of shirtless men were lifting boulders from rubble. And an old man leaning on a staff staring blankly into the distance.

But none of this was as terrible as the center of town. Broken roads converged into a series of wooden spikes. Upon the spikes were charred, naked bodies. And over the bodies were draped flags of a bull, the standard of King Minos and his Minoan kingdom.

Engel turned away in disgust.

"Aye, look away, friend," Sol said somberly. "It should not be for your fair eyes, Engel."

"This should not be for any eyes."

By the end of the village, Sol mused that his brother had followed his orders to the point of derision. Only one structure stood in the entire village. A single stone structure with a statue of a goddess holding a snake in both hands. And on the door was a mural of men jumping a bull. Torinth had spared their temple while burning everything else.

And so it was with the next village. And the next one.

Engel cried but Sol could not care.

Soon they arrived at their base by the castle of Knossos. The great castle perched on a hill about half a league away. The rain and fog was replaced with smoke. The capitol was in flames too. The Tiger King had come. And throughout this valley and along the river Kairatos was Sol's Atalan military in their blue hoplite uniforms. Blue flags with a central yellow sun were hoisted on poles all over their base. They waved in the wind—the Sun King's standard.

Sol and Engel met in an Atalan war tent with twenty of his highest-ranking officers. It still poured and the rain dripped against the canvas. They had removed their coats and wore only their blue hoplite armor, pteruges, and boots. A giant wooden table, similar to the one in the dining room in Azure, lay at the center. And Minoan servants in drab gray tunics—freshly acquired slaves, no doubt—walked around the tent pouring red wine for him and his generals as they sat on wooden chairs. Each cup was first tested in front of the soldiers by a slave, of course.

Sol sat at the head of the table. Engel was by his side. There was one empty seat for Torinth near Sol. The Tiger King was late.

Torches emitted a faint flickering light in the tent. The rain had created a musty wet odor. But this soon changed to the smell of bread and olives as servants brought in silver trays of food.

Torinth finally hobbled in with a wooden cane, along with two other soldiers. Unlike Sol's men, with pressed uniforms, Torinth's armor was dirty. All the men rose and bowed. Then Torinth turned and bowed before Sol. He sat down, tore some bread on a silver plate, and gulped down a silver cup of wine as everyone in the room stared at him.

"Ah, good, they're good, brother," Torinth said with his mouth full, shaking his head, "I must say, they're very good warriors."

"Tell us of your success."

Torinth pushed his plate away, nodded, and leaned back in his chair. He grinned, but then he lost his smile seeing the dwarf.

"We'll have the palace by daybreak," Torinth said.

Then he clapped for more wine from a servant who held a pitcher by the entrance, but Sol put his hand on his arm and shook his head.

"Before you celebrate, tell us what needs to be done."

Torinth signaled with a finger for one of the captains by the entrance to the tent. The soldier walked over and laid some rolled parchments before Sol.

"We're here, eh?" Torinth said, leaning over and pointing a dirty finger at the map. "You see. We've taken this along the mountain range to the west. You no doubt saw some of the villages secured."

Secured.

"Down here through the central valleys are more villages in rubble. I had to run my men through a few of the towns again to clear them completely for the safety of your arrival, of course. Then…" He pointed toward the palace. "Here is Minos. We take the sarding ape's castle and all else falls. We know that there is one remaining regiment protecting him, deep in the castle, but it burns." He smiled wide with his broken teeth. "We're smoking him out, brother." Then he ran his hand through his thin gray hair and thought for a moment, tapping his dirty fingers on the table. "What's that damn town called? Lappa. Lappa, that's what the apes call it. And their port, Phoenix. They have held out in Lappa, thinking that they can rejoin their forces in the far west near Mount Ida. You passed the Mount, but their settlements and bases are on the northern edge."

"We met no resistance."

"Aye. But in the north they think they can regroup and force a second offensive. But what…" He laughed. "What they don't realize, Solinair, is that I've already broken their reinforcements in Gortyna! They have nothing, Emperor. The island is ours."

"Rejoice," Sol said, leaning back in his chair with a sigh.

"Aye!" cried another. "Aye, we are victorious!"

"Aye. Blessed day! Hail Emperor Solinair Solinaray!"

"Aye."

"Aye!"

Then, amid all the cheers, came a quiet voice that said, "You don't need to kill everyone."

Torinth searched the room to see who had uttered the words. He glared at the little blue man sitting beside Sol.

"What did you say?" Torinth asked him.

"We saw the burning villages," Engel said. "You were asked to hold Crete, Torinth, not burn everything to the ground. We also saw the public display of bodies on spits. What you did was savage."

"Why is a footstool talking to me?" Torinth asked Sol.

"He is my chief advisor."

"Sol," Torinth said, running a hand down his face, "I allowed this *thing* to be in my tent. That's enough. I don't need his words. Particularly not after seeing so many of my brave, your brave, men die under the sword from these Minoan animals. I told Queen Cassandra, when she lived, that I could not stand the sight of him."

"Engel, not now," Sol said. He turned to Torinth. "It is in honor of Cassandra, Brother, and for so many more Amazon nymphs, that I ask that you respect his presence in this tent."

Torinth ran his hand along his face again. He shook his head, pounded his temples a couple of times with his fists, and ground his teeth. But then he nodded. He gave a very disingenuous smile to Engel.

"We will secure Knossos by tomorrow," Torinth said. "I have King Minos on the run, but he has nowhere to go. And I know where he hides. Have you amassed the regiments off Phalasarna with General Kaois?"

"Aye."

"Then we should move. Together we will take the castle, burn Knossos to the ground, and return to the harbor. I can leave a remaining regiment under General Alastair as regent to rule over the Minoans until I return from victory over Hellena. Indeed, we should rejoice, Brother. I've taken a land a third the size of Atala in two moons, per your orders. Faster than your orders, Sol. A miracle under your army's grace."

"Aye!" cried a soldier.

"Aye!"

"Very well done, Torinth."

"We must sail for Attica before they even know what's hit them," Torinth added, drinking more wine from his silver cup.

"Now that you have the island, is it necessary to move on to Hellena?" asked Engel. "We can use your victory as a defense for Azure and return in peace. Why continue to advance any further?"

Torinth stared at Engel. Then he hammered his fist on the table and jumped up. Sol rose too. The entire party at the table rose.

"*Does he know how much blood I've spilled!* By the gods, get this rat out of my sight!"

"Calm yourself," said Sol, raising his hand.

"Get him out!" cried Torinth. "Get him out of here. Or shut him up!"

Sol looked at Engel and recalled his look of disgust at the public display of charred bodies. He understood the outrage, but not his lack of tact. And Engel remained in his chair challenging his brother's madness without turning from his glare.

"I will not waste my blood and my soldiers' for nothing, Emperor Solinair!" raged Torinth. "I'm not interested in your companion's reaction to seeing things too strong for his eyes. He should have remained back in his wonderland if he wished not to be in the midst of war."

"I've seen the same savagery in Hades," Engel said unperturbed. "Far worse. But what you did under my beloved king's flag in the villages is criminal."

"I... I... I'm merely asking what time we will strike," Torinth said, running his hand down his face again. "Not criticism from an idiot. Do you wish to continue to deliberate with a blue mutant, Brother? Do you wish me to pull back my army and apologize to an enemy *who murdered your daughter!*"

"*Enough, Torinth!*" cried Sol.

"Casey was killed by the gods," Engel objected, still sitting. He was the only one who remained seated. "Not the Greeks and certainly not the Minoans. And I am the emperor's chief advisor.

That is why I am here. I advise you all to return to Azure after securing this island."

Torinth hobbled around the table to grab Engel and would have had it not been for Sol, who grabbed his arm.

"*Get him out of here, Sol*," Torinth cried.

"I asked for you to respect him," Sol said, holding Torinth's arm and shaking his head. Then he turned to Engel. "And for you to be silent."

"Your brother's probably drunk," provoked Engel.

"*I am not!*" Then Torinth returned to his seat, grabbed his cup, and drank it down. "*Not yet!*" He shook his head violently and threw the cup at Engel.

"Enough," cried Sol, hammering his fists against the table. "No one touches him!" In deafening silence, he turned to Engel. "You're dismissed. Get out, Engel, and return to your tent now."

Engel nodded, bowed, and hobbled out. When he left, Torinth returned to his seat, but his lips continued to quake and his eyes wander.

"Gather the men and return with me to the harbor, Brother," Sol said. "Rejoice. There is no change in our plans. We have the island secured, thanks to you. If you wish to know the time, it is tomorrow."

"I do your bidding, Emperor," Torinth said, bowing to him.

"Gather the men," Sol thundered to everyone, leaning forward and slamming his fists on the table like Torinth. "We set sail from Phalasarna. I won't linger on this wasted island any longer. I want Aegeus's head, you hear me? That is my prize. He's invaded our lands and taken my daughter, not King Minos."

"Aye," Torinth said with a grin. "Indeed, Aegeus's head. And you shall have it, Sol! I swear it."

All bowed before Sol and the meeting was adjourned.

2 1

QUEEN DAINYA

Sol knocked on a wooden pole of Engel's tent. It was late in the evening, and it was still raining hard. The sounds of clashing metal and shouting and the smell of flames permeated the air.

"Engel, I hope I'm not disturbing you."

"No, come in," Engel said, bowing to him. He smiled and gestured for him to sit on his cot. Before Engel could sit on a rug, Sol beat him to it and lay down on the floor. Engel reluctantly sat on his own cot. The tent was meager. It was just a place to sleep, but large enough to accommodate two men.

"You asked for me to be there," Engel said. "I am your chief advisor."

"I'm not here to refute that."

"But you did not approve of my words?"

"What troubles you? Every man invited to the tent had a right to speak his mind, but you provoked him. It's not just what you said, but how you said it."

"Forgive me, my king, but your brother is a butcher. He provoked me. He's an animal."

"We are at war."

"I disagree." And Engel turned and stared at the wall of the tent. "I've been through so much. But what I see here in Crete is worse than war. The things that man who you call your brother is doing I have not seen since the Underworld. This is not in the interests of defending your family. This is far more evil. I wish to never see it again."

There was silence. Some men were shouting, and many were drunk outside. Already they were celebrating the inevitable fall of the island.

"When you asked me to be your counselor after Anna passed," Engel added quietly. "I was honored. Out of respect for the Ambrosia family, I accepted. I may be quiet, but I speak my mind. So now I will to you. The things that you're allowing your brother to do under your standard must end. It's not much different from what Philipp did."

"Don't anger me by comparing my brother to Philipp," Sol snapped. "That tyrant murdered Henri."

"Sol, I grieve for Casey too. Your daughter was my daughter. I raised her. Likely, I am just as angry as you. But that doesn't allow you to do the things you're allowing your army to do. Your brother is not conquering, he's murdering. Under your Sun King flag."

"What's happened must be avenged. The way to do it is to let the Tiger King fight."

"You are the emperor of Atala and king of Azure."

"I am a nothing king, Engel."

"You are not a nothing king, Sol. You are the greatest emperor in the world. You are the Sun King. You must provide us light. When you stop doing that, you might not only live in darkness, but be the cause of it."

Sol looked down and rubbed his temples. Then he, too, stared at the canvas.

"You're worth more to me than any of those men in the tent, Engel. Even my brother. Indeed, you're family. What's left of it. I don't care about Atala. Or about the Minoans. I cared only about Anna and Casey. And you. But, I…you can't talk to me of morals now. Or even about my brother after what's happened to Cassandra."

"Why not?" Engel said, looking down and shaking his head. "I've lost everything too: Avivae, your daughter. I've watched all the past queens of Azure pass over the centuries. I tell you, like Cassandra, they were all my daughters." Then he gazed up at him and, for a moment, his bright blue eyes reminded Sol of his wife's. "But I know what's right and wrong. If you don't, with the power you hold, this world is in peril."

There was nothing but the sound of rain splashing over the fabric of the tent now. Sol listened to it and turned away. He needed the distraction.

"Anna wouldn't agree with genocide, Sol."

"I remember fighting with her over similar things," Sol said, staring at the wall. "I hated her words then as much as I hate yours now. You asked why I came to speak with you? Because I do listen. But how can I fix this? I released my brother because I knew he could do what no other man could do. And he has. He's taken Crete in two moons."

Engel merely nodded.

"So what can I say to make things right for you?"

"End this. Return the army to Atala and stop the fight. That would make you a Sun King indeed. You have Crete. That's enough of a buffer. For what has happened to Cassandra, such an act will be treasured and your strength will hold throughout the world. Otherwise, you go the same way as my dear Dainya. You lead your kingdom to the same revenge that destroyed her in her war with the Hittites over their kursa."

"I've heard of this."

"Did you? What did you hear? Now the fleece stands in our Crystal Palace representing the power of Cassandra, the greatest Amazon queen there ever was. But that same fleece was once the cause of genocide and terror by Casey's great-grandmother."

"Cambria spoke of Dainya and the fleece when we were in Egypt."

"Nephrea's daughter was Dainya when born in Egypt," Engel replied with a nod. "Her name would be pronounced Danaë in Atalan, but we honored the Egyptian. Dainya was Nefertiti and Akhenaten's daughter. But unlike Nephrea, Dainya was raised by me and Jaida. You see, the general Jaida, who never had a child, raised Dainya as her own in Nephrea's absence. Jaida was her mother."

"Why speak of this now?"

"Because you remind me of her. Not who she was, but what you're now doing. For a century, Dainya was a rule abider. She followed order better than any Amazon queen. Until she faced this same darkness. She invaded Colchis." Tears ran down the Mandrigel's cheeks. He brushed them from his face. "Dainya fought the Hittites viciously, torturing and burning their villages —just like your brother, Torinth. Just like you. She created so much terror that the Amazon tried to erase their history out of shame. Just as the nymphs never speak of the atrocities of Harmonia, the nymphs never speak of Dainya in Colchis.

"Of course, what the Hittites had done to Jaida was pure evil. Jaida had been duped, offering assistance in the clouds for a fight that, she had been told, would bring peace between the Hittites and Assyrians. Jaida was betrayed. With Jaida's death, Dainya gathered her nymphs' most loyal. Dainya, of course, won the war. She claimed the Golden Fleece for the Amazons. She would have brought it to Azure Blue had it not been for Zeus and Mount Olympus."

"The vile gods again, Engel?"

Engel nodded. "The gods cannot accept Amazon conquest. So Zeus, with Hephaestus, created the dragon of Colchis. A serpent with sharp teeth and wings that flew to the skies to hunt our nymphs in the North. I knew every one of them that the dragon slew. The monster eventually hunted and killed Dainya herself. Just as the nymphs had terrorized the Hittites, Zeus terrorized the Amazons of Colchis. And another of my daughters was taken from me."

Engel turned from Sol. After a pause, he said with a broken voice, "I know war, Sol. I've seen it for centuries. I also know vile revenge. When I followed Nephrea, she was different. When my Nephree saw evil, perhaps because of the atrocities she had witnessed under her mother, Nephree did everything she could to right evil. She was even whipped and tortured for my people. There was only one thing that could darken Dainya's light. The death of her mother, Jaida.

"Revenge killed Dainya. Not war. The war within, Sol. She cared no longer for her own life or her kingdom. She only wanted revenge. This is the darkness you spoke of to me in Azure after Cassandra died. Dainya brought that darkness to Colchis. And now Cassandra's death has brought darkness to Crete. You two walk the same path of revenge. This will only lead to your ruin."

"I must right what was wrong, Engel," Sol said, shaking his head.

Then Engel shook his head violently. "I cannot follow a leader who rules like Harmonia or Dainya. Revenge will consume you. I can't follow you in this, Sol. I'm sorry. Just as I didn't go with Dainya to Colchis. Instead I raised her beautiful daughter, Delia, and aided her until she gave birth to your lovely wife, Anna. I love you with all my heart, Sol. Believe me. But don't ask me to watch genocide destroy everything you've built and everything you are."

"Oh, Engel," Sol said softly, shaking his head, "I'm sorry, but I can't agree. Not this time."

"I must leave then." Engel nodded and stood up. "I won't serve a king so. But, even now, it doesn't make you less honorable in my eyes. It would only make me less."

Sol placed a hand on Engel's shoulder. "Engel, why did you come here then? You knew of my brother's ways and you knew my intentions. If you're so wise, why come to Crete?"

"I told you. Taking these lands made sense as a buffer to block future war and protect Azure Blue."

"Engel." Sol shook his head again. "I don't believe you. All war is pain."

"This isn't war," Engel replied, shaking his head. "Like I told your brother, this is not war. Casey's victory in the Strait has already crippled any naval advance from the Greeks for years." He smiled sadly and said, "It's been an honor to serve you, Sun King." He brushed the tears from his eyes. Then he kneeled before Sol. "It's been as great an honor, as great as being under Queen Avivae or even the great Queen Nephratee. When I leave, I ask you to think of Dainya and her Golden Fleece. I ask you to search your heart. King Darius, your father and Anna's, used the name *Sun King* for a reason."

Sol remained silent, befuddled by a mix of emotions. He didn't like any of them.

"Dismiss me and allow me to return to Azure Blue."

"Engel, reconsider," Sol said with a sigh and shake of his head. "I didn't come to your tent to dismiss you."

Engel shook his head.

"Aye," he said. "If that is your wish, I dismiss you. For Casey, I can't end this until I meet King Aegeus in battle. But you can return to my beloved land."

Sol took a knee and reached out for Engel. He hugged his friend.

"Like Dainya." Engel said, shaking his head in Sol's arms. "Oh, Sol, it is my greatest hope, sire, that whatever happens to you, you find your light again."

2 2

GREEK TRAGEDY

How odd. The Atalans sailed from Phalasarna straight north to the peninsula of Attica with nearly a hundred red galleys battling few Greeks at sea. When they reached the harbor of Piraeus, some of the Attican ships were docked. And perhaps stranger, the waves were calm without any interference from their enemy, Poseidon.

Rather than battling by sea, the Greeks greeted them on the shore. Here it seemed twenty thousand lay in wait. The Atalans saw lines of soldiers holding a flurry of orange flags. Beneath their standards stood the bronze soldiers, bearing long staffs and shields and wearing bronze helms, breastplates, pteruges and shin guards. They were prepared to be arranged in the dreaded phalanx of Harmonia—spears out with shields protecting them from arrows above or from swords and spears around them. Sol remembered fighting them in this formation in Azerban and Trintz when building his empire.

Sol had brought horses in his ships. His father, King Darius, had used the rapid movement of horses to stampede against the enemy. Now Sol sat on horseback on the sandy beach beside his brother. Beside Torinth stood the red-haired General Kaios. They waited for their army to form behind them.

"Aegeus is a coward, Sol," said Torinth, gnashing his teeth. "He lacks the courage to face us."

"It is their custom," answered Sol, shaking his head.

Three Greek soldiers left the enemy line and rode to Sol. One held an orange flag with an image of an owl.

"We shall make them pay for what they did to the Amazon queen," Sol said. "Is the line ready, Kaios?"

"Aye, just say the word," Kaios said with a nod.

"My soldiers wait in haste," Torinth said with a wide grin. "We shall show them why they fear Atlantis. We will show them the ways of our father."

"Aye," Sol said, staring back at their lines.

The messengers on horseback approached and halted a few yards from them.

"Hail, Atlanteans," said the central man, with a gray beard. He removed his helm, showing his curly gray hair. "We ask you to return to your ships. Because of the Poseidon wave that befell your island, King Aegeus has not battled you by sea. We seek peace. We wish not to fight you at all. But you cannot step foot in Attica."

"But we have, aye?" said Torinth with a laugh. "Where is your cowardly king? Tell him I have his son. Would he like a trade? How about you give me my niece, Queen Cassandra, and I give him Prince Theseus?"

"We hear Queen Cassandra has died, sir."

"Aye," Sol said somberly, not joining his brother's mirth. "Return to your king. Tell him there are no terms. I shall ride through the gates of his kingdom and personally put a sword through him."

"And hurry before the Sun King kills you too," roared Torinth, in laughter, slapping his leg.

They rode off.

"Intelligence says armies in the north are gathering," said Kaios. "We outnumber them now, but not for long. We must strike."

As Sol nodded and watched the messengers ride back, he was

surprised by the sound of a sudden rush of hooves along the sand. He turned and saw a group of nearly a hundred horses fall from the sky. Every man, Greek and Atalan, stared at the winged unicorns filling the field. Then he heard shouts and cheers from his men. It was Amazons atop their monokera, only they were landing on the shore.

The unicorns rode in front of the Atalan lines. They must have looked so strange to the Greeks. Their hoplite armor was bright scarlet and their armor shiny, reflecting the yellow sun's rays. Yet the nymphs' faces were just as fierce as Sol's.

Cambria led them. She stopped before Sol and bowed deeply atop her unicorn. All the while, the Atalan army continued to bash their shields and shout their support.

"My lord," Cambria said with a smile. "I believe you might be in need of some assistance this morning?"

She jumped off her horse. Sol dismounted. The two embraced. That caused more cheering and the thumping of shields.

"You were ordered not to land, Cambria," Sol said. But he couldn't suppress a smile. "You are damned."

"Most of us fought with your daughter defending Azure by sea on the ships," replied Cambria. "We are already damned. And many more of us don't care anymore."

"We're damned anyway," said Hanna. Sol whirled around at her voice in surprise. Then Hanna embraced him. "Sol, every one of us has volunteered to follow Avva's edict, not the gods. We accept our plight. We won't remain imprisoned on our island anymore."

"Of course, we're too far away this time to land in Napea, anyway," added Cambria.

"Hanna, you fight with us?" asked Kaios.

"I'm an Amazon, general."

"We fight under you, or die under you," Cambria said. "You are the king of the Amazon now."

"I never would have thought I'd like seeing women in battle," said Torinth, spitting on the ground. "Hmm. Well, welcome."

Cambria tipped her head to him.

"I don't agree with your landing," Sol said, "but…I could use your help."

"Yes, Sol, you can. Intelligence says kingdoms in the North are gathering armies."

"What intelligence?" asked Kaios.

"Ours," Cambria replied. "We've surveyed the isles by the clouds."

"Welcome," Sol said. He mounted his horse again and said, "Welcome, all of you. It's so good to see friends."

"Prince Gavin sends his regards, Sol," Hanna said. "Your lands are safe."

Sol nodded. Then he turned to his chief general. "Kaios, arrange our guests in their places in the fields."

"Not at the back," quipped Cambria with a broad grin.

"I wouldn't think of it, General."

"Humph, never thought I'd fight with women," Torinth said as the nymphs rode to the line behind them. "Though pretty ones, by the gods, they are, Brother."

The sight of Amazons made him smile for the first time that morning. But then, as he watched the red hoplites ride, with wings folded, and line up with his army, he thought of how tragic it was that they had landed and forfeited their immortality. He lost his joy thinking how tragic everything was seeming to become.

2 3

JUSTICE

Mount Olympus was a golden world reflecting golden yellow off the sun. During the day, it was so bright that one had to squint one's eyes, if not acquainted. During the evening, it was as bright as day. Even after the sun set below, every stone was gilded, reflecting every torch and ray of moonlight. Light reflected along trails and hilltops, beside lush green waterfalls and orchards and valleys. Toward the center was a large lake. Waterfalls cascaded into numerous streams, which flowed down valleys along the crest of the mountain to this body of water. And over the water skimmed yellow creatures the size of one's palm, lake fairies, which jumped, flew, and skipped about the Mount. The fairies were green with human faces. They sang and hummed beautiful music. There were many other wondrous creatures: butterflies of pure light, wild unicorns, mermen, satyrs, and demigods.

Today, everyone gathered on the main outdoor patio. This was Zeus's throne room. It was a reflective marble plaza with very tall Doric columns. In the center was a slick reflective marble floor bordered by a gold ring. Surrounding the floor were gilded chairs, all facing each other in a circle: twelve chairs to mark the chief gods of Olympus. Encircling this plaza were gilded marble structures, thick green vines, and lush bushes. And outside the plaza was a lush jungle of thick green foliage and fruit groves.

All the chairs were occupied this morning except four. Every god and goddess wore long draping white peploi with golden fibulas and golden necklaces with gems and rubies. The head chair was the largest, occupied by an elder with a long white beard, a bare chest, rippling muscles, and a gold crown over thin white hair. Lord of all gods: Zeus. Zeus sat stroking his beard. His eyes scrutinized everything. Beside him was a pretty gray-haired woman. She had a wry smile and watched the others too. And she seemed to be enjoying herself the most: the mother of the gods, Hera. The most arrogant god sat on the left side of Zeus. A young beardless blond-haired man. He seemed irritable, which was amusing as he frequently strummed tranquil melodies on his lyre. He was Apollo. And near Apollo was a tall, lanky, impatient-looking man carrying a staff with two live snakes slithering about the rod in one hand. Hermes.

On the opposite side of the plaza was a strange contrast. Considered the most beautiful woman ever to be beheld, Aphrodite sat with her long flowing blond hair perfectly coiffed, soft pale skin, and a warm smile. In contrast, she sat beside her husband, a disfigured man with a humpback: Hephaestus. He was the only unattractive god in the circle, with a disheveled curly beard and dark, protruding eyebrows. Beside these two was a lady and another man. Both squinted, challenging anyone who looked upon them. They were Artemis, the goddess of the hunt, and Ares, the god of war.

With the same indignant look as Apollo, a goddess with long curly black hair sat beside Hera, on Zeus's right, glowering. She looked upon everyone with disdain and contempt. A small brown owl sat perched on her shoulder. She was Athena.

Outside the circle a hundred spectators surrounded the plaza waiting for the grand trial. Calliope sang; Iris shone bright loveliness; Momus, Morpheus, and even the demigod Pan played music. There were human servants there, too, who had been taken to the clouds by the gods to watch the assembly.

The four gods missing from the circle were Poseidon, Hades, Demeter, and Persephone.

Two of them entered the Court now. Cora was led to the center of the plaza by her mother, Sara, the goddess Demeter. Cora's wrists were shackled in front of her by silver chains. Sara led her through the crowds, hanging her head low and meeting no one's gaze, though many gods glared at Sara. Cora surmised that they blamed her mother, Sara, for her daughter's behavior.

Cora wore the same scarlet dress she had worn into the depths of the sea, now dirty and torn. Her long blond hair was messy and her face was dirty. She was left in the center of the circle, but she defied them by not standing. Instead she lay down on her side on the cold white marble floor. Her eyes continued to blaze red, and many of the gods in her family turned from her. It was the custom for everyone, even Zeus's wife, Hera, to bow before Lord Zeus upon approaching his throne. As Zeus stared down at her, she remained on the floor.

Zeus rose and the crowd behind the circle fell to their knees or bowed. Then he gestured toward Cora.

"It is a sad day, fellow Olympians," Zeus announced. "Today we cast judgement on my daughter." Everyone fell silent. "What say you, Kore? You know the accusations. You battled a god. That is a criminal offense. The price of fighting another god is chains."

"Nice to see you again, Father," Cora quipped with a wicked smile. "I would have preferred it centuries ago."

He furrowed his brow. There was murmuring. He grabbed his staff, fashioned in the shape of lightning, and pounded it on the stone floor for order. Then, with red eyes of his own, he said, "You're fortunate, Kore, I didn't use this on you in Evia."

"I asked you to."

Some in the crowd gasped.

"There's no respect from her," said Athena with disdain.

"She's as unruly as she was as a little girl. She has no respect for any of us."

"Particularly you," Cora replied.

Ares laughed. Then some in the crowd did too, making the crowd become loud.

Zeus turned toward the audience. "Silence!" he stormed. "Calm yourselves. We will hear Kore. Let us hope she gives reason for her actions. Let reason guide justice."

"I hate you," Cora said to Zeus. Then she looked at Athena and the rest of them. "I hate all of you."

After no further words were spoken by her, Zeus turned to Hermes. "Tell her the charges."

The tall, thin god Hermes rose and stood over her, addressing the gods.

"The first is hearsay, I'm afraid. There's no proof. And yet, the queen of the Underworld had the staff. Her possession of it shows her crime. You saw her wield it from the clouds."

"The Scepter of Hades," interrupted Zeus.

"Yes." Hermes coughed. "Or, in this case, the Scepter of Azure."

"I made it for her husband," interjected Hephaestus. "It was meant for Hades. I suppose, technically, it's hers. As you all know, when I gave it to Hades, he chose to give it to Harmonia, the Napean nymph."

"That's how this whole thing started," interjected Athena. "The Napean nymphs. Perhaps we should blame the god of the Underworld for his love for them. And where is your so-called husband anyway, Kore?"

Cora just shrugged.

"My daughter lies before you in chains!" Sara said to Athena furiously, standing up. "She's humiliated. Must you insult her marriage? Isn't her humiliation enough for you, Athene?"

Athena turned as if noticing Sara for the first time. Then she grinned an incredibly ungenuine smile. "I meant no disrespect, Demeter. Only her husband seems to delight in rebellion against us. Pandora. Now his scepter. It belonged to Hades, not to mere mortals. And we mustn't forget the charge, Hermes, that she used Hades' Cap as well. That is another offense that should be logged."

"My husband is not why I'm here, you conceited bitch," said Cora. Some in the crowd laughed, until Zeus glared at them. "I fight on my own behalf. I am here for my actions. I take full responsibility. And I really don't need your defense either, Mother."

Athena stood up in protest, muttered something incomprehensible, and sat back down. Many of the crowd jumped up. Some cheered Cora, which angered Zeus again.

"Silence!" thundered Zeus at the crowd. "May I remind you all that you are here as guests. Control yourselves." Then he turned to Athena and Sara. "We are here to judge Cora, not bicker." He looked down at Persephone. "This is what you do, Daughter. Your rebellion infects everyone. Go on, Hermes. No more interruptions."

"Sorry, Father," Cora said with a wily smile.

"We can only guess that she got the scepter from King Solinair." Hermes lifted his hands, addressing the gods. "I surmise that Cora got it using the helm."

"What say you to this accusation?" asked Zeus. "Did you get it from the king of Atlantis?"

"Who cares?"

"I care!" Zeus jumped up in fury. "It's my law for you to not leave the depths!" He took his staff and pounded it on the ground some more.

"Yes, Father," replied Cora.

"She calls me names," Athena said. "She mocks you. Look at her eyes, Father. Listen to her words. She has something planned in that wicked head of hers."

"Does she frighten you, Athene?" asked Ares.

"You traveled to Amphitrite to battle my brother," stormed Zeus to Cora. "Do you deny it?"

"No."

"You lured him out of the sea and then used your power over the sky to subdue him. Do you deny this charge?"

"No."

"Poseidon was left unconscious on the beach. You dragged him along the sands. Why should I not strike you down, Kore?"

"Strike me down then!" shouted Cora. She kneeled. "I asked you to. You trapped Kronos in my realm. My grandfather. A god who ate those he scorned, including you. Then you call this meeting on the pretense of *justice*. There's no *justice* in our family, Father. There never was. If there was, then—"

"*Silence!*" Zeus's hand shook with the rod. He pointed it at her.

"You can bind me," Cora said, raising her clanging chains before him. "You can hurt me. You may strike me to ashes. But before you do, I ask that you answer me one question. One question I could never ask when I was imprisoned below." Cora squinted into her father's eyes. Zeus nodded. "Why did you abandon me?"

"Enough," Zeus said dismissively, seemingly losing his anger. He sat back down in his throne. "This is a trial. I don't need to rehash the past."

"I think this is a splendid time," Cora objected. "You owe me before you imprison me. Why'd you do it?" Then she turned to Sara. "You owe me an explanation too, Mother."

"I stormed over you," said Sara, shaking her head. "It nearly killed me when you left."

"For a season? One season. One year out of centuries? Then what is it that made you accept the fate of your poor daughter? Hmm? Like you cared."

"It was arranged, Kore," said Zeus, waving his hands at her dismissively. "That's that. We will not talk of it again." Then he turned to Sara. "Sit back down, Sara. I won't hurt her. Repeat the charge, Hermes."

"A violation of your law, Zeus," Hermes said with a bow. "She stole the Helm and Scepter of Hades and used it on another god. She battled with your brother."

"Where is this scepter now, Persephone?"

"In my clothes."

The whole crowd went wild. Zeus rubbed his eyes, tired of calming the crowd.

"Why did you not look for it, Sara?" Zeus asked wearily.

"Hermes and I did," she replied.

"Search her," Zeus said to Ares.

Ares got up and approached Cora. He checked her dress. Hiding in the folds of her peplos, on the right, was a small golden stick. The god of war waved it in the air and it extended to the length of a staff.

"Clever girl," Ares said to Cora. "If only Hades hadn't claimed you."

Cora smiled back.

"Bring the staff to me, my son," said Zeus to Ares.

Ares handed the scepter to Zeus. Zeus took the staff and broke it in two with his bare hands. Then he nodded to Hermes.

"The second is an attack on one of us," continued the messenger god. "Persephone brought the scepter and used it on your brother, Lord Zeus. Using its power and her own, she incapacitated him."

"Battling a god is the highest crime, Cora."

Persephone looked around. She had no friends. All of the gods looked down at her with fear or disdain, all except her mother. But Sara was worse than all of them. Sara pretended to care. Sara didn't even know who Cora was anymore.

"Perhaps the poor girl's lost her senses," said Hera, shaking her head sadly. "I pity her, Zeus. She seems miserable from living in the depths for so long. Don't be too harsh."

"She deserves nothing less than the fate of Grandfather," said Apollo, shaking his head.

"Yes. Chain her, Father," said Athena. "Bind her."

"She has had a hard life," said Sara. "We all should pity her. She had to live under those wood nymphs. And no harm came of her battle with Poseidon."

"Sara!" thundered Zeus. "Cora flooded his palace. Then she nearly killed him."

"But she didn't, Lord Zeus," Sara said. "Poseidon is unharmed. Amphitrite is restored. Cora was distraught over the death of her friend. She's had few friends in her life. And she's had to live with Hades."

"Oh stop it, Mother," said Cora. "Please don't defend me. You hardly care. I ask you again, where were you when I was taken by Uncle? I will never forgive you. You claim it was hard for me under wood nymphs? Nephrea was a better mother than you could ever be." Sara lurched back, opening her eyes wide. "You fetched a nymph to rescue me while you remained comfortable here in the clouds. Then you raised winter pretending to rebel. You're a fraud. A fake. I don't respect you, nor do I love you. Nor do I consider you to be my mother. Just as I don't consider Zeus to be my father. Such a father makes me sick."

The crowd became unhinged. Many cried out in shock. Sara looked at her daughter as if she was mad.

"Listen to her words, Lord Zeus!" cried Athena, with wide eyes, jumping up.

"I told you," replied Hera, shaking her head, "she's not well."

Zeus looked down at Cora in amazement. "Sara is the only one defending you, child… Why attack her?"

Persephone looked up at Zeus with a sly smile, and even the King of the Gods seemed uneasy under that gaze.

Oh yes, I will hurt even you. Even you, you arrogant, vile beast.

"No one cares about me," Cora answered. "Anyone who says otherwise lies."

Zeus addressed Sara: "She's our daughter. What say you? How should we punish her?"

"Exile her," said Sara. "Perhaps to the Indus. Or Nubia. Somewhere far away where we will never see her again."

"That seems fair," said Hera.

"Exile?" asked Athena. "She's already in the Underworld! Father, you can't send her anywhere. She'll simply return. She needs to be chained."

"With Grandfather? Does she really deserve such punishment, Athena?" asked Aphrodite. "If you must punish her, imprison her for a little while. Perhaps after a century, she will have learned her lesson and can return home."

"To the Underworld?" asked Cora with a grin that made Aphrodite quickly turn.

"Father," said Athena. She got up and walked to Zeus. She touched his shoulder. Then she stroked his beard and kissed him on the cheek. Zeus's face brightened in response to the touch of his favorite daughter. "If you don't imprison her with Kronos, she'll return. It seems the only way ... the best way."

"Why do you hate her so much?" asked Ares with an amused smile. "She never did anything to you. Could it be because the king of Atlantis is laying siege to your precious Athens, prepared to take your prized city?"

"Shut up!" Athena turned to the god of war in rage. "What do you care about any of this? You'll get your blood! You don't have to ask for it up in the hills of the gods!"

"But I enjoy it," Ares said heartily, standing up. His eyes burned red. "Please, Athena, come here. Let us embrace. Perhaps a fight with me again—"

"*Enough!*" shouted Zeus. "I said I didn't bring us here to fight. We're here to pass judgement on Kore. And so we shall. Not to fight among ourselves."

Ares bowed his head low to Zeus, but it seemed almost in mockery. Athena turned to Zeus and touched his shoulder again. "For me, Father," she said almost in a whisper. But everyone could hear. "Please. For your people in our new city of Athens. The Atlanteans don't offer libations. They give no sacrifices. They ignore us. You heard King Solinair's blasphemy. She is their champion. Persephone will continue to cause trouble if she isn't chained. But Hera's right too—the poor girl is obviously not well. Too much strain in the depths of the Underworld. Just keep Cora chained with your father for a little while. Even if it is for a little while. Perhaps two or three centuries?"

"What say you?" Zeus asked Persephone.

But Cora didn't feel like saying anything.

"Very well," Zeus continued. "So be it. We pass judgement." Sara began to cry. "I am so sorry, Kore. Before I strike my staff on the ground and make this final, I ask one last time if anyone has any objections."

"I have an objection."

Zeus searched among the gods sitting around the circle. No one said a word. Sara was still crying. The words had come from outside the circle.

The gods turned to see who it was. A tall man in a black robe with a hood over his head entered the circle. He lifted the hood and showed his bald head and goatee.

"Hades?" asked Zeus. "Welcome, Brother."

"I wasn't really invited. But thank you."

"You're late," Cora said, still on the ground.

"Better late than never, Wife."

He walked to the center ring and crouched near Persephone, gesturing to her with one hand. She grabbed it and he helped her up. Then he walked her to two empty gilded chairs.

"What's this!" cried Athena, jumping up. Apollo rose too. "She doesn't deserve to sit!"

Hades turned to Athena and merely smiled.

"What have I missed?" asked Hades. He snapped his fingers. Persephone felt the chains on her wrists break open.

"You shouldn't have come," said Cora with a smile. "I will only hurt you."

"Such is love," Hades said with a shrug.

"Persephone is on trial, Brother," said Zeus, clearing his throat. "She's guilty on two counts. She has stolen what was yours and she has fought Poseidon."

"Did you apologize?" Hades asked, turning to her.

The crowd burst into laughter. But the gods, even those on Persephone's side, remained deadly serious.

"I see," Hades said. "Well, you know, Lord Zeus, that living in filth can cause you to do all sorts of irrational, terrible things. I ask that you take this into account when you pass judgement."

"Our only solution, brother," Zeus said, "is that we must imprison her. Imprison her with our father, Kronos. I have decided not to destroy her."

"How kind." Hades turned to Persephone. "Just say sorry, dear, and we can forget the whole thing. Then you can come home with me to the Underworld. No one was hurt."

"Poseidon was," Athena said. "He was humiliated. She needs punishment."

"Ah, Athena," Hades said with sudden vehemence, "can't you show your allegiance with a little more ambiguity. Do we preside over your justice in the clouds?"

"Father, why even listen to him," said Athena. "He's never here."

"He is just as welcome at this Court as you, child," objected Zeus.

"He listens because I am his brother, you pompous tot," replied Hades to Athena. "I, Sara, Zeus, and Poseidon created everything you enjoy."

"Enough, Hades!" cried Zeus. "Don't speak to her in public in such a manner."

The crowd became unruly again. Zeus struck his staff on the ground repeatedly. Finally thunder erupted in the valley and all were silent.

"Pardon me," Hades said, bowing his head. Then he took the hand of his now unshackled wife. The silence was perfect for Hades to chime in again. "Where is the god affected by the crime, great Zeus? Where is our brother, the mighty Sea God?"

Zeus thought for a moment. Indeed, where was he? Zeus looked over at Hermes. Even the messenger god shrugged.

"No one has seen him since the attack, Lord Zeus," replied Hermes.

"Now that," Hades said with a finger raised, "that's strange, isn't it?" He got up and addressed the circle. "Surely if you intend to damn my wife, the accuser should be here for the sentence. Perhaps he feels guilty."

"He doesn't have to be here," said Zeus.

"Perhaps," Hades said, rubbing his goatee with a smile, "but he shouldn't have interfered with mortals by the Strait. That is also against our laws. Maybe my wife was right in passing judgement *over him*."

"Are you claiming that I didn't consider his actions?" thundered Zeus.

"Of course not," Hades said, holding up a hand, "I'm just saying that Poseidon broke our edict as well. He wasn't supposed to be aiding mortals. And there he was, as plain as day, on the shore of Azure Blue, moving the sea. That wasn't very fair to the Amazon or the Atlanteans. We gods can't be appearing in battle. It's a bit ignominious, don't you think? Not to mention our brother turned his back on his own wood dryads. He fought people from the land he created. Then he slayed their queen."

"What are you insinuating?" repeated Zeus.

"He's claiming that Persephone punished Poseidon for the sake of justice," said Apollo. "Which is a completely ridiculous assertion."

"Hades, this meeting is about Persephone, not about Poseidon."

"With all due respect, Brother," said Hades with a half bow, "this trial is a farce." And he returned to his seat.

The crowd could not be controlled. Zeus glared at his brother with venom. And Zeus's eyes burned red. His face contorted into a mix of confusion and rage. Lightning flashed and thunder cracked above them.

Cora cocked her head to her husband in amusement. "Do you have it?" she whispered in his ear.

"How dare you!" raged Zeus.

Hades put up a hand again. "Forgive me, great Zeus. But I fail to see the point in this trial, unless it is to humiliate my wife."

"We are here to pass judgement on her!" Zeus shouted, jumping up. "She has attacked a fellow Olympian."

Hades shrugged. "All right, then do your bidding, mighty Zeus." He pointed to the crowd behind him. "You needn't bring all of them into it. It merely embarrasses—"

"Do you wish to be on trial as well!" thundered the King of the Gods. "She used your scepter!"

Hades did not answer. Instead he turned and whispered to his wife. "I do this, Kore, for my own hatred, not yours." He looked at his brother as he spoke into her ear. "If you change course now, I can return us home. But as to your plans…"

"Today, I love you, Husband," Cora said, patting his hand.

"A fool's love for both of us."

"Silence!" stormed Zeus, standing and pointing at the couple. "What are you murmuring to each other? I embarrass her? You embarrass me, Brother! How dare you call this trial a farce!" He looked ready to charge him.

"You are not understanding my point," continued Hades. "The whole thing—"

"Speak no more! Do not push my hand to do something I'll regret. I can't believe the blasphemy you are speaking publicly from your mouth."

Hades got out of his chair and fell to the ground, bowing low in reverence before Zeus.

Cora rose. She patted him on the back and walked past him to the center circle. Hades did not rise until beckoned to by Zeus.

Zeus quieted his rage and his eyes returned to blue, gazing at Persephone again.

"Lord Zeus, you asked if anyone objected," Cora said, now standing and addressing the crowd. "I don't object to your sentence, as I fully admit to guilt." The crowd quieted. All stared at Cora. "I ask one thing before my sentence, then I will go willingly. Do you grant it?"

"Why are her chains broken?" asked Apollo.

"She hardly needs to be treated like a dog, Phoebus," said Hades.

"Quiet!" shouted Zeus. "This is my last warning, Hades! Speak no more." Hades nodded. Then he turned to Cora. "You already asked one question."

"Now I ask for final words. I know my sentence. Let me speak my mind, before you all damn me. Don't speak until I am finished. No one. I will say things that could anger you. Wait until I'm done, then I will go willingly beside my grandfather. Do you agree, Father?"

Zeus squinted and stared at her. Then he nodded.

The crowd turned silent. Persephone turned to them. She walked in a circle around all of the gods and goddesses of the court as she addressed them, even the bystanders behind them.

"You all know that, as a child, I was taken out of Azure by Hades on his chariot and imprisoned in the Underworld. I spent many moons, without knowledge of time, in a cell. Hades would come to me and force me to do unspeakable things. Then he would feed me. It was torture, but soon the opposite—when I obeyed him. When he was kind, I found he could offer delicacies and riches beyond anything any mortal could ever dream of. I became somewhat content, but still very alone. I sought companionship.

"My husband and I witnessed the turning of time in misery. Then came the Amazon queen. Nephrea intended to stop the winter in Gaia by rescuing me. When Nephrea came, a part of the small heart that I had left in Azure Blue was lit again. I saw that someone in this cold world still cared for me through her sacrifice."

"It was not you, Mother," Persephone said, looking at her mother bitterly. "And, certainly, it was not you, Father. You abandoned me. Demeter only pretended to rage to cover her guilt. But Nephrea was willing to give everything for me."

Sara jumped up in objection, but Zeus ordered her to sit back down.

She walked around the marble floor. Calliope and Pan sang quietly of the past to the crowds. And many gods spoke among themselves about their own memories.

"I realized how flawed we gods are. I had always demanded respect and libations from mortals as a child, but after a short time in Tartarus, I realized that we didn't deserve any worship. Not one god has ever walked this Earth that showed more self-lessness than my guardian, my Nephrea. She deserved every sacrifice in the world. She gave me the strength to rise up against my husband. She allowed me to risk everything in order to be free. And so I fought back against my husband and avenged my abduction, damaging his perfect replica of Gaia. I froze the machines that cooled us. And I stopped the supply of food and drink that had enabled us to live like the spoiled tyrants up here on Olympus.

"My husband tortured and imprisoned me again for a year after that act. But even that punishment did not stop this new flame that burned in my heart. I learned to pity Hades. I realized that he was as miserable as I was, living an eternity in the underground and loathing it. In all those eons imprisoned, and later freed, underground, my hatred for him lessened, while my anger at you, all of you, only grew.

"There was a new respect for my husband. Of course I still hated him, but I understood him. Hades, thought to be the most vile and cruel snake by all of you, at least prized truth. He was not spoiled and pampered. He lived in dirt and understood pain. He gained respect for me, too, after my acts of rebellion. And I gained respect for his reign. But what's more, the resemblance between him and me that I adored the utmost—and this is most secret—the greatest secret that he holds deep in his chest…" She turned to Zeus. "Is that Hades, great Zeus, hates you more than anyone."

Zeus struggled to not rise. Far worse, Hades did not stir, object, or even look away from Zeus.

"Hades loathes you, Father. It is only your pride and arrogance that blinds you to this truth. And why wouldn't he? First you forced him to live in the dirt. Next you took Harmonia, the only woman he ever loved."

The audience shouted and jeered. Zeus hammered his staff against the ground for order, and protesting her words, as they raged.

"I object to that," Hades finally interjected, raising a finger. "I love you too, Kore."

"No lies, husband. Lust is not love."

"Ah, but you are the loveliest goddess on Olympus." Then Hades smirked at Aphrodite.

"Prophecy told me that my husband's and my lot would turn if I waited for Cassandra," continued Cora. "So, I endured the pain. I waited centuries. That, perhaps, was the greatest torture. My only hope was the conviction that one day I'd hurt you, Father. Every day of pain made me think that."

"Why, Father, hear anything further from this gorgon!" Athena jumped up, along with Apollo. But Zeus had promised. And, according to his own laws, he'd abide by his agreement. Though he twisted and turned in his chair impatiently, waiting for her to finish.

Cora looked at Hades. Her husband nodded in encouragement.

"Poseidon now lies imprisoned in the Underworld," Cora continued matter-of-factly. "My husband and I chained him at the bottom of Tartarus beside your father, Kronos, Zeus. Unlike you, we saw no need to bother with a false trial."

The uproar became terrible. People screamed. Others shouted and jeered at Persephone. Zeus's hand trembled holding his lightning scepter. He stood up.

"A promise is a promise?" Cora added with a big smile.

Zeus looked ready to break her in half. He nodded as he ground his teeth. Hades held an odd look, almost fear, as he stood up with the rest of the gods.

"I had to, Lord Zeus. For he is the only one who could have stopped me."

There were more shouts and jeers. The crowd became so loud that they couldn't hear the gripes of Athena or Apollo any longer.

"Father..." Cora raised her hand, silencing the crowd. She smiled wickedly. "I leave you. This time, *I* abandon you. And as a parting gift, I am going to hurt you. I am going to hurt all of you in the same way that you hurt me. It will sting. It will cause great suffering, more than even you, terrible Zeus, would sanction, but such is my only way to avenge the death of my beloved

Cassandra Ambrosia. This is her sacrifice. She was better than all of you. This is for you, Casey."

There was silence.

"I only ask…" She turned from them and looked up to the sky saying quietly, more to herself. "That my God can forgive me."

She turned to Hades and held out her hand. "Give it to me now, husband."

With incredible speed, Hades threw open his black coat. Inside the coat hid the long silver trident of Poseidon. He threw it to Cora. He reached toward Zeus and called out for his scepter. The golden Scepter of Azure, which had lain broken on the floor under Zeus, slid across the marble and became whole in Hades' hand.

Cora raised the trident over her head and thrust it down into the center of the circle. The gods jumped back in shock. It sank down deep into the marble. Cracks formed along the center floor and the earth shook. Then she thrust the trident repeatedly into the ground screaming:

"*Thanatos!*"

Then, like the madwoman Hera believed her to be, she cried again and again:

"*Thanatos, Thanatos, Thanatos!*"

The ground exploded. The earth shook so violently that it knocked down everyone, even the gods. Many in the crowd screamed. Then people around the circle ran for their lives as the gods turned on one another.

Ares tackled Apollo before he could touch Cora. Then Athena came to Apollo's aid.

The king of gods flew to Persephone. "*What have you done!*" Cora did not defend herself. She was too busy hammering Poseidon's trident into the ground. As the whole mountain caved under her, she saw her father's lightning scepter raised over her head. It came down on her, and she waited to be cut in half.

Another staff blocked it.

"*Do you think I will let you destroy the only thing of pleasure left to me in this forsaken world!*" cried Hades, blocking the blow. "She is all I have, Brother!"

"*You both will destroy all of us!*" raged Zeus.

"It's been my dream!" Hades roared.

Cracks appeared throughout the valley. Water jumped from cracks around the central lake and poured over the top of Mount Olympus. The waterfalls siphoned water from the lake and poured it over the mountain.

And Cora would not stop her thrusting.

"*Thanatos!*" she screamed in an almost possessed madness:

"*THANATOS! THANATOS! THANATOS!*"

"I shall break you in half, Hades!" thundered Zeus.

And indeed, the great King of the Gods took Hades and hurled him nearly fifty feet from the circle. The Dark Lord landed, stunned, in a valley, in a clearing between trees. Zeus flew to him, but upon landing, the two gods were thrown into the air as the ground below them broke apart.

Athena and Apollo charged Cora. Athena took out a javelin and nearly speared the queen of the Underworld. Apollo removed a golden glowing sword and raised it, ready to ram it into Cora's chest. But then Persephone looked up to the sky with fiery eyes blazing. A cloud, something never seen over Olympus before, and never seen again, formed. Then lightning, not from a staff, nor from Zeus, but from Cora's scorn, struck Apollo and Athena.

Hera, the queen of the gods, tackled Cora. She grabbed her throat, choking her. The one goddess out of all who had feigned calm seemed to be the most crazed now. Hera squeezed so hard that it felt like she would snap Cora's head off. But the grain goddess, Sara, defended her against Hera, and the two elder goddesses fought.

Cora saw Ares recover from the ground and strike at Hephaestus. Even the old man and the loveliest blond goddess wrestled Ares. All the while the ground crumbled around them. The crowd—every man, satyr, merman, and demigod that had witnessed the trial—were crushed by falling rubble or buried under the crumbling Mount.

Zeus and Hades continued to fight. Their violence only tore the mountain down faster. Cora saw lightning strike Hades and nearly destroy him. Then Hades froze the ground around Zeus to trap him with his mighty staff. He grabbed Zeus's head, attempting to decapitate the King of the Gods.

They sank further through the storm clouds by the top of the Mount. The storms below Olympus only caused further destruction. Boulders were carried off in torrential wind. They fell, fell, and fell, crumbling over the Isle of Napea. The sun's rays turned green. The rocks mixed with the blue and green world of Azure until they sank in a bubbling, fiery sea. The energy from a mountain falling was so great that fire exploded in the water, competing with the waves. Flames mixed with steam as Hades fought with Zeus.

Cora grabbed the trident and continued to thrust it at any rocks near her. She thrust even as water flowed over her, covering her ears.

All became quiet, but she could still see her family, in the distance, fighting under water.

Cora finally let go of the trident, extending her arms.

She let herself sink. She hoped she would drown. Immortal or not, she hoped her lungs would fill and she would just pass away.

She thought of Cassandra. And in all the chaos, that re-sparked her anger. This was how her nymph daughter had drowned.

"Thanatos," Cora gurgled in the salty water. "Thanatos," she bubbled. "Thanatos."

All turned dark at the bottom of the sea.

We will never be free, Nephree. Never.

24

THE FLOOD

The salpinx was blown. Torinth gathered the cavalry.
Then the Tiger King's foot soldiers started their march in a turtle
formation—shields surrounding his soldiers, led by spears—while
Torinth raged on horseback, gesturing wildly at the enemy. Sol
sat on horseback beside generals Kaios and Cambria, watching.
He and his men would stay back during the initial assault on the
shore.

"The men are ready," said Kaios. "A glorious day, Sol!
Behold, your brother has victory in his heart."

The Tiger King rode alongside his phalanx as they marched;
then he sped in front of them, headlong into the Greeks' own
turtle formation. Such a strike was against all Greek protocol, for
it left Torinth's horsemen vulnerable. Countless blue Atalan
hoplites fell as archers threw a volley of arrows and foot soldiers
speared them. But it wasn't enough to stop the mad general.
Torinth rode straight into them. He was thrown from his horse
by the impact. But his violence and speed broke the first phalanx,
and the Greeks were forced to fight a bloody battle within their
own defenses.

"Do you see, sire!" shouted Kaios. "Your brother was born to
fight."

The mad Tiger King managed to get back on his horse and lead his phalanx straight into a hole in the Greek army.

Sol pointed to another line of Greeks, standing closer to the walls of the city.

"Unleash the beasties on them to clear our path," Sol ordered Kaios. "As the tiger beats back their first defense, break a hole so that I may move on the city walls. And be quick. Their reinforcements come by land in the north."

This was known due to aerial surveillance. Reinforcements were rapidly approaching from the northern city-states and, if they arrived, the battle could quickly turn in the Greeks' favor.

"Aye, emperor," Kaios said with a nod. "We shall stampede."

"Do it now," Sol said, squinting with hatred at the bronze lines. "Let them run from Torinth to their burning ships," he said, still watching his mad brother's fury. "Then we go to the walls and I shall meet up with King Aegeus personally. Whether he chooses to fight or not."

"Aye, my lord," Kaios said excitedly.

"Go now!"

Kaios rode hard to a series of olive groves on a hillside, where the farthest encampment of Atalan soldiers waited. Sol pulled out a scope and gazed at the hill. Kaios disappeared for a moment. The ground shook. Soon Kaios reappeared with chariots behind charging elephants. Blue-armored hoplites rode atop the beasts too.

"Once the beasties were my greatest fear," Sol said, with a smirk, to Cambria. "I had nightmares of those monsters invading my camps. Now I bring them to Hellena."

Elephants stampeded so quickly that some of the enemy lines could not regroup and were hit from the side. Those that turned watched their spears break like twigs. Greeks ran and broke ranks. No matter how seasoned and disciplined, they could not withstand this barrage.

"You've given up your immortality, Cambria," Sol said, pulling his reins toward the city walls. "Fitting. Your friend is Persephone, the goddess of the dead. The gods have taken my wife and my daughter. Let me now take their favorite Greek men. We will take their souls and send them to your goddess as sacrifice for what they did to my Cassandra. Then we can give libations to Persephone upon their ashes."

"We'll defend you from above, Emperor."

"And I shall see you below. Yah!"

Sol pulled his reins and rushed in the opposite direction from the stampeding elephants. Raising his hand, Sol gathered his elite cavalry and rode to the now undefended side of the city walls.

Solinair's cavalry barreled into the shields of the enemy. Then, when cracks appeared, the king's seasoned soldiers, some older than Sol, rode through. Sol dismounted and hacked and thrusted his enchanted Mandrigelian sword at the Greek hoplites. Sol was an expert swordsman and now, with the death of Henri and Milo, likely the best in the world.

Time passed. All afternoon. Then a fog rolled in.

As surprised as the Greeks were by the fury of the Atalans and their mastodons, Sol was disillusioned by the Greeks' stubborn resistance. Sol had planned to divide and conquer his enemy before nightfall. A quick victory was the only victory. Night would bring a hard fight and allow them to possibly regroup.

It was twilight when Torinth came beside Solinair's personal guard in the thick fog.

"Brother! A brutal fight!" shouted Torinth, out of breath, grasping Sol's gloved hand. "I'm impressed by these Greeks."

"You're hurt."

"It is nothing," Torinth said, grasping his bloody side. It wasn't nothing. There was fresh blood along his right flank, and he was pale. "I've cornered most of them by the sea, Sol. If you ignore the stench, you can smell the salt! They will have nowhere left to go but the water, where they belong."

"You've fought well. Our father would be proud."

"Aye."

They grasped hands again.

But the old man winced as blood dripped along his right arm.

"Blow the salpinx," Sol raged to his men nearby. "Get our men in formation once more. We need to kill or force the rest back into their city walls."

"It is difficult to see in the mist," objected a nearby soldier.

"Do as I say," Sol said, "or they'll regroup by morning with reinforcements."

Then Sol jumped back, surprised, as Cambria landed beside him. He hadn't seen her coming in the mist. Then another surprise when a Greek charged through the fog and lunged at her. She dodged it, withdrew her Mandrigelian sword, twirled it around, and struck the young man square in the stomach.

"Sol!" she cried, pulling out her blade. "The fog is thickening and we can barely see anything, even from above. We've almost cornered them, but we should stay where we are until it clears by morning."

"How do your people fare?"

She removed her helm. Sweat covered Cambria's head. Her long blond hair was soaked and unkempt. Crimson mixed with blond on her lower curls. Her red armor was stained a darker red. But there were no visible injuries, only a thin slash of blood along her right arm.

"We've lost many," Cambria said, climbing back on her unicorn. "But I think it will soon be over. For Casey, we can win this."

"For Casey," Sol said with a nod. "Have you seen their king?"

"You don't see him there by the wall?" Cambria pointed. Sol looked but could not see anything.

"He's out!" Sol cried in excitement. "You see him! How many defend the wretch?"

"A small group," Cambria said. "But they're well trained. And there are many soldiers behind the city walls. They think we intend to attack the city tonight. They don't know our plan to set up camp by the shore. But thinking we will not strike until nightfall is keeping the king's defenses down, for now."

Solinair nodded.

"I can't see anything through this!" exclaimed Torinth nearby. Sol could only see his shadow. "Horse's ass! Where, by the gods, is my horse's ass!"

Just then a Greek ran through the white smoke. Torinth met him and hacked wildly with his sword.

Solinair found his horse. Then he rode beside Cambria.

"Take me to King Aegeus."

"Sol!" she said, shaking her head. "No. Not tonight. He's too well guarded. We should regroup and hold our position. Strike by morning. The mist is too thick."

"It's too thick for them too," he said, shaking his head. "Take me there now, or he'll hide behind the gates."

Cambria looked down in thought. "You should remain here. He could gather many more numbers by the wall and trap us. If he does, you might win the port, but he'll kill us."

"Cambria, if I don't chase him now, he'll run. I won't let him run like Morteus. We kill him now and end this. Killing their king will seal our victory. Attica might even surrender."

"Let him go," said Torinth with a laugh, shaking his head. "You can't stop him. His will is what took a continent. Aye, he is a Solinaray."

"Just one moment, then," Cambria said in the thick mist. "Many of my nymphs are resting on a hill. Stop and allow me to at least fly back with them to provide you defense. Please, Sol."

Everything seemed to come down to this last charge. Battled and bruised, he was exhausted. But he would avenge his daughter.

"I can wait, Cambria," he said wearily. "Aye, I can wait. But if you don't return soon, I'll strike on my own."

Cambria nodded and quickly launched up into the air. Then Sol did what he loathed. He waited.

Wails could be heard. Then he heard shouts. There were snorts from horses, the sound of hooves, the roaring of flames, the clang of metal, and the splintering of wood. He smelled burning flesh, blood, and ash. But he couldn't see anything.

Occasionally a soldier would come charging at him through the smoke. But then the clouds returned. It was worse than fighting at night. At least then, one could ride by torchlight.

After what felt like an eternity of waiting, Cambria fell through the mist again. This time, with her came the sight of many wings in the haze—her army of Amazon. Now, with their support, he squinted into the fog, pulled on his reins, and charged.

He was amazed at the ferocity of the Amazon. He had never fought sword-to-sword with them in battle, always with their arrows above. But these Amazon fought with the same bravery and heart as his elite guard.

In time, he met the king's royal guard. He recognized the pompous jewelry and rich opulence of his new enemy. Many of them wore real gold instead of bronze.

The nymphs landed beside Sol and fought blade-to-blade. These Greeks were the best. But so were his guard and the Amazon. Many that Sol knew personally fell by his side. But, in time, they charged through the enemy line.

The fog cleared. Off in the horizon, the sun had not fallen yet. It was twilight. A yellow and red glow formed, made redder by all the smoke.

Sol could see his prize. The stone castle walls were close. The city of Attica and its Acropolis were now in striking distance. But he did not care to take the city. Not tonight. Tonight, he wanted the head of their king.

As he gazed at the stone walls, he was hit in the head from behind. His helmet was thrown off by the impact. He found himself on the ground, thrown from his horse. Then he felt warm liquid run down his forehead. The assailant was promptly killed by one of his guards, above him, but some of the Amazon soldiers had to help him up from the ground. As he wiped blood from his eyes, he spotted a man with long graying blond hair and ornate gold armor fighting. King Aegeus.

Sol pushed off the nymphs helping him and lunged toward him. The brazen attack forced his soldiers and the Amazon to join the terrible fray. Frustratingly, hack by hack, he could not reach his prize.

Aegeus was not a coward after all. The king fought without his helm, battling any soldier approaching him with bravery and honor. But respect meant nothing to Sol now. It was because of this man that his daughter had died.

Aegeus lost two guards beside him, one struck down by Cambria. Then Aegeus's royal sword was split in half upon contact with Cambria's enchanted Mandrigelian blade. Aegeus fell on his knees before them.

Sol finally stood over the king. Sol's eyelids were heavy. He was winded, sick, and in severe pain. More blood wet the right side of his face; he tasted the salt on his lips. Then, as Sol stood over the fallen king, he was hit again from behind, this time a sword thrust through Sol's flank. Guards battled the assailant, but now Sol could barely stand.

Sol limped weakly to Aegeus. He flicked blood from his eyes. Aegeus remained on his knees.

"You have my kingdom," Aegeus said to Sol. "I surrender all of Attica."

"I had it when I landed!" Sol said. He shook his head, fighting pain and unconsciousness.

"We don't live to fight, like you Atlantean," Aegeus said, raising his hand. "Spare me. I never meant to cause the terrible fate of your daughter, sir."

"Does he beg, Sol?" Cambria asked in wonder.

Solinair became so dizzy that Cambria had to catch him before he fell over the defeated king. All darkened for a moment. Then Sol found himself on his knees, leaning over Aegeus.

"I am defeated," Aegeus said. "Spare my life, Emperor. I know my neighbors. I can see to it that Attica remains safe under your reign, great Emperor of Atlantis."

Solinair raised his bloody sword over the Athenian king. But he was unsteady. He raised it high, but before he could thrust…

The ground shook. The shock was so great that it knocked Sol over. Then there was thunder, but it did not come from above. It sounded like it, strangely, came from below the ground. Then another quake. Then another. Each quake was so terrible that not just Sol, but Cambria and many other Azure knights struggled to stay on their feet.

Thunder and lightning cracked in the night sky. The sound of explosions echoed throughout the valley. The lightning shone through the twilight, and Sol could spot thousands of his men now battling by the shore.

"What's this?" asked Aegeus, wide-eyed.

Cambria and the other Amazons searched the valley with eyes wide open in shock.

Amazon nymphs flying above shouted to Cambria and Sol, pointing toward the beach.

"Sol, look!" cried Cambria. Cambria had to help him stand to see.

Red ships were being capsized by a tremendous wave. His fleet, a fleet that had taken countless years to build, was gone in an instant. Then more water barreled toward the shore. It was a rapid surf that seemed to have no end. The water continued to rush along the shore, soon covering the ports and beaches and crashing over the armies still battling. Then the wave rushed over trees and fields. As it crashed, it threatened to drown everyone in its wake.

Sol squinted, too shocked to believe what he was witnessing was real. He thought perhaps his pain had made him black out and he was dreaming all this.

"What's this?" cried Aegeus, leaning toward Poseidon's wave. "What is happening? A sign from the gods?"

"I believe this is *justice* from your Greek gods," Sol muttered, still staring. "This is how my daughter died." Then he looked down at Aegeus. "And so shall it be for you." With this, Sol thrust his sword deep into King Aegeus's neck.

The terrible quakes roared again. Everyone fell on the ground, this time from an even greater tremor. When they rose, many pointed in horror as a rush of water over a hundred feet high had traveled the three leagues from the beach and was now hurdling toward the city.

"Get to the sky, Cambria," Sol said, too weak to stand. "You and your Amazon can escape this."

"Not without you, Sol," Cambria said, shaking her head.

"Let me die with my men," Sol said, shaking his head. "Leave me."

But it all was too much. Sol was too sick. All turned dark as night, and he was consumed by the darkness.

FIRELIGHT SHONE UNDER SOL. He blinked an eye open. He thought perhaps this was the black River Styx and he had finally been taken to the ferryman. But he smelled iron and the familiar filth of battle.

Both eyes opened to a struggle below. What had been a battlefield was now a sea of thousands struggling to stay afloat. The water had moved from where he had killed Aegeus all the way to the very gates of the city. And even in the midst of the flood, men still fought atop splintered wood. But everything under torch fire was being washed away. Unlike all of Sol's other battles, this was a fight without a victor. Soldiers from all sides were simply drowning.

Under searing pain, Sol's heavy eyelids closed again.

He saw an image of himself in bed and the great King Darius standing over him. Then it was Henri. Then his beloved Anna. And, finally, his beloved Casey. He let the ebb and flow of the flying unicorn lull him in the midst of cries from the suffering below. And every time it turned black and full of darkness, he felt calm. But every time he opened his eyes, he felt pain, heard desperate cries, and felt only sorrow.

2 5

THE PRISONER OF PHALASARNA

ENGEL LOATHED SAILING. USING SOL'S ROYAL SEAL, HE HAD BEEN given a large galley, comfortable enough for any sailor, but Mandrigels—though they made wonderful climbers and builders —did not make good seafarers. Engel struggled to not stumble, amid nausea in his gullet, as he felt his way down the wooden hall to the brig. The smell of rotten fish didn't help his sea sickness either.

They had sailed from Phalasarna a day ago. He was happy to be away from Torinth's vile presence, but he already missed King Sol. Just as he had become a fixture in the Amazon queen's Court over the centuries, he had become a constant companion of the Atalan emperor.

He stood before the guard by the brig. He hadn't seen his prisoner yet.

"Strange fellow," said the guard in blue hoplite armor. "He claims he's a prince, but all he does is brood on the floor. His clothes are like a peasant's. And why didn't this Greek *prince* send for his people to come and rescue him if he's so important?"

"They don't know he's here," Engel said. "Open the door."

"Aye." Then he stared at Engel's clothes with a smirk.

Engel had chosen his finest chiton, a formal blue chiton made in Azure by nymphs, and even a long golden necklace. He had combed his thin hair back and straightened his thick brows.

The thick wooden door creaked open. Inside was just as dim as the hallway with a single torch on a sconce. There, leaning on a filthy cot with the smell of excrement, was the prince.

"Shout if you need anything, Captain," the guard said, chuckling as he shut the door behind him.

Theseus glanced over. Then he quickly turned back again. "A Mandrigel?"

Theseus still wore brass hoplite armor, now quite tarnished. It was royal enough, with gold by the sides, but—between scraggily hair and dirt on his face—he looked, indeed, like a peasant.

"Aye, I'm a Mandrigel," Engel said with a nod.

Theseus opened his eyes wide. "I haven't seen one since—"

"Mangornia," Engel said, forcing a smile.

"Mangornia," Theseus repeated, nodding slowly.

"I come for information, Prince Theseus," Engel said. "I am Engel, chief advisor to Emperor Solinair. I'm the captain of this ship and I'm here to free you."

"A blessed day, then," Theseus said, finally rising from his cot. "Chief advisor, eh? You must be the dwarf that advised Queen Cassandra."

"The fallen queen, yes."

"I heard this," Theseus said with a long sigh. "I am so sorry. You don't know how much. I was too late."

"No, I'm sorry. I heard that the two of you cared for one another."

"We barely knew each other."

"But she slept alone with you one night."

Theseus lifted an eyebrow at Engel.

"Once there were Imada spies in the Crystal Palace of Azure, Theseus," Engel said with a smile. "They said they knew everything that transpired. But they never knew more than I did, I can tell you."

"Yes, I was very fond of her, Engel. And I'm very sorry for her death."

"I know. You're a ruffian. But, like Casey, I like your spirit. If things had been different, you two might have been close. She really was my daughter. I cared for and raised Casey ever since she was a baby. I heard of the reason why you set sail to Azure from Attica, Theseus. It is for that reason that I stowed you aboard my ship. And it's because of it that I'll free you."

"For my freedom, I'm at your service. But I warn you, little man, your people—your emperor—may not favor you for it. Where are we heading?"

"Did you see my brother in Mangornia?" Engel asked, ignoring his question. It had been eating at him since he came aboard the ship. "Intar is my brother's name? Did you see him?"

"Yes, I met Intar. He asked about you too."

Engel squinted at Theseus. He wasn't sure he believed him. "How did you escape the Underworld?"

"I'm a scoundrel. That's how I survive. I stowed myself, invisible, on Hades' chariot until Persephone, the demon goddess of that world, found me. That woman is so wicked. She wooed me and claimed she'd been waiting for me. She had foreseen that I'd come with her husband's helm."

"The one Casey gave you for the fleece."

"Yes. Persephone found me, clever witch, by asking the guards to search for any new footprints by the Flume of Thyra that weren't accounted for. When the guards found my footprints, they found me. They brought me, alone, to her bedchamber at the top of the Dark Tower. She hid me there for a few days from her even-more-evil husband. She fed me delicacies. She treated me like a king. Indeed, her room was like that of a queen—no, grander—with an actual stream flowing through it. Just as you asked of Intar, she asked me about Cassandra. It seemed Cassandra was all she cared about. And after I had lain with her for a few nights, after she had her way with me, when I was no longer of use to her, she flew me to Mangornia, claiming that she could bring me to Attica from there." He shook his head with a big sigh. "That was a trick. It was the wrong direction. Then the goddess fooled me again by stealing my helm. I learned that the only use she had for me, aside from carnal pleasure, was recovering her husband's helm. In her warped sense of justice, she figured she'd let her enemy, a Greek hero, survive by banishing me to Mangornia.

"Though wondrous your valley was, Mandrigel, I didn't travel through the Underworld just to be trapped there. That's when I met your brother, Intar, and he told me of the three witches. They helped me out."

"How? Hades trapped the Stygian witches too."

"They were trapped because they were blind. They knew the way all along, but they needed someone to accompany them and be their eyes. They asked to use my eyes. With my eyes and their knowledge—and my protection, as they claimed—they found secret and narrow passages only they knew to avoid the Styx and Elysium and help me get back to Hellena. And they told me that, just as Persephone had predicted me coming, they had predicted a hero would arrive to free them." He shook his head violently and cursed at himself. "Some hero. I've let those evil harpies loose in Hellena again. What a terrible price."

"My people are all right?"

"Yes."

Engel took a deep sigh and nodded. He leaned back against the ship's wall. It was the best news he had heard in a long time.

"You bring me good news. I'm sorry I can't return the favor, Prince."

"You needn't tell me." Theseus hung his head. "I know about Atlantis. Unlike my father, I've been there. King Aegeus is a smart and just king, but he does not know your ways. I warned him. I knew that if Azure Blue was invaded, Emperor Solinair would do everything he could to hurt us. And now that Cassandra was killed, I can guess that he will not only invade, but kill my father and burn my kingdom."

"He will."

But Engel felt bad for this Greek. If what he said was true, he was not only a hero to the Greeks, but a hero to Atlantis too.

But he failed. Still, many heroes fail, don't they? Isn't it their acts that make them heroic, not their results? His efforts were no less than trying to stop a war and save the world.

"I do have some good news for your emperor, Engel," Theseus said. "Something I know will interest him. His wife, Queen Avivae, lives. Persephone asked me to tell Casey when I reached Azure. Now that I can't tell her, I can tell you. Tell your emperor his wife is alive."

"Avivae lives," Engel said, opening his eyes wide. "Are you certain?"

"Yes. The goddess thought the news of Casey's mother being alive would make Cassandra happy. Avivae lives... well, if you can trust Persephone. She, of all people, could have lied. But I don't think she'd deceive her beloved Cassandra. She said something about how Queen Avivae must live. Persephone herself wasn't certain why, but she knew she had to protect Avivae and keep her alive for your people. I tell you, that goddess only cared about the nymphs and Cassandra. She was under the impression that Cassandra would somehow defeat the gods and free her. When Persephone finds out that her beloved Cassandra has drowned, who knows what terrible thing that harpy will unleash upon this world."

"Avva lives." Engel shook his head in amazement. Indeed, he'd have to get this news to Sol. It could be the one glimpse of light that could save his king.

"Where are you taking me?" Theseus asked.

"Hmm? ... We sail for Azure Blue."

"Your emperor will execute me! I wish you'd reconsider. Give me a raft, and I will brave the sea alone and return home."

"I can't, Theseus," Engel said. "But you'll be under the care of a just prince, Gavin."

"Isn't Prince Gavin that fiend Torinth's son?" snapped Theseus. "No. If you care so much about me, let me run. You said you'd free me. Let me go overboard."

"Gavin's also Solinair's adopted son. The prince is a just man. And..." Engel shook his head morosely. "If you had arrived faster, I believe you would have fallen into favor with Sol too. Oh, this tragedy is unbearable." And, indeed, Engel fought back tears. "It's so sad that your plan didn't work."

"Yes. Plans are meaningless. All that matters is that I failed."

"Not to me," Engel said. "If Gavin agrees with Torinth in his view of you, I'll simply stow you away again. I won't let him harm you."

"Why do you care about me?"

"You poor man," Engel said, shaking his head. "For what you did. But more so, for my Casey. Cassandra told me she fell in love with you." Then… Engel hesitated. Tears formed in his eyes. In a broken voice, with sorrow mixed with rage that surprised himself, he said, "She was pregnant with your child."

Theseus stiffened with a look of shock. Engel couldn't take it. He ran out of the cell and didn't look back. And as the door closed, he didn't hear a word from his captive.

It tore at Engel. He had kept this secret hidden from everyone, only for it to emerge when he discovered that they had captured Theseus.

Against the door, Engel wept more. From the corner of his eye, he saw the stupid, burly guard chuckling. So strange that men viewed tears as weakness.

Then there was shouting from the deck above. And the sound of running footsteps.

"A Poseidon wave!"

"By the gods, we'll capsize!"

"Brace yourselves!"

Before Engel and the guard could climb the ladder to exit the hatch and see what had caused the pandemonium, Engel was violently hurled against the bulkhead. He crashed so hard against the wood that he blacked out for a moment. When his eyes opened a rush of water poured through the hatch. He and the guard were trapped. What was worse, he was fighting against inertia that continued to push him against the wall. Engel, though detesting being at sea, had been on ships before, but never had a storm hurled a ship with so much force for so long. And it didn't stop pushing him against the wall.

There were no sounds above now. But there was a tearing sound that sounded like splintered wood, as if the whole ship was about to break in half.

Engel looked back at the brig. "Give me the key!" he said to the guard.

"We have to get above," shouted the guard, shaking his head.

"There's nothing up there but rushing water!" cried Engel, pointing. "Give me the key!"

The guard reached in his tunic and handed it to him.

Engel fought the constant inertia of the ship, crawling against the bulkhead until reaching Theseus's cell. Then he unlocked the latch and threw the door open.

He heard the guard scream. Engel looked back, but Theseus had slammed the cell door closed.

"What's happening!" Engel cried.

"A flood wave," said Theseus, searching his cell with wild eyes. "Likely my father's wave."

"Aegeus?" asked Engel, befuddled.

"No. Poseidon."

"Poseidon is your father?" Engel shouted in amazement.

Theseus searched the room again and nodded. Then Engel's ears popped.

"We're sinking under water," Theseus said.

As quickly as they had been thrown, the inertia of the wave stopped and Engel and Theseus were tossed back in the other direction. The walls cracked and water started rushing in from all directions.

"What can we do!" cried Engel.

"Calm yourself. If we don't sink to the sea floor, there's still a chance."

If we don't sink to the sea floor!

When, finally, Engel could do nothing, he wondered about the wave. How could such an enormous wave occur? They weren't near the shore. Their ship was between Crete and Azure, in the middle of the deep ocean, nowhere near a beach. How could such a giant wave appear in the middle of the sea?

The cabin filled with water so fast that Engel found himself treading water. Soon they would reach the ceiling and would be submerged. But then…it stopped. Engel looked at Theseus. Theseus's teeth chattered. In fact, his olive skin was pale and his lips were turning blue. The water was icy cold.

"We have to try to swim out, Engel."

"You said we were sinking."

"Yes. But if we had sunk to the bottom, I think the water would have filled the room or the cell would have broken. Either way, we'll die in the cold if we don't try."

Engel nodded. He helped Theseus push open the door. Engel was shocked to see that there was no hallway outside the brig, only splinters of wood. They were outside facing a blue sky with the bright yellow sun above.

Theseus pushed himself out and helped Engel onto the ship's deck. They floated as if on a large wooden raft. Engel looked all around them. The rest of the ship was gone. Everything was gone. But the sea was still rough, likely from the violence of the first wave.

Theseus gestured to Engel to hold on to the broken, splintered wood jutting out from their broken barge. Then came another wave. This time, they rode above it. Then another. But as each successive wave came, the water became increasingly temperate. Then the sea finally stilled.

After some time in silence, Theseus turned to Engel. "You shouldn't have unlocked my cell." Theseus stared blankly at the horizon. He took a deep breath and uttered, "I don't deserve to have survived."

2 6

IT'S ALL GONE

Sol opened his eyes to torchlight and a gentle breeze. He found himself lying in bed wearing a thin white linen tunic. Through a row of columns he could see an outdoor patio. It was evening and torches lit the outside too. He looked to his side and saw his blue armor, worn but cleaned, on a stool. He turned to his side and groaned. He could not take a deep breath without intense pain. And his head ached terribly. He ran a hand along his head and felt a long gash over the right side. His hair was shaved there and he felt stitches. Someone had sewn the skin.

Along the brown stone walls was a mural. There was a man with a dark bird head. And beside the man was a line of servants, bowing and fanning him. Above the line of servants and the bird man was a single orb. And around the picture were strange animal figures: a monkey and a lion. He had seen these sorts of images before. This was Egyptian art.

Egypt? How? All he remembered was looking down on the flood in Attica. How could he be in Egypt? It was so far a journey by sea.

A woman in a tight linen dress walked into his room carrying a beige ceramic pitcher. Her face was thick with kohl. She bowed before Sol and smiled.

"Keetaru solver Beenik?" she asked. "Beenik? Beenik?"

Sol squinted at her, not understanding her words. She shrugged and poured liquid from the ampulla into the cup by the side of his bed. Then she bowed and left.

Egypt? How was he in Egypt?

⸻

"PHARAOH," said a man looking down on Sol. Sol squinted. It was Sadiki, the vizier to the pharaoh of Egypt. But more welcoming was his companion. A short blue fellow with a big grin. His dear friend Engel.

"Sadiki? Engel?"

"Sol, you don't know how happy I was to hear you survived," Engel said with a smile. And the Mandrigel placed his small stubby palm over Sol's hand. "But you're hurt. Just rest."

"Where are we?"

Did he need to ask?

"You've reached the land of Kemet," Sadiki said. "Your Amazon returned you to our river to mend. You've been asleep for a long time. We will care for you. This is now your home."

"What happened?" Sol asked, lifting himself up but then wincing as a searing pain fell over his side, and he quickly lay back down. "Is Cambria here? What about my brother? Engel, why weren't we taken to Azure? Or Azerban?"

Engel lost his smile for the first time. "You need rest, Sol."

"Engel," Sol said, snatching his wrist. "Why aren't we in Crete? Or Atala? Tell me."

"He won't stop," Engel said to Sadiki, shaking his head. "He'll keep fighting until he gets his answer."

Sadiki nodded. The woman who had come in earlier rushed over and fell to her knees before Sadiki with a silver cup in both her hands. Sadiki took the cup. Then he offered it to Sol.

"Wine," Sadiki said. "Red wine. Pomegranate wine from Atlantis. Drink. Rest."

"Answer me," Sol said weakly, pushing the silver cup away. "Tell me. Why am I in Egypt? Why not home? Or Phalasarna?"

"Phalasarna is badly damaged," replied Sadiki. "Your port is no longer safe for you to return."

"Then why not Arbor Dunn? Jedithian? Why would Cambria bring us to the Nile?"

"It's gone," Engel said, quickly shaking his head. "There are no ships. No ports. There's barely a city left in Crete. The island barely survived. Most of the cities were along the borders. As you know, the island is mountainous. Most of the shore is completely destroyed."

"Then why not Azure Blue?"

Engel hung his head.

"Engel! Tell me!"

"It's gone, Sol. Everything. We don't know how or why. The nymphs that survived took off from the stables during an explosion. They said the entire Mount erupted. It exploded and fell upon them. There are only a handful of nymphs left. The majority that survived had battled with you. Cambria. Hanna. A hundred or so nymphs. But the palace, everything, all of Azure Blue, by the gods, Sol, is gone."

Sol must have been staring at him. Engel met his gaze, but his eyes watered. Then Engel looked away and just shook his head.

A wave of nausea came on. Then an intense searing pain along his back.

"You might not be able to walk if you don't rest," warned Sadiki.

"What of my brother! Torinth? My god, Engel, what of our prince? My son?"

Engel kept looking down. He quickly shook his head.

That was enough. Torinth was dead. Apparently, so was Gavin? Sol's daughter and adopted son were dead. Anna was dead. His kingdom was in ruin. Everything had been taken from him.

"Your continent of Atlantis has sunk into the sea, Pharaoh," Sadiki confirmed stoically.

Sol heard it, but he wasn't listening anymore. He turned from them. Engel gently embraced him from the side and wept. Sol didn't. He didn't even answer them when they spoke. The words just became noise. He allowed his nausea and pain to envelop him. Then that blissful darkness fell once more.

2 7

VISITORS

Solinair did not eat. He slept, only fitfully. But he wouldn't eat. He wished that all would end. The darkness and shadows that he and his dear Mandrigel had spoken of now fully encompassed him. He lived without reason to live. His home was gone. His family was no more. And now, truly, he was nobody.

He didn't believe it. He thought that perhaps this was Elysium. He had always been fond of Wasset. It wasn't that far from his imagination to believe that he had been killed in Attica and that now he had simply been taken by the ferryman to live an eternity as a ghost in the Underworld.

Engel visited often. He even tried to force liquid into his mouth. The Egyptians tried to funnel medicine into him too. He refused, spitting it from his lips. Some men came in with long robes and tall blue hats and stabbed his skin. They were priests and they poured things into his skin. He allowed only that, for that was painful. He would accept pain as punishment for his sins.

One morning—he assumed it was morning since the light from the outdoor patio blinded him—he awoke to a woman weeping. When he cocked his head, he saw that the bright yellow sunlight lit her face to a faint blue. And she had long black hair with slightly pointed ears. Sol stirred at the sight of her, thinking for a moment that it was Anna. She opened her bright blue eyes. Then he recognized her face. This was not Anna. It was her best friend, Hanna.

"Oh, Sol. Please eat. Please." Tears streamed down the nymph's face. "Please eat for us."

"Why?"

"For Avva. For the remaining Atalans. For all of us. You are our king. We need your leadership now more than ever."

"There's nothing left. Everything was taken, Hanna."

"Many of us live. Cambria leads. She is gathering us from every corner of Gaia. Some left after Avva's edict. Now we shall all be together. But we need your direction."

"Remain here in Egypt. There is nothing left for us."

"If that is your order."

"I have no orders. I am no longer your king."

He felt liquid touch his lips. He quickly coughed it up.

"*Leave me!*"

She didn't. He didn't know for how long she remained, but when he opened his eyes again, she still sat at the foot of his bed. But now there was darkness outside the patio.

Even when it was light again, she still sat there. She sat by his bed as if in vigil. Sol thought it was Anna again. He even called for her. She would look over at him and the vision of a nymph beside him permitted him small joy.

Then, perhaps later that day, or another, he recognized that the woman beside him wasn't Hanna or Anna. It was Cambria.

It was dark outside once more.

"Anna lives, Sol." No, that wasn't Cambria. That was Engel talking, in tears. All was dark, but he heard his voice. "She lives. Live for her."

Anna lives. Lies. Now you lie to me to keep me alive?

The priests cut his skin more. Was it for torture?

All the visitors came and went, just like the light from his patio. Soon they blurred together.

He saw the illusion of King Morteus sitting by his bed, a

chubby old bald man. The vile fool was standing over him and laughing as they cut at the skin on his arms. He had once met the villain with pride. Now his endless mockery of Sol, he felt, was well deserved.

"Anna lives."

"Lies!" he shouted. "Do not lie to a nobody king!"

"She lives. Theseus told me. Live for her, Sol."

"All I ever did, ever, was live for her. All I ever did was do that."

"How dare you!" he heard Cambria's voice snap. Then, in a broken voice, "Everyone we have left, all our Amazon, look to you for help. I crowned you. And now you give up? I haven't given up. How dare you let yourself rot away like this!"

Sol laughed. He laughed with his eyes closed, for he wasn't even sure if Cambria's voice was real. Was it Cambria, or was it his mind admonishing himself?

Where does this end? When does this fight against pain end?

When I pass, shall I be in pain forever? Is that my deserved punishment?

"You are the emperor of Atlantis."

"I am the emperor of nothing!"

28

EMBER

SOL AWOKE, FEELING CONFUSED, SITTING ON THE HARD WOODEN floor of a large room. Sliding doors opened onto a patio overlooking dense woods. Birds chirped and he glimpsed a blue sky through branches, but it seemed to be getting dark outside. The trees were so dense that it shadowed the outdoors. Such a forest wasn't Egypt. This was Shadow Forest in Atala.

And he was in Henri's home. Sol's home when he was a boy. Iron swords, shields, and armor hung along the walls. He smelled meat and baked bread. Pots and pans lay along a single wooden table, and a hearth was in the center of the room beside a single wooden door.

Sol was surprised to find a man with long black hair and a beard sitting on the floor leaning over the hearth.

"Young man," the man said, looking into the flames, "is this any way to repay me for offering food and shelter from the cold?"

Those words had been imprinted in Sol's mind and would stay with him as long as he lived. They had been said to him by his foster father, and later chief advisor, Henri Untair, when he was a stray boy. It was after Sol had brandished a knife at him. Sol had been only ten years old.

Sol sat up straighter and was surprised to feel no pain in his back.

"Thank you," muttered Sol.

"You don't look good," the man said, shaking his head but still staring at the fire. "Like a mess. I'd have cleaned you up, but you might have bit me." He laughed. "You're more like a wolf. Well…" He kindled wood in the hearth. "At least you thanked me."

And Sol remembered those words too. They had been the first words spoken to him by his father.

"Henri?"

The man cocked his head back and squinted as if considering the name.

"I've lost everything."

"And I welcome you, boy."

"Why?"

When the man turned all the way around, Sol lurched back. There sat Henri Untair with a long dark beard running down to his stomach and thoughtful eyes. Indeed, it was the Magi. Henri's ghost? Perhaps. But this was a young Henri without gray or white hair. He seemed real, as if he was alive again.

"Come sit by the fire with me." And Henri turned back to the flames.

Sol sat on the ground beside him.

"Is this Elysium?" Sol asked.

"No. Ember."

Ember? Where is Ember?

"Everything is gone," Sol said, running his fingers down his long hair and shaking his head. "Castle Cove. Anna. Cassandra. Azure. You. I've lost everything, old friend."

"That's why I welcomed you into my home."

"I don't understand. The gods took Casey. They destroyed our home. Why continue to fight? What's the point in any of it anymore?" Sol waited for a reply, but he didn't get one. Henri continued to just gaze at the fire. Sol sighed. "Why am I here?"

"You come in dirty, whipped, and scorned. And so I welcome you to my home once more."

"But why?" Sol looked down and shook his head.

"For me."

Sol raised his head and furrowed his brow. In Henri's profile, Sol saw him smile.

"Once I took in a prince. He came to my home. A nomad king's raiders had plundered the boy's castle, tied him to a tree, and made him watch the beheading of his own father, King Orin. Then they raped his mother, Lyra, and his sister, Alia. The boy escaped. But he was sold into slavery to a blacksmith in Sinteria. There his back was scarred by a scourge. Witness the scars on your back. That boy was you, was it not?"

"I know it, Father," Sol said, nodding at the ground again.

"I was already old, alone, ready to retire from a long life of service, when you came to my door. I never had a family. Darius and General Onos were my family, I suppose. But I left them to retire here. I wanted to live the rest of my life alone in the woods. Until I met my stray wolf. You, Sol. I took you in for me. And when I took you in, I took a nothing prince and made him a king."

"You made a nothing king," Sol said, shaking his head.

For some reason, saying those words to Henri, though he had said it so often in his convalescence, made him weep. He hadn't cried like this in front of anyone since he was, perhaps, as young as in this memory, but the tears came down hard. And he saw tears fall down Henri's cheek too.

"When you feel this emptiness," Henri said sadly. "Coldness. When you are enveloped in shadows. As darkness threatens to consume you, there is only one thing that can re-spark the flame in a cold world. Do you know what that is?"

Sol shook his head. Henri touched his hand and squeezed it.

"Why do you not know? Why is it so easy for you to understand revenge and hate, but not love?"

"Why am I here?" Sol asked, shaking his head.

"Anna. You need to help my daughter, Anna. The two of you can start together anew."

"No!" Sol shook his head and jumped up. "No! I won't do it. For what use? With everything that was sacrificed, why continue this struggle? Everything was for nothing. Just to get the gods to break everything down all over again? Why? Why did we ever fight? Tell me why I should do anything?"

"Sit."

"No."

"Sit down!" Henri scolded, not in the way he spoke to a king, but in the way he once disciplined an unruly young boy.

Sol reluctantly sat down beside him again by the fire.

"Look into the flames, son. Every flame is like a battle. Some you win, some you lose, but the fire remains. Watch quickly!" Henri threw wood on the fire. "There! The flood destroyed Azure and our home. Perhaps if I threw enough wood, the fire would blot out everything. How many fires did this hearth burn when you were a boy? How many times did you sit for its warmth? When you die, the flames end. Life is the same. And in the morning, after the fire is doused, it is lit anew. Each of these days is like your children. And tomorrow will come your children's children. They are added to the smoke, ash, and embers of the generations that came before you. You say to me that all is lost. You say that you are nothing. And yet, here you are." And he poked his shoulder with a finger. "Behold, here I am. In Ember."

"Neeteru Belok Dispin."

Henri paused in silence, as if trying to understand his own words.

Sol shook his head and said, "Such wisdom is useless."

"Anna flames. Seek Anna. Light this fire tomorrow. For her. I welcomed you to my home for her. I didn't come for you. I never came for you. I came for me when you were a boy. Then I came for my daughter now. Seek her flame, son."

Sol shook his head.

"Then don't," Henri said with a shrug. "Count your days

numbered like in the eyes of fools. So many do this and are eventually consumed in hatred, fear, and pain. Such idiots fear darkness and live in it. Your life has been so hard, Sol. I know it. But do you truly believe, son, that the alternative was ever this?"

Henri leaned forward and swept his arm across the fire, knocking the wood down and dousing all the flames. Everything turned pitch black.

"Is everything gone?" Henri asked in pitch darkness.

He laughed.

Neeteru Belok Dispin.

29

BENNU

"Nephthys destroyed the continent of Atlantis out of rage over the loss of your daughter." This was not Sadiki. This was a new voice. Sol recognized it as the voice of the pharaoh of Egypt. "We know this from Bennu, perched in your room. Take a look. We have Magi who can speak with the fowl. He also tells us that Avivae is kept beneath the world in Amarna. The bird has seen her. She's a prisoner and held by Nephthys—the goddess your people call Persephone. This is not deception. Avivae lives. Based on what your bird has said, we are now certain of it."

Sol squinted his eyes to a blinding light. Above him was a man wearing dark kohl. He wore a tall blue hat. Along his neck was a row of golden necklaces. Sol knew this man. It was the pharaoh of Egypt. Behind him was the flickering light of torches. And still further behind was a group of men in Egyptian priest robes.

"I spoke of this a year ago," the pharaoh said. "It was not a lie then, and it is not a lie now. Your wife lives. Your kingdom is gone, but you are still an Ambrosia king related to the great Nefer. Look over near the wall and witness your standard, King."

And the pharaoh of Egypt gestured to the other side of his

bed. There, perched upon a pole, with rainbow-colored wings and a blue chest, was a phoenix.

"How long have I slept?" Sol asked.

"Nearly a moon," the pharaoh said.

"How could I survive a moon?" Sol shook his head. Then he winced.

"We hold ancient remedies from the temple of Sekhmet. The priests have been feeding you. But we'd much prefer you get up and eat, my friend."

"I've lost everything."

"Some of your friends have survived." The pharaoh shook his head. "And your wife is alive. I promise you that. At first, we wondered at the meaning of Bennu's words after returning to our palace. I sent priests to speak with him—ancient Magi from the Indus who knew the tongue of fowl. We believe Thoth sends him from the depths. He knows of the importance of Wasset and, we believe, he was told by our gods that you would come. Bennu told us what we suspected. Your wife is still alive."

Sol tried to sit up in bed, but he was too weak. The pharaoh jumped up and helped him back down. "Rest," he said. "If today is the blessed day that you choose to rise, please give your body time to mend."

"My back and head aches," Sol said. "But I feel more weak than in pain now."

"Yes, you must eat."

"Bring me Hanna and Cambria, please Pharaoh," Sol said. "If I haven't imagined them. And…thank you. Thank you for everything."

"They live. They've been by your bedside every day."

The pharaoh squeezed Sol's hand and left the room.

THE NEXT MORNING, or perhaps a few mornings later, Cambria was the first to visit him. This was after Sol had finally allowed himself to drink some milk. She walked in wearing the scarlet armor of the Amazon. She even had her helm on. She looked fierce and angry.

But before the bed, she kneeled and bowed.

"General," Sol said.

"You shame me," Cambria said, standing up beside his bed. "I had always looked up to you. But letting yourself pass like this and giving up was shameful. I know you are not well, but I also know you haven't been trying to get well."

Sol smiled. Cambria flashed a quick grin. "But I'm pleased that you are getting better, Sol."

"You've been gathering our people?"

"Aye." Cambria sat by his bedside. "From every corner of the world. Some nymphs had already left Azure after Avva gave her edict years ago. We found some in the North by Colchis. One settlement is believed to have been formed by Dainya. There the nymphs had never left. We've also sent some to the North along Etruria. And even further north into the frigid lands of Thule. We head in that direction, where man will not know us. But…" Cambria shook her head. "There are so few of us left. The gods finally managed to destroy us."

"I heard it was Cora," Sol said with a nod.

"Some say, but we don't know for sure. If it was her, then the goddess of the Underworld is truly the most despicable being in Gaia. What sort of god loves us and then plots revenge that leads to our destruction?"

"She destroyed Olympus."

"She destroyed Azure Blue."

Sol nodded. Then he winced in pain from his back. "You will continue your search?"

Cambria walked over to the outside patio. The view was beautiful. In his convalescence, Sol had not seen that his room was on a patio perched on a hill overlooking the entire kingdom. He could see all of Wasset and, along the horizon, even the great Nile.

"We don't belong here, Sol," Cambria said. "I remember what Jaida told me of the Egyptians and their treatment of

Dainya when she was a baby. Now we are their guests. But they won't want us to stay for long. But I … I really don't know where we belong. Luckily for us, we are a warrior race. Man will hunt us. But we will fight." Cambria looked back at him. "We go north. In Thule it is less populated. In Thule, we can survive."

"I've fought my whole life, surviving."

"Then why'd you stop?" And she glared at him. Cambria turned back to the view. "I hear your Avivae lives."

"I had thought that it was a lie to get me up."

Cambria shook her head and walked back to him. She sat beside the bed and touched his arm. "Avva lives. Engel said that the Greek prince, or now king, Theseus Aegeus, who had traveled the Underworld, told him that Persephone imprisons her. She claims to protect her—some great protection that infernal harpy could give anyone. But this Theseus—"

"Theseus Aegeus? A prince of that fiend we fought?"

"Yes. Calm yourself. Engel said Theseus came to Azure to warn us of the invasion. To stop it. The prince was on our side."

"Where is this prince? I'd so like to kill him."

"He thought as much before we found Engel. He fled before we spotted Engel's broken ship on the sea. Of course, if Theseus returns to Attica, he is the rightful king. Though he will be busy doing a lot of rebuilding. Cora's destruction didn't only destroy Atlantis, it damaged every settlement along the shore."

Sol nodded. Then he fought nausea from intense pain.

"He loved Casey," she added.

"Who?"

"Theseus. Engel told me that Theseus loved Cassandra. He came to see her to not only warn her of the invasion, but to see her again. It is tragic. And… there's more. Perhaps Engel will tell you the rest."

"It seems all those that love us do everything they can to hurt us."

Cambria nodded. "When will you go, Sol?"

"What do you mean?"

"When will you go and see her?" Cambria said with a smile. "We all know the only thing that awoke you was her name."

"She is the only reason I've ever lived. Even before all this. You know the peril I was in when she saved me in Crescent Blue. It started there, when she saved us. There would have been no empire without her."

"Then I bid you the best of luck." Cambria rose. Then she added formally, but with a smile, "I am overjoyed that you're feeling better, Amazon King. Now that you're well enough, I ask for orders. Tell me what you wish of me before you leave?"

"Take my seal and my crown."

Cambria lost her smile and shook her head. "I can act as regent, if you wish, until you return."

"I won't return. As you guessed, I'll go to the depths. I probably won't survive the journey."

"You are the greatest king there ever was," Cambria said, bowing again. "We Amazon have refused to have men live with us over the centuries. I don't think you understand the significance of the funeral when my people accepted you as ruler and we gave you the crown and scepter. It was not only out of mourning. You shall be remembered, King of Atlantis. We will sing of your honor and achievements, never of the things that were outside of your control."

She touched his hand and squeezed it.

"Take care of Hanna," Sol said. "And dear Engel. And take care of yourself."

"I will tell everyone you're better." Then she smiled and left the room.

Sol turned. He clutched his side in pain.

There, on a small wooden table, perched Mainax. Sol could not speak to birds, but it seemed the phoenix was waiting to tell him something.

GOODBYE

"THIS IS MADNESS, SOL!" CRIED ENGEL. "STOP HIM, HANNA."

Wasset glowed in torchlight under a full moon. Engel leaned on a column, wearing a white chiton, with his arms folded, staring down at the city. But Hanna said nothing. She just sat beside Sol's bed with a joyful smile. She seemed content that he had been up and about for the first time in days. Now Sol sipped boiled cabbage soup from a small wooden bowl in bed.

"She says nothing because she knows there's nothing stopping me," Sol said, sipping more soup.

"Because you're a fool."

Sol laughed. "And you're the only subject who has no fear when insulting his king. If a subject in this Court called the pharaoh a fool, he'd lose his head."

"So now you've decided to be my king again?" quipped Engel.

"I know he'll go, no matter what I say, Engel," Hanna said. "But what is this nonsense about descending down a hole? That's how we lost Avva."

"If they can truly speak to Mainax, like Henri, they claim that somehow, the Underworld will unveil itself to me under Amarna, and Anna will be there."

"By falling down a chasm?" quipped Engel. "And what if Inghorn hits a rock?"

"It is what the pharaoh and his priests claim, Engel," Sol said with a nod.

"Amarna is so far from the Underworld," Hanna said. "How could she be here? Did Cora take her all the way to Egypt?"

"When are you going on this fool's errand?" Engel asked.

"When I can walk without a cane."

"Well, that won't be for at least another week," Hanna said with a sweet smile, touching his leg. "Go when you have the strength."

"Do we have more wine?" Sol asked.

Hanna rose and nodded. Then she walked around the bed and poured wine from an ampulla into a silver cup.

"Humph. It's too dangerous," Engel said. "I think you shouldn't try it."

"Seems we disagree often. But if I can bring Blue back to you, you won't think that anymore." Sol sipped the red wine. It tasted like the wine in Azure. "Umm, this is very good wine."

"They call it Shedeh," Hanna said. "Legend says that Nephrea brought Shedeh to Amarna from Azure. It is our Atalan red wine, Sol."

"It tastes like Azure." He smiled sadly with a nod. "Aye, I miss it already. Not the wine, of course. Well, that too. But, Azure. It's so odd how much you miss a place once you've lost it. This wine…" He tapped on the silver cup. "Is strong but sweet like an Amazon. Like my beloved Anna. Perhaps that's why I like it?"

"You said the pharaoh warned you not to do it," Engel persisted.

"Well, you two saved me from death already."

"At least bring some of the guard," Hanna said. "Cambria's willing to go with you. I'll go too. Many of us are willing to descend into Amarna."

"Hmm. No. Just as Anne forbid you to fly up the Mount

when she rescued Cassandra, I must object to anyone following me. It's too dangerous. I go alone."

They both nodded. Then Mainax fluttered on the table beside him.

"Anyway." Sol turned his head to the bird. "I won't be alone."

"If she's there, Sol, bring her back to me," Hanna said, grabbing his hand. Then Hanna mused, seemingly more to herself, "Avva would be so amused to learn that I came to a land even she had never seen."

"Aye," he said. "I know how much Blue would want to see you again, Hanna. But, Hanna, Cambria is relocating you north. Everyone is to leave and head north. It's possible, even if I succeed, that I may not ever see you two again."

"We will wait as long as we can." She hugged him. "Give Avva my love."

"How do you know I'll find her?" Sol asked, amused.

"Because you are you."

"Humph, well, he isn't strong enough to walk just yet," Engel said with a snort.

"Why should you care?" asked Sol, scooting up. "Does it relieve you that I'm not leaving yet, Engel? Are you actually going to miss me when I leave?"

"Aye, my king. I'll miss you." And the Mandrigel forced a smile.

31

QUAKES

Avva's hair was wrapped in the fashion of her ancestors, as she folded her arms around herself to keep warm, staring out into the cold, endless dunes by the porch of her house. She jumped when Mainax landed on her shoulder. Her phoenix had been missing for the longest time.

"Mainax," Avva said, petting the bird. "I've missed you."

The phoenix flapped his wings wildly on her shoulder.

"What's the matter?" Avva asked. She petted his feathers and whistled to try to calm him. But he jumped in the air, flapped his wings, and landed on her shoulder again.

"You didn't happen to bring food?" asked Avva with a chuckle. The bird rustled some more. "Oh, what's the matter? Hmm?"

As welcome a sight as the phoenix was, Avva would have preferred Cora. Her goddess was late. Avva had wrung out every last emergency drop of pomegranate juice from the dried-out Myrle berry orchard. Now she waited for the goddess to return.

Her house quaked. Avva held a wooden column until the movement subsided. The shaking had started again yesterday, but none of it, thankfully, was as bad as it had been a few days after Cora left. That initial shake, nearly a moon ago, had made

Avva think her house was going to cave in. Hasevalah had never had quakes before. That worried her. And thinking about Cora's look of worry before she left—well, that worried her more. Cora seemed to be getting more and more restless—like Mainax now.

Then Avva finally spotted her. She shielded her eyes, with her hand, from the light above as a horse made its way down toward her. But Cora always came from the opposite direction. And this horse reflected more of the light. Was it another god? Avva squinted harder. Then she couldn't believe her eyes. There was a glistening horn on the head of the flying horse. It was a unicorn! But how?

"Who's that, Mainax?" Avva asked, furrowing her brow. "Did you bring her with you?"

There was another quake. This one was so strong that it knocked her off her feet and she tripped over the wooden planks. Then she heard the strangest sound of her life. The sound of a salpinx echoing in the empty desert. Behind the single unicorn came a glowing chariot led by four horses. Then a person, far behind, whose body seemed to levitate in the sky.

First to land was a white monokera. It was Inghorn. Avva froze at the sight of a man in sky blue hoplite armor, who was holding the reins: her husband, Sol.

"Oh, Sol!"

But there was no time for a reunion. As Sol landed, he cocked his head behind him. A glowing gilded chariot landed on the sand. A goddess wearing brown leather hoplite armor and a quill of arrows on her back leaped from the chariot. The goddess rushed with incredible speed and grabbed Sol.

"Sol!"

Then came a small bird about half the size of Mainax. When it was near the ground, Avva recognized it as an owl. Mainax surprised Avva as it launched from her shoulder and attacked the owl. A shriek was heard, and the phoenix burst into flames, falling to ash. Before the owl landed, it transformed into a woman and crouched on the sand, standing over the ash. As she straightened, glowing gold hoplite armor shone on her.

"Bring the barbarian to me," said the woman in gold, removing her helm and revealing long curly black hair. Then she turned to Avva. "Seems we've found the conspirator, Artemis."

"It's too easy, Athena," Artemis said with a nod.

"Stay away from her!" cried Sol. But Sol couldn't move. He was held in Artemis's arms.

"We should have checked Egyptiotes and the girl's tantrum-hole long ago," said Artemis.

Sol slipped out of Artemis's grasp and brandished his sword. Artemis backed up, seemingly surprised, but then laughed. He hacked at her and would have sheared off the goddess's arm if she weren't a goddess. The sword contacted her wrist guard and did nothing. Then the goddess shoved him, hurling Sol's body across the sand.

"Stop!" cried Avva. "Stop it. Leave him alone!"

Sol gazed at Avva, on the ground. He ground his teeth and glared at Artemis. Avva shook her head, knowing her husband too well. Sol charged the goddess again. He raised his Mandrigelian sword. Artemis blocked the blade again, this time striking it hard enough to split the enchanted sword in half. Then Artemis grabbed Sol, wringing his neck.

"Please," Avva said. "Leave him alone!"

Cora said I'd see Sol. Is it to watch him die?

"Release him," said Athena, raising her hand dismissively. Then she squinted at Avva. "Don't kill our bait. We're not here for either of them."

Then a shirtless man with winged shoes landed beside Artemis and Sol. He glowed like Athena, but his reflection came more from his bright white chiton and pale skin. He was lanky with delicate features. Avva surmised this was Hermes.

Mainax shrieked in the sky, flew down, and perched on Avva's shoulder again.

"Unnatural fowl," snapped Artemis.

Another quake made Athena lose her arrogant smirk. But then she straightened and turned to Avva. "Queen Avivae of Azure Blue, I presume. We never met. Daughter of Delia and descendant of Harmonia Ambrosia, do you know who I am? I've watched you from your Mount since you were an infant. And now, I hope I am the first to tell you that your home, Azure Blue, is gone. It has sunk into the sea."

"*You cursed vile monster!*" cried Sol, fighting in Artemis's grasp. "*Keep your hands off her!*"

"I haven't touched her *yet*, man-nymph," Athena said, cocking her head back.

Azure Blue is destroyed?

"Your friends are your enemies," Athena said, turning back to Avva. Athena squinted her bright blue eyes with an infernally wicked grin. "Has your grain goddess sheltered you from the news?" Athena laughed. "I'm sure the liar did." Then she passed Avva and opened the wooden door to the cottage. "Sister? Are you here? Quaint hovel, wood nymph. Oh, sister, are you in there? Come out. I'd like a word with you."

Another light flashed above Avva. For a moment, Avva hoped it was Cora, but this one looked like reflected wavy lines. As it descended, she saw it was a golden chariot, led not by horses but by two winged snakes. Dragons.

Hermes looked up. "She's found us, Athene," he said.

Athena scowled at the incoming chariot. "Go to her. Cursed old woman! Tell her to turn around or I'll turn her around myself."

The ground shook again.

"We should be helping Lord Zeus below," Hermes said, shaking his head.

"Apollo is fighting them." Then Athena looked down on Hermes and snapped, "Go tell her to turn around, I say! I have no wish to fight her mother."

"She is stronger than we are," said Artemis, staring at the descending chariot. "And, on our side or not, she'll defend her sarding grain goddess again."

"There's three of us," answered Athena.

"Oh, Sol," Avva cried out. "I love you."

"Aye, I love you so much, my love," he said with a pained

smile. The witch Artemis still held him by the neck. "Finally seeing you brings me happiness, Anna. Even if this is our last day."

At that, Athena looked away from the approaching dragons at Avva. Then she slapped Avva across the face. Avva was knocked many feet across the wooden patio from the impact.

"You sarding turd!" cried Sol. "Don't touch her!"

"I should touch you!" said Athena, spinning around. "You do not know the extent of my hatred for you and your wife. You two shut it and stay quiet or the next strike will be your death! How dare you raise arms against my men. My people were building a city under my name. But at least now, be comforted in knowing that people will forget your Azure Blue and Atlantis."

"Let me squeeze him to death, sister," hissed Artemis. "Please."

"Not yet," Athena said, raising her finger.

Hermes plummeted to the ground. He hit it so violently that a crater formed around him in the sand. And with that explosion landed the terrible serpents. Engel had told Avva, as a child, the myth of the goddess who flew on a chariot of snakes: Demeter, or Sara, Cora's mother.

"Leave this place!" cried Sara. Sara had a regal look that was so at odds with her fiery red eyes and the cold, empty desert. She wore a white peplos and gold around her neck, with jewels along her ears and wrists. The jewelry shone in the light. And yet, as regal as she appeared, her gaze was fitful. She kept looking around the sands as if waiting for someone to pounce on them.

"Next will be you two," Sara said, gesturing to Hermes, who still lay in the ground. "Get out! Go and leave this place or he will come for us and chain us too!"

"Zeus!" cried Athena. She seemed almost brought to tears. "Is Father chained, Demeter? Is he chained in Tartarus!"

And with that came more tremors. Sara searched all around the dunes again.

"Where is Kore?"

Artemis shook her head.

"I rushed to warn you, you fools," Sara snapped. "Not fight you."

"What's happened below, Sara?" asked Artemis.

"There's no time to explain. Don't doubt my daughter's fury. She's bent on killing every last one of us, whether it destroys her or not. Why taunt her with her playthings? Leave her pets. We must head back to Hellena to regroup."

"We should kill them," Artemis said. "Leave their dead bodies as an example. I'll break his neck. There is nothing that should stop our revenge on this man and nymph."

With speed Avva had never seen, Sara rushed to Artemis and knocked her grasp from Sol. Both Sol and Artemis fell to the ground.

"Athena, you're wise," Sara said, glancing back at her. "Why are you doing this? You must understand that we have to leave now."

"The plan was to take Avivae," Athena said, shaking her head. "She obviously means the most to Kore. Perhaps take her with us now."

"Hades already thought of that. He's helping her. He knows you followed the human down here. That means Cora will know too. Leave them, I tell you."

"If we leave, we take her," Athena said, turning to Avva with those eerie red eyes.

"Then you're a fool!" Sara said. "We must plan in Argos away from here. It's done with my daughter."

"All we do is fight because of these two," Athena said. "Even now."

"They have nothing left," Sara said, shaking her head. "Leave, I tell you. With Poseidon and Zeus chained—"

"They destroyed our home!" cried Artemis. Then the goddess fell on her knees on the sand and started to weep.

Then another quake, this time so strong that everyone, even the horses by the chariots, fell to their ground. It was so powerful that part of the roof of Avva's cottage, which she had lived in for so long, caved in.

"It's over!" cried Sara. "That is it. There is the sound of Lord Zeus being chained beside Poseidon. Run! This is her domain! Run now, or my daughter and her beastly husband will come down and hurt and bind you all too!"

"He's chained!" cried Athena, now breaking down too. "Father is chained! How could they do this? How could they do this to our blessed Zeus?"

"Ares is against us too," Sara said with a nod. "They planned everything."

Athena turned, with fiery eyes, to Avva. Her sorrow seemed to have turned to fury. In terror, Avva's legs involuntarily backed her up against the wooden wall of her cottage. She hadn't been driven by any force other than Athena's gaze. Athena's eyes had turned as red as Cora's. So had Artemis's, and she glared at Avva too. Then Hermes rose from the sand. He turned on Avva. All the gods turned to Avva with demon eyes as if everything was her fault.

"We will kill her," said Athena, narrowing her eyes. "Kill the Ambrosia queen. If we're too late and nothing's left to barter for Father, let us share with Kore the pain she's given us. Kill her nymph friend."

"Gladly," Artemis said with a smile, letting go of Sol. Sol ran to help Avva, but Artemis grabbed Sol again and threw him to the ground. As Artemis and Athena rushed Avva, Sara stood before them once more.

"Back away! These two mean everything to her," Sara said, shaking her head. "Leave, I tell you! Why do you think she's kept her alive all this time?"

Artemis charged Avva again. She grabbed her ankle and twisted. With her grasp, she probably would have easily snapped her foot, or even cleaved it off, if it weren't for Sara's blow to Artemis's head. Sol shouted Avva's name again. Then Hermes rushed Avva. Again, Sara took the lanky winged-foot god and hurled him from the cottage.

Both gods turned on Sara and tackled her.

"You always took kindly to them too!" Artemis said. "Perhaps we should shackle her mother to this desolate pile of rubble."

But it took both gods to wrestle with Sara, such was the power of Demeter.

That left Athena alone.

Athena walked slowly to Avva with fiery, burning eyes. That's when Avva saw a reflection up in the sky. It was a single horse rushing down. A black horse led by a girl in a tattered red peplos. But there was no way her champion goddess would have time to save her.

Athena lifted her arms and grabbed for Avva, but Mainax leaped from Avva's shoulder and pecked at the goddess. Athena flung a hand at the phoenix as if trying to swat a fly. Then Mainax burst into an exploding flame. Athena fell to the ground screaming and clutching her eyes. The explosion was so violent that it lit the goddess's face on fire. Athena writhed on the floor, using sand to try to douse the flames.

Cora landed.

Athena's face was scorched, but her eyes—which had been gouged out by the fire—quickly reformed before Avva's eyes. Now, although blackened with ash, the goddess got up and charged Avva again.

"Get out!" cried Cora. Persephone grabbed Athena and threw her many yards from Avva. Then Cora leaped on Athena.

Persephone did not wrestle Athena; she grasped Athena and pulled her arms and legs with her bare hands. Cora literally pulled Athena's limbs out of their sockets and thrust her arms into the goddess's chest and abdomen, tearing her flesh to pieces. Blood flowed over Cora, covering her face and body. It was so terrible that everyone halted and stared at the violence.

Then she ran to the wrestling gods. She took her protector, her mother, and threw her off them. But she didn't have to fight. All three, including Sara, backed away from her. Cora's body and face were now covered in Athena's blood, the crimson matching her burning red eyes.

"Get out! Get out!" Then she said to her mother, Sara, *"Leave my realm! All of you!"*

"I came to protect the Ambrosias," Sara objected.

"You came too late! Get out before I tear you apart too."

Athena slowly materialized, but she sat breathing heavily with her head in her hands, weak and shaking. She transformed into an owl and flew off into the bright white light of Hasevalah. Artemis ran to her chariot. Hermes was right behind her.

Avva ran to Sol and he scooped her up in his arms. For the first time, she noticed that her husband limped. He was hurt, but not by the gods, from some other terrible fight.

"Oh, Anne," Sol said, kissing her lips and cheeks. "I found you."

"I love you, Sol," she said, kissing him. "I love you so much."

Avva looked over. Both Sara and Cora were staring at them.

Sara did not appear much older than Cora. Such was the magic of the gods' immortality. They almost looked like twins. But whereas Sara wore jewels and a great white peplos, Cora was covered in blood and tatters.

Cora's eyes changed. They returned to azure blue.

"I never wanted things to be like this, Kore," Sara said, shaking her head and looking down.

"Father is chained," Cora said to Sara, continuing to watch Avva. "Poseidon remains with Zeus. I will allow you, Demeter, to run before Hades catches up to you. Hades and I know your allegiance. You have my mercy for protecting my family, but we will not befriend you. And when we ascend from the depths and take power over Athens, know that you and I are at war. Now get out of my realm."

Sara looked as if she was about to speak, but instead, she climbed aboard her serpent chariot. Then she raised her head high as her snakes slithered over the sand. She took off into the air and flew to the sky of Hasevalah.

"You were right, Cora," Avva said, smiling at her and choking on her words. "You were right. He came. He came for me! I should never have doubted you."

"Aye, Anna. I'm so happy. And now you, my beloved nymph, will leave me."

32

THE SURVIVORS

Avva rose early and walked onto the wooden patio outside, staring out at the sands as she did every day in Hasevalah. But today, she feared that it was all a dream. That Sol wouldn't be there when she went back inside. She had spent most of the night enjoying watching her husband sleep. Just being near him and listening to his breathing was the greatest joy she had felt in so long. Now she did what she must have done for the past year. She stared at the endless sandy horizon. Had it been a year? She couldn't tell time in this wasteland.

"Blue?"

It was Sol's voice. He walked out and stood beside her on the wooden deck, placing a hand on her shoulder and pulling her to him. Then he ran his hand along her back.

Solinair wore his blue hoplite armor. He had come yesterday, as if to fight a battle. And, she supposed, they had witnessed one.

She closed her eyes and leaned her head against his chest.

"You're here," Avva said. "It must be a dream. It makes me so happy."

"Aye. Everything is like a dream here, isn't it?"

She nodded.

"Your world is beautiful, Blue. Cold but beautiful. What is this desert called?"

She opened her eyes and gestured to the sand. "Cora calls it Hasevalah. In the ancient Napean tongue it means *gateway*. For me, it's been a prison, like when my mother imprisoned me in a tower as a child. Cora even claims, like my mother, that she was protecting me. Well, after yesterday, I believe that. But it has always been a cold prison to me."

"It is beautiful," Sol said, staring out along the valley. Then he squinted at a figure standing in the far distance. He gestured to her.

"Persephone," Avva said with a nod. "Cora's been just standing there the whole night while we slept. I've never seen her act like this. I went out a few times on the sand. It's bright here almost all the time, you know. She turned, but never faced me. She stands without moving, staring out into nothing. I don't think she looks at anything. She just stares."

"She destroyed everything, Anna."

"Don't," she said, shaking her head and leaning back into him. "Don't talk about that again. Let me just feel your touch. Your warmth. Let me just share a little happiness now."

"Aye," he said, kissing her cheek. "That is what I have said to myself ever since you left. A little happiness. The thought of you after you left was painful because I couldn't be near you. But those thoughts were my only happiness. You've haunted me, Anne. And all I've desired since you left was to be with you."

Avva shook in his arms. Tears fell, but she didn't want to cry. Even tears of happiness. Or sorrow. Because her feelings were mixed. Cora hadn't told her about Cassandra. She hadn't even told her of the Greek war. When Sol had told her everything last night, like now, Avva had felt the strangest mix of sorrow and joy. She wondered if her friend in the distance, her best friend for so long and now, perhaps, her greatest enemy, wept too.

"I have you," Avva said. "What more can I ask for?"

"And now we must leave."

"Where?" Avva asked, cocking her head at him. "You say our home is under water. Where can we go?"

"We can't stay here. Unless you wish to be at the mercy of that harpy."

"God Sol, she hasn't even washed the blood from her face. The sight of her face and her clothes covered with blood is as shocking as when her eyes burn red. I've seen her rage before, but never like this. She just stands there." Avva tore herself from his grasp. "This was the longest time we've been apart." Then she looked up at the bright light above. "She prepared me for it. She deceived me, telling me it would take a long time to get you. That was her excuse for gathering so many extra provisions. It took her many visits to stock up." She turned and gave her husband a sad smile. She lost her smile and shook her head. "But she never told me about Casey. Sol, I think she loved Casey as much as we did." Then she turned again to the silhouette in the distance. "You confused goddess, I can't imagine the struggle in your head."

"You sound like you feel bad for her, Blue. She kept you prisoner. Destroyed our home. Then she destroyed our people."

"She loved Azure Blue more than any other place in the world." Avva shook her head sadly. "I'm sure of that. Only her hatred for her family was greater. I think she's losing her mind. Perhaps I am too. I can't accept what you've said. I can't even accept that you're here. You have to realize my only company's been her for so long. I'm... very confused. I care for Cora. And... Cassandra. Oh god, Sol, Casey."

Then she cried tears of sadness again.

"Aye, Anne," he said, hugging her.

But Sol never cried. So Anna cried more for him.

"Rage isn't enough," Avva said in a broken voice. "Nothing can be done to take away this pain. That terrible thing Cora did for Casey's honor, for us, to destroy our home!" Avva shook her head. "Why? Casey's gone, Sol. None of it can ever be taken away. And destroying Olympus won't stop that pain. If only I could have told Cora that. If only she had spoken to me."

"Aye, Anne," he said, holding her tightly again.

"Everything's changed so suddenly, from a prison to this." She looked into his eyes and kissed his lips gently. "I just need time. Perhaps I shall go mad like Cora. It's too much. I have you, but… I can't leave. Not yet."

"We'll go when you're ready."

He kissed her on the forehead and she nodded.

When embracing wasn't enough, Avva walked over to Inghorn. She petted the unicorn. "Hey girl, I've missed you too."

Inghorn whinnied.

"An incredible steed," Sol said, accompanying her. "She's the only monokera willing to drop down into the abyss with me."

"But she wouldn't drop into the Stygian Hole. Strange."

"Unlike the Stygian Hole, there's light under the hole in Amarna. I think that's it. And they're smart. I know your unicorns can't talk, but they know far more than they let on. She was willing to do it to find you again."

"But how did you know where I was?"

"Mainax. I followed Mainax. Like you did when you found Casey."

Mainax was perched on Cora's shoulder now. He had flown away through most of the night, then returned to keep the miserable goddess company. Occasionally, Avva saw Cora pet the bird. For some reason, that felt heart-wrenching.

Avva cradled the unicorn's head in her arms. "Is… Sol, is Inghorn the last?"

"No. There are a few who survived in Egypt. And a thousand more of your people. From Egypt, they will travel north under Cambria's command. And yours, when you're ready."

"Cambria's strong."

"I hope you can regroup with the general. You are still their Amazon queen, Blue."

Avva nodded, brushing Inghorn's feathers. "And our son?"

Sol quickly turned from her.

"Oh Sol… how terrible."

"It's okay," Sol said, shaking his head and staring at the

ground. "All will be all right. We have each other, Anna. I had a vision when I was sick. It was Henri. But I swear, Anna, he was really there. He told me to find you. As he always did, he picked me up when all was lost."

Anna held him in her arms again. "We'll have a funeral to remember everyone," Avva said. "A ceremony marking the day in memory of the tragedy."

"There was already a great ceremony for Casey," Sol said, nodding. "Just as there was a grand one for you."

"But you and I should honor them alone too."

"Aye." Sol hobbled from her grasp and over to a column, and he leaned on it.

"So much has happened," Avva said, shaking her head. "Why? Why did you bring our people so far west to Hellena? What was the use in a fight so far away?"

"Our daughter."

"You sought revenge?" asked Avva. Then she nodded, gesturing to Cora. "Like her."

He nodded.

"Brave Inghorn," Avva said, running her fingers along her feathers again. "You didn't know what lay beneath the hole, just like in Azure, huh, girl? Hmm? But you went in the darkness for me?"

"Engel warned me as much, Anne," Sol said.

"About Inghorn?"

"No. The wise man told me we should back off from war after we conquered Crete. He told me to stop the fighting. He was right."

"Oh, please tell me if Engel is alive? Or…perhaps…don't."

"He lives."

Avva gave a long sigh of relief.

"Who else?" She petted Inghorn's feathers, gazing at her blue fingers along her white, feathery hide. "But…don't tell me who's gone, Sol, tell me only who lives."

"Your dear friend Hanna. She misses you."

Another smile. *The sweetest of all of us.*

"Casey's best friend, Lalaina."

"Sandra."

"Falena."

He rattled off many names. The names didn't surprise Avva, the list did. It was too short.

Avva looked at Cora again. The goddess turned her head for a moment, but when she saw Sol look over, she quickly turned back. Persephone spent the rest of the day like that, staring into nothingness, ignoring them. Yet after the second night, the demon goddess left more food in the kitchen for when they awoke.

33

UDAT AL MAWT

On the third day, as another short evening in Hasevalah passed, there was a knock on the door. Sol woke Avva, pointing at Cora at the threshold holding a lantern. The goddess had finally washed the blood from her face and changed into a clean red peplos. Her blond hair was neatly clasped in a ponytail.

"You two must go by daylight. I'll need Inghorn. You may take my flying konobera back up the hole in Amarna and see your people. I can no longer provide for or protect you here."

"You've protected her enough," Sol snapped.

"I betrayed you and your people," she said with a nod. But it wasn't up for discussion. Cora closed the door behind her and left. Avva jumped up from bed and ran outside.

"Cora, wait."

Cora stopped. She still held the lantern, lighting her path in the darkness. It reminded Avva of when they first met. "You have no business taking my unicorn."

Cora laughed bitterly. "I hold every right, nymph," she said. "Antilus was claimed by me long before you were born, when I met my mother. And Inghorn is Antilus's daughter."

"Where are you going?"

"Why should you care?"

"Cora… it's okay. You can talk to me."

"No, it isn't okay," Cora said. Her eyes reddened. "It will never be okay with us again, Avva."

"You freed us."

"You forgive me then?" she quipped, cocking her head back. Her eyes were still red.

"No. But after spending so long with you, you could at least say goodbye."

"Goodbye."

Then she turned and approached Inghorn, who was near the cottage, in the darkness. Sol came and stood beside Avva. Cora petted Inghorn under the light of her lantern. The redness faded from her eyes again.

"At least tell us where you're going?" Avva said.

"It will not sound sane."

"What's sane here?" said Sol.

"I'm going to the clouds to find my mother."

"Using Inghorn?"

Cora nodded, still petting her feathers.

"How will you find a dead pharaoh?" asked Sol.

"There is a diagram on every sarcophagus in every tomb in Egypt. The diagram shows two paths to Duat. I used to think the upper line represented this desert." She shook her head and finally turned to them. Her blue eyes flickered in the torchlight. "No. This is a false belief of the Egyptians. I searched and starved along this sand, searching for her, for years. These icy sands where I hid you, Blue, go for thousands of leagues. One day, when searching for my mother, it dawned on me that Hasevalah was actually the lower line on the map. The Egyptians had called that line "fire." After burning my skin, I realized the sand burns cold. You know this. This frigid realm is the lower line on their diagram.

"There is another legend that my Nephrea was seen leaving her people in the sky. There is a light that formed in the clouds upon her disappearance. In order to find Nephrea, I ascended, forming the hole at Udat al Mawt, and tried to fly up to that light and find her in the clouds right after she disappeared."

"You used your hands to form the hole," Sol said.

"That is an Egyptian myth," Cora said, shaking her head. "I emerged on the surface and created the chasm the same way my husband did in Azure. I broke through the ground using his chariot. After I created the hole at Udat al Mawt, I drove my husband's chariot to the clouds. There I saw a shiny structure. An isle in the sky that floats above Amarna and is as bright as the sun. But the konobera are not strong enough to fly all the way up to the floating city. They can fly out of the Underworld, for sure, but they don't have the power you had with Antilus, Avva, when you flew through the Olympian storms. I've been trying to make the journey by monokera ever since."

"Your Nephrea won't be there, Cora," Avva said, shaking her head.

"You really aren't here either," Cora snapped angrily. "If you had any pride, the king and queen of their sunken kingdom wouldn't speak to me."

"How can you be so cruel after all you've done to us!" Sol snapped.

But Avva quickly interjected, "Why didn't you take a monokera up there before, Cora?"

"I did. The island in the sky disappeared when I returned with a unicorn from Azure. Now, after Casey passed, the light has returned to Amarna. It calls for me now." Cora mounted Inghorn and ran her fingers over her soft white neck. "Now that I did my cursed deed, I have Inghorn."

"You knew Sol would bring a unicorn here, didn't you?" asked Avva. "That's why you built your house near the hole?"

"No. I built this house centuries ago to live near my mother in Egypt. I had hoped to find that city in the clouds and waited for years. But the light never returned—until the flood." She looked at Avva and finally gave her a hint of a smile. "After you showed courage in defying my family, I rescued you and brought you below Egypt to protect you. My family was far too conceited to wander these parts or even know about Udat al Mawt. Only Hades and I knew. That is until you, Sol, led them right to her."

"Goodbye," Cora said, turning from them. "I've reunited you. As my mother would say, may your water rise and sprout forth an ample harvest. Despise me you should, but I wish you two well, all the same."

"At least hand us your lantern," Sol quipped.

"You won't need it, barbarian." Cora tossed it onto the sand. "The sun's about to rise, and you'll leave when I go. Now that Zeus is chained, she no longer needs my protection from him in the depths. We are all free."

And at that exact moment, the sun of Hasevalah flashed bright along the valley. For in this desert valley, there was no sunrise. Only instant light.

Cora rose above them with Inghorn flapping her great wings. Then she said, "Avva, I swear, I didn't deceive you. I didn't know what would befall Cassandra. But I always foresaw the need to protect you. At first, it was out of respect and love for your spirit and blood. I suppose it might have been to see what I see now. You two reunited gives me a small shred of joy that I'll cherish and protect the rest of your days."

After that, she soared up to the bright ceiling of Hasevalah and disappeared.

34

HER HUSBAND

"Kore, my love. I should never have doubted you."

Cora blinked her eyes as a bald man with bright blue eyes, a goatee, and a sly grin leaned over her. He went in and out of focus. Then she smelled burning meat. Waves of nausea hit her. And his goatee and bald head spun around her in circles making her feel sicker.

It was bright around Hades. The light shone brightly around him. But Cora couldn't remember where she was. She only remembered falling. And… burning.

"What?" she asked, flittering her eyelids again. "What'd you say?"

Then… she opened her eyes wide. A severe shearing pain ripped through her body, shook her, and surrounded everything. She heard a scream. She recognized it as her own voice. It was so shrill that Hades dropped her and covered his ears with his hands. Horses trumpeted and snorted and then hooves raced from her. There was another yell from her mouth. The intense burning surrounded her, more pain than she had ever felt in her life. It was as if her whole body stood in the middle of fire. All turned dark… Then something held her again. She realized with revulsion, as she opened her eyes, that it was her bastard husband, but she was too weak to get out of his disgusting grasp. Worse, her legs and arms were naked and charred. Smoke rose from her body.

He draped his black hooded cloak over her body. Then, when she was strong enough, he helped her rise onto her knees.

She looked around and saw that she was on a sandy, desolate desert. Then she spotted the great river Nile off on the horizon. Egypt. Amarna? She had seen the river when she had emerged from Amarna and flown to the bright light in the sky. That light in the sky was gone.

"We rule the world now, Kore," Hades said with his arm around her. "I came to accompany you to our new kingdom. When I arrived, I had to dig you out of the ground. But your unicorn was still in one piece."

"My kingdom lies at the bottom of the sea, bastard," Cora said. She searched the dunes looking for the Amarna hole. She couldn't find it. How far had she fallen? "How'd you find me?"

"I watched you fall. You fell so fast that your body ignited in flames."

"Are my nymphs safe?"

"If my lovely Persephone wills it."

"I will it." She pushed him off her. "But I'm not *your* Persephone."

"You have many enemies now. Following Apollo's lead, Imada plans to hunt the wood nymphs. They're using the ancient ways to gather intelligence. And many of them continue to enter Tartarus—what's left of it—to save my brothers. They wish to undo everything you've achieved and, at what it cost you, we can never allow that. Although Mount Olympus has sunk in the sea and Zeus and Poseidon are chained, there's hardly peace in the world."

"I only care about Nephrea and her kin," Cora said, rising. But as she stood, she fell. Her infernal husband helped her up again. "I hate you and have no wish to be anywhere near you. Enjoy your power alone. You heard what I said about our love.

You never loved me. You never loved Azure. You loved only Harmonia and your power. I was mere amusement."

"Well, I'm far too immersed in blissful gratification at the moment to be pricked by you. Or to expostulate." Then Hades looked up at the sky, amused. "Did you find what you were looking for? An isle in the sky, you called it? Did someone throw you off? Seems you created a new crater."

"I jumped."

"I see. Did you leap away from your so-called nymph-mother, Nephrea?"

"She wasn't there," Cora said, looking up at the bright sunlight. "There was nothing up there but false gods, like all the members of our horrid family."

"I see." Then he gestured to his chariot led by four konobera standing in the sand. "Come then. Climb aboard my chariot. I shall fly you anywhere you'd like, Kore. Perhaps we can go together to Athens where we may conduct more of your glorious revenge on the Greeks."

"Leave me alone," she said, shaking her head. She turned her back on him and hobbled to Inghorn, who stood nearby. Thankfully, the monokera was unharmed.

"You wish me to leave you here in the desert?"

"Aye." She ran her hand along the unicorn's feathery wings, and Inghorn neighed.

From the corner of her eye, she saw him watching her. She closed her eyes tight and took a deep breath, leaning against Inghorn's wing, still bearing pain. But the pain would be over soon. Jumping off the barge in the clouds had been a really stupid thing to do. But so was living. Her mother wasn't up there. Only an image of her, a tease so terrible that it made her want to stop everything and not live anymore. But she couldn't *not* live. Even if she fell leagues in the air from the clouds. Apparently, even that fall couldn't kill her. Nothing could kill her. And that was, perhaps, her greatest curse. She was an immortal goddess, after all.

"Goodbye, Wife," he said finally. "For now."

Cora turned. Hades looked down, seemingly in thought, for a moment. Then he quickly shook his head and jumped in his winged-konabera chariot and flew off.

35

THULE

For many moons, Cora lived along the Nile like an Egyptian, changing her garb to a thin linen dress and wearing dark kohl over her eyes and a hair-dress to cover her conspicuous golden-blond hair. She watched over her nymphs from a distance. Then Queen Avivae and King Solinair gathered their people together for a large exodus out of Egypt. Cora still shadowed them, even then, but never revealed herself. Hades watched over them too, protecting them with his Eruboi, for the Imada and the gods of Olympus sought their revenge.

It was far in the cold northern lands of Thule on a frigid evening, decades after the flood, that Avivae Ambrosia fell sick. She had lived a long mortal life and, in many ways, in Cora's eyes, had been happier in her later years than when she had lived in Atlantis. When she was dying, not only her nymphs, but a long cavalcade of humans from the northern countries, came to watch over her. Cora visited too, using her helm of invisibility to be at the bedside of the last Atlantean queen. She sat by her and touched her, trying to use her power to revive her. But a mortal's life was destined to not be eternal. At the chosen hour, even Persephone could not revive a mortal. Instead, sitting by her side, she took her hand and spoke parting words.

Cora asked Anna for forgiveness. Anna whispered that she forgave her.

How could Cora ever be forgiven?

And now in the dark afternoon, alone before a snowy tomb, Cora kneeled weeping for her. Anna had been provided a large stone monument deep in the woods. The nymphs had buried her body under a stone tomb to shelter her from the cold. The ground had been so frigid that they had to wait for it to thaw before placing her mummified body underground. For many years, Cora had tried to worship a new god: the rays of the sun, Nefertiti and Akhenaten's Aten. Now, before Anna's grave, she cursed Aten or any god who could permit Anna to die. And she cursed any god that would allow her—a monster—to, all the while, still breathe.

When she stopped weeping, she looked up at the clouds. Some of them were her own. An icy wind blew across her face. She clasped her hands together and said, "Forgive me, Nephree. Forgive me. Please, by God, if you can hear me, forgive me." She looked down at the stone monument. "Anna, my edict remains. As long as I shall live, I will protect Sol and your people."

Then she thrust her right hand deep into the mud before the tomb, bearing searing pain as she dug through frozen stone, deep into the solid earth. The ground was so iced that it felt like she was thrusting her hand through solid rock, but she withstood the burn as it tore the skin along her fingers. She brought up a fistful of dirt. The mud and grime mingled with her blood. And as she looked down on her torn hand, she held the wish she always had —that her hand, like Anna's, was blue.

"I sacrifice for you. You may have forgiven me at your last hour, Anna, but I know you can never forgive me for what I've done. I destroyed Atala and your people. But kindness is a trait brought down, generation after generation, from my dearest mother, Nephrea. And for that, I love you, Anna, all the more."

I forgive you, Cora.

Cora spun around. The words had been so clear that she thought an Amazon villager had spoken them in the woods. But she was alone. Could it have been the wind? Or was it simply an illusion or something she wanted to hear? The voice was not Anna's. It sounded like… Nephrea's.

I forgive you.

"Why, Mother?" she asked, shaking her head. "Why? How can anyone forgive me for what I've done? Why would you forgive me?"

Because I love you.

"Why do you care about me, Mother!" Cora cried, standing up. "You send me words of comfort now? There's no comfort in this world! I'm a demon from the depths and should never have been born. Here lies your kin, buried in foreign lands after her home sank into the sea by my hands. I can't revive her or Azure from the grave."

Neeteru Belok Dispin

Those Egyptian words were breathed by the same voice through the breeze. But these words were more ancient than Cora's Egyptian tongue, and she didn't know what they meant. But she knew it was Nephree. She didn't know how, but through all the planes of worlds, across impossible distances, Nephrea had uttered words of comfort to her after so many centuries of silence. This was her mother. Somehow in Thule, this evening, in the farthest northern regions of snowy Gaia and at Cora's worst hour, Nephrea had come down to speak with her. Cora knew it was her. And why? Because Nephrea had always cared more for Cora than for herself.

Cora rose bitterly before the grave, nodding and wiping her tears with her clean hand. She listened for a long time, staring at Anna's tomb, but her words of comfort ended. If her mother had, indeed, come for her, she now was gone.

"Grandma Anna?" It was another voice. This one sounded like a child's.

Cora turned and a small girl wearing a thick fur coat similar to her own was standing behind her. Sunlight shone forth between clouds, revealing a face that looked eerily like that of her beloved Anna. The girl's arms were full, holding cakes and a silver cup of white liquid. She presented it to Cora.

Cora shook her head. Then she quickly hid her injured hand in the sleeve of her thick furry coat.

"Momma wanted me to offer you choai. Here." Then the little girl gestured for Cora to take all the things in her hands.

"I'm not your grandmother, child."

"Who are you?"

"A friend."

The girl shrugged and walked to the tomb door. She laid the breads near the door and put down a silver cup of milk. Then she got on her knees and bowed before the door three times and said: "Blessed Freyja, goddess of grain, our protector, care for my grandma. Protect Anna Ambrosia under your wings with your eternal love. Bring her to the golden realm of Valhalla. Or take her to your blessed azure fields of Folkvangr. Neeteru Belok Dispin."

She bowed a last time and rose to head back into the woods to the camp.

"Wait," Cora said, on one knee before the child. "What were those last words you said?"

"Hmm?" asked the little girl, looking up at her with bright blue eyes.

"What did you say to your grandmother? Those last words?"

"Neeteru Belok Dispin?"

"Yes. What does that mean?"

The girl looked down for a moment, furrowing her brow. Then she said, "It's words by our ancient mother, Nefertiti. I think it means nothing never is, or something like that. Grandfather said it means there's no such thing as nothing."

Then the girl jumped and laughed as a bird fluttered on her shoulder. It was Mainax. Mainax had been with Anna all her last mortal days in Thule. Now the phoenix had fallen from the dark, cloudy sky and landed, fluttering over the little girl's shoulder. But she didn't stay on the girl's shoulder; she moved over to Cora's. The girl clapped.

"Oh, Mainax," the girl said. "Where've you been? Did you return Grandma to the golden sands of Valhalla again?"

The phoenix cooed.

Then the girl squinted at Cora. "Who are you? Are you a ghost?"

"No. My name is Persephone."

"I've heard of you. My grandfather, Sól, spoke of you when he addressed the elders at the chief hall," the girl said with a nod. "He said the spirit of Persephone freed us."

"Seems time changes many things," Cora quipped quietly to herself.

Mainax cooed again and the girl laughed again.

"Mainax likes you."

"I'm sorry for what happened to your grandmother."

"It is the way of things," the girl said with a shrug. "You know, just two moons ago, my friend Iris was attacked by a pack of wolves. Can you believe that? And a black witch named Menilda fought our guards by the doors of our great hall. Life can be hard, you know."

"Yes."

"I think you're a spirit of the dead. But a good spirit. I've never seen you here before, Persephone."

"You can call me Cora. That is what your grandmother called me. What is your name, child?"

"Cassandra."

Cora jumped back. But the girl didn't notice her reaction. Cassandra turned before Cora could respond and headed back toward the village through the forest.

Cassandra.

Avivae's granddaughter was named after her lost daughter. Cassandra was a name that, in these parts, had grown to represent great heroism. A name more revered by the nymphs than even Persephone—and rightfully so.

"I hope I'll see you again tomorrow, Cora," Cassandra hollered in the woods. "Momma wants me to lay more chaoi every night for the rest of the week." Then the girl giggled again.

"I suppose you can eat it, if you're hungry. Whether you're a spirit for Grandma Anna or not."

I forgive you. Because I love you.

The words stirred again in the wind as Cora watched the girl walk on a path between thick trees. Mainax fluttered his wings as if hearing it.

I forgive you.

"Well, I can't say I'd have forgiven you, Mother," Cora said quietly, shaking her head. She watched as the girl's heavy fur coat disappeared behind tree trunks. "But we always fight, don't we, Nephree?" Rays of yellow peeked through gray clouds. Mainax cooed by her ear. Cora petted the bird.

The bird took off soaring high in the air. It gave a shriek as it passed by the light of the sun.

"Aye, my God, I love you," she said with a nod, squinting up at the sky looking for her bird. "I love you more than anything."

THE END

Cora and the nymphs of Azure continue their Greek mythological mayhem in the epic fantasy "Azure Series":

- CORA: RISE OF THE FALLEN GODDESS
- AZURE BLUE
- CORAL RED
- HARMONIA (prequel)
- PRINCESS SOJOURN (prequel)

ALSO BY A. L. HAWKE

FANTASY: THE AZURE SERIES TRILOGY

- CORA: RISE OF THE FALLEN GODDESS
- AZURE BLUE
- CORAL RED
- HARMONIA (prequel)
- PRINCESS SOJOURN (prequel)

URBAN FANTASY ROMANCE

- MY EVIL EYE
- THE GUARDIAN
- NECTAR OF AMBROSIA
- CORA

PARANORMAL ROMANCE

- ALONDRA
- BROOMSTICK
- WINDSTORM
- THE HAWTHORNE WITCH

- SHADES
- HAUNTING JOY
- PHANTOM MASQUERADE

SCIENCE FICTION

- CANDY SAVANT
- MOTHER SAVANT

Books available at https://alhawke.com/books

PARTING WORDS

What did you think of *Coral Red?* By placing a book review, you can inform others of your thoughts and help spread the word about my book.

Want more? Periodically I like to send news regarding current or new projects. If you'd like to be privy, I encourage you to sign up to my email newsletter. Your information will remain private and you can cancel any time.

Sign up at www.alhawke.com or scan the following QR code:

ACKNOWLEDGMENTS

I couldn't have shaped my finale to this epic fantasy series without the continued keen-eyed scrutiny of my beta reader George B. It was further improved and polished by Stephanie Ward's copy edit and proofread by Alexa B. And the painting depicting Cora's fury was fashioned beautifully by the cover artist Sean Counley. This concludes my Azure Blue trilogy. Thanks to all of you!

ABOUT THE AUTHOR

A.L. Hawke is the author of the bestselling Hawthorne University Witch series. The author lives in Southern California torching the midnight candle over lovers against a backdrop of machines, nymphs, magic, spice and mayhem. A.L. Hawke writes fantasy and romance spanning four thousand years, from pre-civilization to contemporary and beyond.

Visit A.L. Hawke at www.alhawke.com

Email: contact@alhawke.com